OFFER THE DEMON

BY

SHIELA STEWART

THE DEMON SERIES – BOOK TWO

CB

Decadent Publishing
www.decadentpublishing.com

This book is a work of fiction. Names, characters, places, and incidents are the products of the author's imagination or used fictitiously. Any resemblance to actual events, locales or persons, living or dead, is entirely coincidental.

Offer the Demon
Copyright 2012 by Shiela Stewart
ISBN: 978-1-61333-293-1
Cover design by LFD and Cribley Designs

Published by Decadent Publishing Company

Look for us online at:
www.decadentpublishing.com

Printed in the United States of America

~DEDICATION~

To every woman out there who has been told she couldn't do what she desires to do. Stand up tall, be proud, and live the life you want to live. You and only you have control over your life. Live it!

Chapter One

$\mathcal{H}$e screamed.

They always screamed when the shadows came to take them away, take them down. The sound reminded her of nails on a chalkboard. That guttural screech, like a cat when its tail is caught in the door, vibrated in her bones, sank into her soul, and tormented her in her sleep. She would never get used to it.

Never!

As the shadows dragged the man's soul away, she took a step back, one thoughtful step away. He had a tainted soul, and he deserved to die. Yet he was still human, even though he held other human beings in the lowest regard. He was still flesh and blood despite the fact he'd taken three lives. Now, he would be eternally damned for his sins.

Aurora couldn't help but feel remorse for what she had done. It had been she who'd taken his life away. She, the Reaper of Death.

What a burden to carry.

She longed for a hot bath, a strong drink, and a smoke. Damn it, why had she picked now to quit, when she'd just begun a new phase in her life? It wasn't as if it could kill her. That thought alone disturbed her. There were very few things that could kill her. Cigarettes weren't one of them. Why had she given them up?

Rolling her shoulders, she decided *what the hell*. Conjuring up a cigarette, she lit the tip and pulled in the rich tobacco. She smiled. Now that was much better. She indulged on the cigarette, savoring every bit she could get before she stomped it out beneath her foot. She felt much better.

Another night over, and she couldn't be happier. Taking one last look around, making sure no one would see her, she vanished into the darkness.

Aurora Starr was a demon with a conscience, and it weighed heavily on her mind. Setting herself down in her house, she drew in the familiar scents, glad to be home.

"I ran your bath and set out a nice glass of wine for you."

Hunter, once her father's loyal servant and best friend, now worked for her. He had to be as old as time, yet he didn't look it. He wore his brown hair slicked back from a rather stern, bony face. Beneath it lay a gentle man. "Bubbles?"

"Of course," She beamed then took a quick step back when he leaned in closer and sniffed. She knew damn well what he smelled, and she cursed herself for not ridding the scent of the cigarette from her clothes. "Your father won't be pleased."

"So don't tell him." Heading to the kitchen, Aurora figured her request would not be granted. "How old is this cake?"

"I purchased it just this morning."

She grabbed a plate to save herself an argument with Hunter and sat at the table to enjoy her snack. "You're going to tell him, aren't you?"

"I'm afraid so."

Without setting her eyes on him, she waved her hand and sealed his mouth shut. "Try it now."

Undaunted, Hunter pulled up a chair across from her and simply stared at her.

She continued to nibble on her cake, trying not to let Hunter's penetrating stare break her. As a child she had loved to play games on him. She just couldn't resist. He would wake in the morning to feet that belonged to a chicken. Or she would wait until he stepped into the shower, hiding by the door, and turn the water into jelly. She simply loved teasing him to see if once, just once, he would lose his cool. But he never did, and like now, he waited with complete patience. It simply infuriated her.

Snarling, she removed the seal from his mouth. "I hate when you do that."

"I know." His thin lips lifted into a sneaky smile.

She licked her fingers clean. Feeling sated, she pushed from the table. "At least let me have my bath before you tell him I slipped and had a smoke." She didn't trust the silence when he simply nodded his head.

So what if she had a bet with her father to see who could go the longest without a smoke. And so what if the loser had their powers temporarily stripped. It was worth every drag she had taken from that cigarette, and she had no regrets.

She climbed into the steaming hot bubble bath. Sliding down, she let the heated foam lull her into contentment.

Her job wasn't exactly easy. The stress alone gave her reason enough to need a cigarette. One little cigarette after a hard night's work wasn't so bad. Her father wouldn't punish her for one single cigarette. Wishing for a glass of wine laced with blood, Aurora leaned back and enjoyed the moment.

She was a grown woman after all, able to chose for herself, make decisions for herself. From the time she'd been born, her life had been mapped out for her. When she turned twenty-one, she had to do her Master's work. She hated that word, *Master*. He wasn't her Master, she was her own master. But she enjoyed life, and she loved her parents dearly, so she did as expected.

She gathered souls for Satan.

That had been the agreement between her parents and the big guy known as Lucifer. They'd be granted a child, and when old enough, that child would become his collector.

So here she was, twenty-one and under complete control of Satan. Oh, how she wanted to break free of it, if only for one day. Sighing because it would never be possible, she gulped down the last of her wine. She needed more. With a snap of her fingers, she stared at an empty glass. She tried again. Still nothing. Hunter had obviously told her father of the cigarette, which meant her father had cast the binding spell on her to prevent her from using her powers. Hunter would pay for this, one way or another.

Sulking, she slid down lower into the bubbles.

"Damn it, Daddy, I only had one."

CЗ

The facility was jam-packed, as it had been for three weeks running. People were scared to go out, scared they would be next on the list, scared *it* would come after them.

It was Death.

In the past few weeks, people had begun dying unexpectedly. Heart attacks, choking, convulsions. Some said they died out of fear. Their fear came in the likes of a dark angel, a name they claimed fit the shadow that lurked in the dark, taking lives. Some said her long black hair came to her feet, similar to a cape, and helped her to fly off into the sky. Others said she had the looks of a beast cloaked in a black robe, the hood draped over her head. One look at her would be your death.

Scott Monroe didn't believe in any of it. He didn't believe that some dark cloak of death lurked about, taking lives.

There had to be a rational explanation.

Yes, people were dying—okay, lots of people were dying— but that didn't mean some dark force was involved. You take in account that these people were: junkies, derelicts, and alcoholics who had abused their bodies with chemicals. Heart attacks, seizures, and strokes were not unusual. People like that just didn't have a long life expectancy. It had simply been their time.

That's where he came in.

Owner of The Monroe Rescue, Scott took in everyone and helped to rehabilitate them. Oh, he knew what people thought of his facility, and they'd tried so many times to shut him down. But he always came through, thanks to a nice chunk of inheritance. Funding his own facility went a long way toward keeping the wolves from the door. The city couldn't pull back their funding to shut him down.

Still, there were those who tried. Saying he allowed drunks and junkies to stay hooked, that he fed their addiction, giving them a place to stay to get high. Those people had no idea how far off they were.

Yes, he welcomed junkies, alcoholics and so on, but he never, never allowed even one drop of alcohol in his place, and drugs were strictly forbidden. Each person stepping through the doors received a thorough examination for paraphernalia and hidden bottles of booze. If any were found, they were confiscated. If the person agreed to stay, they were given a bed to sleep in, a meal to fill their belly, and counseling. Some benefited from his facility. Some didn't.

Scott had come to realize over the years that you couldn't save them all. Still, he gave it everything he had. The young were what disturbed him the most. Innocent children thinking once couldn't be so bad. Once *was* bad. Worse, it could kill. But they were lured into a lie, being told it would give them so much more happiness. Instead, it gave them only pain.

He'd seen so many walk into his facility, strung-out, jittery, and begging for help. He did his best, did what he could to give them the help they needed. Unfortunately, some couldn't be helped, and it never got easier to read about, or hear that one of his people had succumbed to their addiction.

In the fifteen years since his father had opened the facility, Scott had seen a lot of misery. Too many people that had given in to the demon known as addiction. Others that had waited too long to get help, their bodies worn down by the chemical abuse. His father had been one of them.

Dustin Monroe had been addicted to cocaine and heroin. By the time he'd agreed to get help, his body had suffered badly. Dustin wanted to prevent it from happening to others, and so he'd opened The Monroe Rescue. When his father became too weak to run the facility alone, Scott took over. Dustin had been sixty when the years of drug abuse finally claimed him, sixty when he'd taken his own life.

Scott missed his father dearly.

Once a famous rock star, Dustin Monroe had had it all. Fame, fortune, and friends. Unfortunately some of those friends had aided in his addiction. Some had not. With the help of his father's band mates, Scott continued Dustin Monroe's quest to help others fight the demon that had killed him.

Looking around the crowded facility, Scott hoped his father would be proud of him. What started out housing fifty now housed over a hundred, and some days, the place was packed. As was the case tonight.

Shutting down the lights, he listened to the quiet. Tonight they would sleep peacefully. Tomorrow would be another day.

Chapter Two

*A*urora slept to give herself peace. She didn't need it, but she liked at least that tiny ounce of normalcy. She could go for days without sleep, if need be, but she rarely did. Though she may not be human, she did her best to portray one.

As she climbed out of bed, dressed in a cute pair of cartoon-banana pajamas, she felt his presence. Taking a seat, she began to brush the long strands of dark hair she cherished.

"Come in."

Her bedroom door swung open and her father took up the space. He was always, and would always be, the most handsome man she would ever know. He had jet-black hair, so black it looked like satin. His face was firm with defined cheekbones, and a strong chin. His eyes were black, not deep brown or dark blue. Black. He was a tall man, a strong man, a loving man. He was her hero, but she was very glad she'd inherited her mother's golden eyes instead of her father's black ones. Less intimidating.

The way her father looked at her now, he definitely was intimidating. Too bad for him she'd inherited her mother's stubbornness. She rose, standing on her tiptoes to give him a peck on the cheek. She wished she weren't so short. With an innocent smile on her face, she stepped back.

"Hello, Daddy. I've missed you." Running her hand along the navy jacket he wore, she smiled sweetly. "My, don't you look handsome today. Business meeting?" Her father owned Starr Enterprises and had more than enough money. She'd grown up in a mansion and never wanted for anything. Being an only child, she'd been spoiled rotten.

He kept his dark eyes trained to hers, his face emotionless. "Sucking up won't help you one bit."

She drew her lips in a pout, which usually worked on her father. "But, Daddy—"

"No buts. Come. Sit."

Not this time apparently. She did as he asked and sat beside him on the bed. "I only had one."

"Yesterday, maybe. What about the days before that?"

"Yesterday was the first time in weeks. If you don't believe me, have a look yourself to see if I'm lying." She stared into her father's eyes and opened her mind.

He shook his head. "We had an agreement."

"I know." She sighed. "It's just so hard."

"I know it is difficult." He smoothed the hair from her face. "But it will be worth it in the end."

"The end of what? It's not as if they're going to kill me. I'm not human." As always when she talked about not being human, the pain shone through in her words.

Taking her face in his hands, he held her in place. "No, they can't kill you, but they have other effects. They stain your teeth, taint your breath, and emit an odor that is less than appealing."

Her face brightened. "That's the beauty of having magical powers. I'll just use a glamour and everything will be fine."

"You know better than that, honey. We don't use our powers needlessly any longer."

She pursed her lips, frowning at her father. "Aren't you supposed to be the big mean Draco Starr, the fear of mankind?" She'd heard the stories. She knew what he'd been like before he'd met her mother. Ruthless, merciless, and unforgiving. He was anything but that now.

He kept his gaze firm. "That is in the past."

"Before I whipped him into shape."

Standing in the doorway of Aurora's room, her mother smiled. She wasn't tall, but she made up for her height in her body. It was strong, lean and very shapely, just like Aurora's own. As she stepped into the room, her long, curly black hair swayed with the movement. She kissed her husband, smiling, then kissed Aurora's head.

"Did the two of you straighten things out?"

Aurora scrunched up her face. "Yeah, he put me in my place."

"That's all right. You both can start over from today, since your father strayed as well."

Aurora's eyes shot to her father. Seeing the stern, wide-eyed look he gave his wife, she snarled. "You had a smoke?"

"No." He looked from Aurora to her mother. "No, I had a cigar and I only did that because one of my employees just had a child. I couldn't refuse a new father's joy."

Aurora waved her hand at him. "A smoke is a smoke, whatever form it comes in. You rotten man you, chastising me when you'd indulged yourself. You are in so much trouble." Waving her hand erratically at her father, she realized quite disturbingly that her powers had yet to return. "Damn it, Mom, he's got my powers blocked."

"No, dear, I have."

Aurora turned to her mother with confusion. "You?" Her mother practiced magic, had done so after learning her birth mother had been Wiccan. It surprised Aurora that her mother used those powers on her.

"Yes, and you'll both get them back tomorrow."

"Daddy—"

"Don't look at me. I've never been able to convince her to see things my way." He placed a hand on Aurora's shoulder. "One day. It won't be so bad."

Aurora snorted. One day was an eternity when you worked for Satan.

"Someday you'll see what we're trying to do is only for your good." Kissing her head, her father stood. He took her mother's hand in his and they left the room.

How many times in her life had she heard that one?

CR

"Is she still pouting?" Hunter asked as he set two cups on the table filled with coffee.

"Yes. She'll get over it." Draco lifted his cup as his wife sat beside him. "How was she last night?" Whether his daughter liked it or not, he worried about her.

"Unsettled. Displeased." Hunter wiped the already sparkling clean counter. "This isn't easy for her."

Draco laid his hand over his wife's. No words needed to be said. They both felt bad for it. "We know."

"Regrets?"

Draco turned to Hunter. "Some, but not of her. She's our life. Without her...well, we're just not complete." Despite the eternal love between him and his wife, it had become quite apparent after three years of marriage that something had been missing. Children. And due to his wife's partially human side, Satan forbade Draco the creation of a child. So they'd done what they thought had been best: they'd pleaded.

It had taken time, too much time, to convince Lucifer to grant their request for a child. They could have adopted. There were so many needy children in the world who didn't have homes. His wife had been one of them. Adopted as an infant, she'd been raised by kind, loving parents. But he and Missy weren't normal people. They weren't human. A human child would never have been able to cope with what they were.

So they'd bartered—yes, bartered—with their child's life. But at the time, they saw it as only a small price to pay to have a child of their own. They'd hoped their daughter would understand. Right now, Draco wasn't too sure she did.

"You will inform us if you see signs of it getting to be too much for her?"

Hunter nodded. "What will you do if it does?"

Draco's eyes met Missy's. They'd both agreed that if it ever became too much for their daughter, they would take over. At any cost. "We'll take care of that."

Chapter Three

The heat was nearly unbearable. Scott wiped the sweat that trickled down his face and turned up the air. It seemed silly, and certainly not very environmentally conscious, to have the windows open while the cool air ran in the car, but damn it, he was hot. He couldn't roll the windows up. He wouldn't be able to hear it if someone needed help. Twice a week he hopped in his car and cruised the city streets looking for those in need. He'd started because so many people were dying. He refused to believe the rumors that some dark angel scooped up bodies and took them as her own. There had to be another explanation.

As he drove down the dark, quiet streets, he kept his eyes and ears open. If someone needed him, he could be there in a flash. Rolling his shoulders, trying to work the kink out that had been nagging him for days, Scott moved slowly from stoplight to stoplight. A sound, distant, faint, had his ears perking up. Slamming on his brakes, he exited the car to see what direction it came from.

North.

Climbing back in the car, he drove toward the screams.

Pulling to a stop near a deserted section of town, Scott raced into the darkness, with only his fists as protection. The heels of his boots ground into the gravel, tiny rocks shooting out behind him as he ran. Though faintly, he could see something in the shadows.

He skidded to a halt, dust forming a cloud around his feet as the dark figure swooped up and over him. Craning his neck, he tried to follow it, but it disappeared before he had a chance to get a good look at what it had been. What he'd seen made him wonder. The long hair that flapped like a cloak as it took off seemed strikingly similar to the rumors that had been going around. Could it be the Dark Angel he'd just seen?

Impossible. There was no such thing.

The whimpers drew him back. Taking a deep breath to calm himself, he hurried down the alley and saw a shadowed figure lying on the ground. It was a woman, curled up into a ball, shivering and moaning. Crouching down, he spoke softly. "Are you okay?"

Her head lifted, eyes wide. "She almost had me. I heard her words, but she didn't speak, her mouth didn't move," she babbled, her eyes wide as she scanned the alley. "She said I needed to pay for what I'd done, needed to pay for my sin." The tears came now, hot and heavy. "I didn't mean to drown him. He just kept crying and crying and I couldn't make him stop. I just couldn't make him stop."

Scott took the young woman in his arms and held her while she cried. When the tears finally subsided, he led her to his car, and to his shelter. While she drank the hot coffee he'd offered her, Scott called the police. What else could he do?

He sat with her as she gave her statement, told the police that she'd had a child two weeks ago, but couldn't afford to keep him. She didn't know where to go for help, so she helped herself. She'd filled the tub with water, and laid her infant son inside. She'd walked away as he drowned.

Scott felt pity for her at the same time it angered him. The woman had to be ill and would probably do time in the psych ward. Especially with her babbling on and on about the Dark Angel that had come to call. They'd asked him what he'd seen, but Scott could only tell them that he'd seen something he couldn't identify. It could've been a bird. But in the back of his mind he wondered. How many birds wore perfume?

ଓଽ

Though she wished with all her heart this would be her last, it was inevitable she'd have to take another because she'd failed to take the first one. Aurora waited for the call. She hated the intrusion in her mind. Unfortunately, she couldn't do anything to stop it. Satan didn't pick up a phone and call. He used her mind to tell her what needed to done.

As she sat atop an old warehouse, looking out over the city, she wondered who the man had been, the one with the halo of blond hair. Could he be an angel sent to stop her and save the souls she dammed? Or had he simply been a man who had stumbled upon her? She couldn't be sure. One thing she did know, he had seen her. Not enough to recognize her or make out her face, but enough to know she was real. Not many did.

There were some that claimed to have seen her. She enjoyed the write-ups of her description in the paper, but none of them came close to her real identity. Often they weren't taken seriously, as the only ones who claimed to have seen her were homeless, drunk, or on drugs. The sightings were brushed off as mere hallucinations. She wondered now if that would still be the case. She needed to be more careful. She couldn't afford to be seen. The punishment would be unbearable.

The tiny jolt inside her mind startled her. Aurora tried not to resent it, yet she did. From past experience, it would get worse. The intrusion only got louder and more painful. Ignoring Lucifer's call had dire consequences. The price was too high for her to toy with.

Standing, she let the power of Satan's voice carry her to the next victim. A serial rapist. Another tainted soul.

The middle-aged man clamped one hand around the poor woman's throat while the other shot under her skirt. The young woman cried, frozen to her spot.

Aurora opened her mind, reached inside the man's chest, and watched his eyes shoot wide. He gasped once, twice, before releasing the girl. He fell to his knees, clutching his chest. The young woman didn't bother to look back. She just ran.

Setting herself down, Aurora came face to face with the attacker. "It's time you paid," she said using only her mind and the power within her to twist his heart. Only a thought, a mere thought, and she could make a human beg for his life. The slime whose life she held in her hands begged with raspy breath. His pleas would go unanswered.

"Forever you are damned. An eternity you will pay."

His hands clasped to his chest, he gasped, sweating profusely. She watched as his heart gave out. He fell to the ground, nothing more than another hideous soul she'd been sent to gather. Yet she felt so dirty. Why?

Stepping back, she waited for the call, and as usual, ten seconds after the life-force had been drained, the shadows fell. His soul did not go quietly into the night. It screamed and screeched, clawing, digging into any shred of life it could still grasp. But as diligently as he fought, the shadows were much stronger. With one last attempt to escape, the man clawed at the ground as the shadows swallowed him up. His fight was over.

A silent tear slid down her cheek. She shouldn't be crying for a man that was vile, dirty, who invaded women in the most hideous way, yet she still cried. As she took off, flying high into the night sky, she let her tears fall.

○ɜ

Aurora appeared in the house, feeling less than jovial. The sight of dozens of colorful balloons taking up most of the space in her living room amused her but did little to lighten her mood. However, the chocolate cake sitting on the coffee table helped. Pushing her way through the balloons, she took a seat on the floor and cut into the cake.

Taking a huge forkful, she shoved it into her mouth and sighed. "Thank you, Hunter."

Through the crowd of balloons he appeared. "My pleasure."

He handed her a glass of chilled milk.

How he always knew when she felt low puzzled her, yet he did, always had. "There are few things better than chocolate cake," she mumbled through her next bite. "Not even blood or the finest slice of raw steak can compare, and that says a lot coming from a demon." Smiling, she stuffed more cake in her mouth. "Have some."

Taking a seat on the sofa, he dished out a slice for himself. "How did it go tonight?"

"Rough." She swallowed some milk. "The first one got away. Well not really. Someone showed up to save her. Blond guy, tall." She nearly said cute, but she figured Hunter didn't need to hear about that.

"Did he see you?"

"Only briefly. Not enough to make out my face or anything." She cut another slice of cake and greedily dug in. The chocolate did wonders for her sour mood.

"You need to be more careful, little one."

"Yes, *Dad.*"

Hunter narrowed green eyes and jabbed his fork at her while he spoke. "You have a father, a perfectly good father. I am only doing what I know he would want me to do."

She scrunched up her face and toyed with her cake. "How do you always know when I'm feeling blue?"

"You've been blue since you started collecting souls for Satan. And I've known you a long time. I know everything about you."

She looked at the balloons. He didn't know everything. Did he know she cried in her bed sometimes, wishing she were human so she could lead a normal life? No, he didn't. "You are too good for me, Hunter." She gave him the brightest smile, despite her sorrow.

"About time you admitted that." Leaning over, he kissed her head before he left the room.

Sighing, Aurora picked at the dish. Thankful she couldn't get fat, she sat back and began to devour the entire cake.

Chapter Four

The shelter was packed full, once again. The noise level probably would read well above the allowed decibel point, if anyone bothered to check. The lounge area was full of worried patrons, and only one thing worried them: the so-called Dark Angel.

Climbing up onto a table, Scott clapped his hands. "People, settle down now." He clapped his hands again, finally drawing their attention. "I know everyone is worried, but there's no need to be."

"You saw it. You told the police you saw her. The Dark Angel."

Scott sighed as he stepped down from the table. Turning to Percy, one of his regulars, he stayed calm." I didn't see anything, Percy."

"You lie." He pointed his bony sixty-five-year-old finger at Scott. "You lie. You tell us not to lie, but you lie."

Scott had a feeling his guards were going to have to break up the situation. "I saw a shadow, nothing more. That doesn't mean anything."

"The hell it don't. It's the Dark Angel, and she's come a callin'," Percy stated firmly, jabbing a finger at Scott.

The crowd began muttering, cheering him on, agreeing with what he had said. Holding his hands up, Scott tried to calm them all down. "There is no such thing as the Dark Angel."

"Explain the deaths," someone shouted from the crowd.

Scott took a deep breath. It wouldn't do any good if he showed them his frustration. "There's a perfectly rational explanation for them."

"Okay, let's hear it."

He drew in another breath and resisted the urge to run his hands through his hair in frustration. "They were old." *Oh, wow, is that the best you can do?*

"Devin wasn't old."

Scott turned to Percy again. "No, I suppose not, though with everything he did to his body, it's no surprise." He was doing terribly.

"So, you're saying that because we're weak, we're all going to die." That had the people gasping and muttering amongst themselves.

He'd lost control of the crowd and they were beginning to panic. "No. Now you're putting words in my mouth." He calmed himself, used his best reasonable voice. "What I meant to say is, the more you abuse your body, the weaker you'll be. Devin didn't want help, but if you take it, stick to it, you'll all live longer, healthier lives."

"Your daddy didn't," Percy reminded him, as he stuck a stale cigar between his yellowing teeth.

Scott's heart clenched in his chest, a pain only the loss of a loved one could produce. "No, he waited too long to get help, but he lived longer thant he would have if he had continued to abuse drugs."

"You can't know that for sure. People are always saying this is bad for you, that's bad for you. Well, hell, if we lived by that rule, we wouldn't be eating, drinking, or breathing." The crowd agreed. "They say smoking is bad for you, yet I ain't known one person who died from it."

"Statistics show—"

"Screw the statistics. There are people who smoke drink and do drugs and have lived long, happy lives."

Scott let out that frustrated breath. He was steadily losing the battle. "That may be so, but the chemical abuse to the body weakens it. If they hadn't done that to their body, they would have been healthier."

"Save the preacher act, son. I ain't buyin' it anymore." Percy turned to the crowd. "Who's with me?" The crowd let up a loud cheer.

"No, wait!" Despite his plea, Scott figured that he had lost the battle on this situation. Hell, he hadn't even had a fighting chance going in. What would his daddy think of him now? He watched the people milling about, talking amongst themselves, discussing what they would do. He only hoped some of what he'd said had sunk in.

Who was he kidding? They hadn't listened. Too many of them didn't listen. When they walked out of his shelter, they were lost to him. He could only do so much.

Signaling to the guards, who were busy keeping an eye on the situation, Scott informed them he was leaving. Maybe he could be of more help on the streets.

03

She didn't want to do this, but the damn voice in her head screamed at her to take him. He was only eighteen. He had a long life to live yet. So she rebelled.

"Why? Tell me why he has to go? He's so young." She clutched her head when the voice grew louder and more demanding.

DO IT!

"What if I refuse? What if I say no and walk away?" She suddenly fell to her knees as the pain sliced into her. Like fire erupting in every molecule of her body, it took more than her breath away. She grabbed her head, her eyes tearing up as the pain radiated throughout her body. Aurora gasped. Clinging to the edge of sanity, she cried out,. "All right, all right, I'll do it, damn it! I'll do it!"

She took in a huge gulp of air when the pain subsided. The

thought came to mind to call him several nasty names, but she didn't think that would go over well. Instead, she stood, dusted off her black jeans, and turned to her next victim.

He was so young, only three years younger than she. Much too young to die. The voice inside her head reminded her that the young man had just robbed a convenience store and had shot and killed the owner. Not his first offense.

"With help, he could turn out to live a better life."

Take him now! the voice screamed at her, filling her body with pain.

Having no choice, Aurora stepped up to the young man as he counted his money. She would make this one quick. He didn't need to suffer. The wind swooped down, blowing her hair to fan her face. She touched the young man's shoulder.

He spun around, and his face froze. What he saw wasn't human.

"I'm sorry." Opening her hand, she blew a cloud of dust into his face. In a matter of moments he would fall into a deep sleep and never wake.

He made a choking sound, his hands reaching for his throat as the air refused him. As he fell to his knees, gasping, she heard the crunch of gravel behind her.

Spinning around, Aurora saw him, the blond angel that had come to the rescue last time. She lifted off only seconds before he reached her. He was most definitely a man, a human man, a gorgeous man.

Spotting the child on the ground, the blond man dropped to his knees and took the boy's head in his hands. He held him as the shadows took the soul away.

"Who the hell are you?" he screamed into the warm dark night. "Why are you doing this?"

She stood atop the building, invisible, cloaked in the shadows, and watched as the handsome man did everything in his power to revive the boy. She couldn't answer the cries of the blond man, couldn't go to him and explain. Instead, she looked down at him silently as he cradled the lifeless body. She stayed where she was as the man called for help, watched as the police arrived, asked their usual questions, and cordoned off the scene. She was transfixed by him. Something about that blond hair drew her in, making her want to risk it all. She followed him, cloaked in invisibility. When he pulled up in front of a tall building, she settled on the roof of his car and waited.

Stepping from the car, he paused and looked around, then shrugged as he closed the door.

Oh my, Aurora thought, he looked much better close up. She smiled as she watched him saunter—and he did saunter, a slow, easy gliding of feet—into the building. He was tall, strong, and gorgeous. Curious, she looked up at the sign over the top of the door. *Monroe Shelter.* What kind of place was this? The temptation to step inside, unseen, and see what went on nearly took over, but she knew the rules. They didn't spy on people. She huffed. Rules. She was sick of them. They were running her life.

Well, maybe the time had come to make her own. Take over her life, and have some fun. She wanted to partake in everything normal people experienced. So what if she wasn't exactly normal? She could pretend. What harm would that be?

Scanning the areas of the city, she spotted a club that seemed to be hopping. Waving a hand over her body, she dressed herself in a tight blue mini-skirt that showed off a great deal of leg, and a shimmering white tank top, revealing more than she should. To hell with it. She wanted to have fun. Winding her hair, she clipped it to the top of her head and let the length fall over her shoulders. It was party time.

Setting herself down in a vacant stall in the ladies room, she ran a hand over her body before stepping from the stall. The loud, hard music seemed perfect for the atmosphere. Flashing lights shot out of beams on the floor, mirrored balls hung from the ceiling sending glittering lights on the dance floor. She had never seen anything like it.

How could she? She'd been sheltered from the time she'd been born. She hadn't been allowed to go to a normal school, she hadn't been allowed any friends unless they were approved by her father, and rarely were they. The only time she'd been able to go out and enjoy the world had been when she and her mother would go shopping.

Watching the people dance, mingle, drink, and simply enjoy themselves, Aurora realized just how much she had missed.

She had a lot of making up to do. Back straight, she sauntered out onto the dance floor and mimicked the moves of everyone else on the dance floor. Men slid up to her, bumped into her, all clambering for her attention. She loved it. They bought her drinks she eagerly drank. They offered cigarettes she took and enjoyed. She'd never felt a man against her before. The one that held her now as they danced to some slow tune seemed nice enough, if she were looking. But, of course, she couldn't. Not with a human, at least.

For hours, she danced, drank, smoked, and had the time of her life. At last call, she thanked her dance partners and vanished the moment she was out of sight. She'd had more fun in a few simple hours than she'd had her entire life.

Tired yet feeling absolutely glorious, she set herself down in her bedroom. She figured Hunter would be long asleep by now.

She was sadly mistaken.

"Where were you?"

"Out. Having fun. Don't ruin my happy, Hunter. Be gone." Waving her hand, she sent him to his room. Kicking off her heels, she dropped face-first onto the bed.

For the first time in her life, she felt free.

Chapter Five

*W*aking, the light from the window piercing into her eyes and skull, Aurora grabbed a pillow and pulled it over her head. She felt horrible, utterly horrible. Her tongue felt like sandpaper, her throat raw and tasting as if she'd eaten an ashtray. Her head throbbed something fierce and her stomach rolled. Well, this wouldn't do. Waving her hand, she prepared to heal herself, and nothing happened.

Cursing silently, tossing the pillow aside, she opened her burning eyes. "I should have known."

"Feeling a little ragged, my sweet?" Sitting in the very chair Hunter had been in the night before, her father smiled devilishly back at her.

The sly smile on her father's face spoke volumes. She was in for it. Easing up, she took a moment to breathe through the nausea. She suddenly realized she hadn't changed out of her clothing from the night before. "I don't like you." She pulled the blankets up, glaring at him.

"I know you love me." Rising from the chair, his large frame moving in unbelievable silence, he sat on the side of her bed. "You've been naughty, Aurora."

Though he looked calm, she heard the temper behind his words. She matched it with her own. "I am so going to kill Hunter for this."

"Leave him out of this. You got yourself into this alone."

She pushed from the bed. The room spun. Yes, yes she had, and she'd had fun doing it. "Damn it, I'm a grown woman, and it's my prerogative if I want to go out and enjoy myself."

"Yes, but within reason."

Pulling the clip from her hair, she let it fall like a black cloak to land past her hips. "Within reason. It has always been within reason. Well, I'm sick of reason." Walking to her washroom, she poured water from the tap. Holding her long hair to the side, she dipped her mouth under the stream. She needed an ocean of water to drown out her thirst.

She felt it the instant her body healed and let out a sigh of relief. "Thank you." She didn't spare him a glance as she walked to her dressing table, sat, and picked up her brush. "I just wanted to have some fun, a tiny bit of normalcy in my life."

Her father came up behind her and, seeing his reflection in the mirror, she refused to meet his gaze. "You will never have what is considered normal."

Relenting, she leaned back and rested her head on his chest. As always, he wrapped his big, strong arms around her. "I know, but it's nice to pretend once and a while." Her mother would understand.

"Yes, she probably would." He shook his head when she glared at him. "Sorry, it slipped."

They'd agreed early on that none of them would invade the others' mind. Their private thoughts were to be just that, private. Yet occasionally, each one of them would slip and let the veil down to hear each other's thoughts.

"She would also tell you not to be reckless."

"I wasn't being reckless," she sighed. She'd just wanted some fun. "I've been...lonely."

He turned her to face him and knelt down at her feet. It was a move so classic of him when he was trying to be tender. "Come back home with us. Your room is waiting."

Aurora appreciated his sentiment, but she'd wanted a place of her own and had managed to convince both her parents she would be fine on her own. They had only agreed if Hunter came along. So she'd given in. "I like it here, living on my own. I appreciate the offer. I just need some friends, that's all."

He stroked her face delicately. "You could never tell them who you really are."

"I know." And that was the crux of it.

"You might slip up."

She lifted her eyes to meet his. "Do you, when you're having a board meeting, or inspecting a new building?" She saw the recognition in his eyes. "I'm careful, Daddy. I learned from the best."

"Now you're just sucking up."

She smiled a wide, toothy grin. "I know. Is it working?"

Laughing, he kissed her head. "I only want what is best for you, my sweet."

"I know." She'd always known.

"Stay cautious." He stood, giving his black jacket a tug.

"Always." Smiling, she stood to kiss his cheek, and barely reached his chin. "When will I ever grow?"

Bending down, he kissed her cheek. "In my eyes, you'll never grow."

She frowned. "I'm not a little girl anymore, Daddy."

"I am aware of that. Though you've grown into a beautiful young woman, you will always be my little girl." He kissed the top of her head. "Now, go shower. You smell horrible."

Cষ

The place seemed too quiet. Scott was used to the noise, the clatter of dishes, the chatter of voices. Everyone had gone into hiding today. They were all spooked, and as long as his thoughts were his own, he could admit he felt a little spooked as well.

What had that been in the alley? What had swooped over him only to disappear into the darkness? Surely she couldn't be real. Could she?

No, humans weren't able to fly. She had simply been a hallucination. If only he'd been able to make out her face. He berated himself for falling into everyone's trap. She couldn't be real.

Pushing from his desk, his work done, Scott pulled open his office door and nearly jumped out of his skin.

"Oh, I am so sorry. Are you okay?"

He felt foolish, but not so foolish that he didn't notice the raven-haired beauty in front of him. She had hair as black as night, and long enough that the braid she had her hair twined in fell over her shoulder, nearly to her waist. Her eyes were an interesting shade of gold, with tiny flecks of brown around the edges. She had a delicate, bronze-toned face. And now that his heart had settled down to a gentle patter, he found he could speak.

"Yes, I just wasn't expecting anyone. How can I help you?"

"Do you work here?"

"In a manner of speaking. I own the place." He held out his hand. "Scott Monroe. And you are…?"

She took his hand. "Aurora Starr. I had no idea this place even existed." She turned to the long corridor that led to the shelter's recreational area. "What do you do here?"

"Are you in need of help, Miss Starr?" Why did the name sound so familiar?

She turned back, her face captured in a smile that made the gold even more prominent in her eyes. "Is that what you do? Help?"

"I shelter addicts in need of assistance. I help them break free of their addictions. I also house the homeless when needed." She certainly didn't look homeless with those designer shoes she wore, which probably cost at least a month's rent.

"How interesting."

Interesting. He wouldn't have called it that. "Do you need assistance, Miss Starr?"

"Oh no, no I was just curious. I've never noticed this place before. Thought I would come in and check it out."

He sighed again. "Well, we're not a department store, but if you would like a tour I would be happy to oblige you."

Once again her face lit up with her smile. "I would love one, thank you."

Stepping past her, he could smell the scent of soap, nothing more, simply soap. Odd how it managed to tangle up inside of him to make his body ache.

The scent stirred something in his memory.

"We have the capacity to house two hundred. Though we have yet to fill it, we've come close." He led the way. "There are bedrooms down the hall to your left as well as upstairs. Each unit has ten beds. All of them are open, no hidden spots for people to hide in." He had made sure of that. "The kitchen and banquet room are usually filled." He opened the door enough for her to see inside. "Especially around the holidays." He finished as he turned her back to the recreational area. "Upstairs is the healing section. Patients who need more care are looked after up there."

"That must cost a fair amount," she said as she looked at all the faces in the room.

"I've plenty to spare."

She turned to him with complete surprise. "You pay for this all yourself?"

Her wide-eyed innocence amused him. "Yes, mostly." He didn't think she wanted to hear all the details of where his money came from and who helped out.

"Do you run it yourself?"

He smiled down at her and found her naïveté sweet. "I have people who help me. We have doctors and our counselors work with the people four days a week, not to mention plenty of kitchen staff as well as nurses. I also have guards, as you see, standing by the door. They help me in case a situation gets out of control."

"How interesting."

"These people struggle every day to beat whatever addiction has them imprisoned. It's not exciting to watch a junkie willing to do anything for their next score, including selling themselves, or an alcoholic who is vomiting blood yet continues to reach for the bottle. Some of these people are homeless and haven't eaten a decent meal in months." When he'd hoped to make her squeamish, he saw she kept a straight face. If anything, he thought he saw understanding.

"Do you always help them, Scott?"

"No, unfortunately, I don't. If life were that easy, we wouldn't have half the problems that plague our society today." He walked her to the front entrance. "May I ask what your interest is in this place, Miss Starr?"

She turned to him, her amber eyes illuminated in the bright sunlight that streamed through the glass doors. "Please, call me Aurora. Before I knew how passionate you were about this place, I'd planned on asking my father to buy it."

He crossed his arms over his chest. "Is that so? Well my place is not for sale." Not for all the money in the world.

"Pity." She fumbled with the gold stars in her earlobes.

Starr, Starr, the name finally clicked. "Would you happen to be referring to Draco Starr?"

"Yes, I would be."

"That's why your name sounded so familiar. You're his daughter." He cocked his head. "Not much press on you. Why is that?"

She smiled such a sweet innocent smile it made his heart flop in his chest. "I like my privacy." Pushing the door open, she walked away.

Scott watched her leave, baffled by her, yet intrigued all the same.

Chapter Six

Once a week they came together for a family meal. Her mother insisted on it after Aurora left home. And once again Hunter seemed reluctant. Despite him being around…well, she really didn't know how long he and her father had known each other, Hunter always felt his place was as a servant more than family.

She'd known him all of her life, and thought of him as her family. At times, he'd been her salvation. Playing ball with her in the back yard, swimming in the pool her father had finally given into installing after months of her begging. And whenever she'd been blue, Hunter had always been there for her.

"Come on, old guy. You're part of the family, like an uncle. In fact, from now on I am going to call you Unkie Hunter." Her arm around his waist, Aurora gave Hunter a teasing kiss on his cheek.

Straightening his back, he shot her the most disdainful look she had ever seen. "I wish you wouldn't."

"Now, now, Unkie Hunter, you know me better than that." She leaned her cheek against his arm. "I never do as I'm told." Aurora smiled as she sent them both to her parents' home.

If a man's castle were his home, her father should be king. When he'd decided to settle down, end his days of evil and destruction, to find his perfect soul mate, her father had had this estate built. And a grand house it was. Ten bedrooms, a lounge with a fully stocked bar, and a game room. It boasted a large dining hall, not to be outdone by the huge library, where her mother often sat to read. The sitting rooms were elegant and large as well. Looking at the place, one would think her father had planned on having a big family. Unfortunately, her mother had only been able to carry one child. From what Aurora had been told, it had been a hard and difficult labor and had nearly killed both of them.

Her mother's story had been just as exciting as her father's life. She'd run away from an abusive fiancé and had found refuge here, in the mansion. She'd had no idea her host had been a demon, or that she, too, was a demon. It took an incantation to bring the hidden demon in her out, and after finally accepting what she'd become, she and Aurora's father had fallen madly in love. It still blew her mind that her mother was part human. Aurora wished she'd been given that gene, more so than the demon gene.

Standing now in the grand dining hall, she felt a tiny bit of homesickness as she looked at the huge table and its perfectly-placed china. Gold candles were place on the table in crystal dishes. Beautifully arranged fake flowers sat at the center of the table. They had to be imitation, as flowers emit a certain aphrodisiac to demons. The amount of food set out could easily feed a small army.

"Wow, Emma has outdone herself this time."

"Hmm, yes."

"Hello, darling." Her parents entered the room. Her father stretched his arms out to her. She went to him, feeling at home as he wrapped them around her body. "Hello, Hunter."

"Sir. Missy."

"I've decided that from now on, I'm going to call him Unkie Hunter," Aurora boasted as she tipped her head back to allow her father to kiss her cheek. "It's catchy, isn't it?"

"I can see it impresses him a great deal."

Hunter grunted as he took his seat at the table.

Smiling, Missy turned to her daughter. "So, how has your week been?"

Taking dishes handed to her, Aurora filled her plate. At her mother's insistence, they ate human food as often as possible, though the meat was not always cooked thoroughly, to satisfy their demon side. "He brings them in, I knock them down."

Missy looked down at her plate, cleared her throat. "Aside from that, what have you done?"

Aurora handed dishes to Hunter as she spoke. "I met an interesting man the other day."

The clatter of a fork on china had her turning to her father. "Not in that way, Daddy. I know the rules. I am a demon and I can't let anyone know what I am, nor can I become involved with a human," she recited with a hint of attitude. "He owns a shelter. He takes in addicts and homeless people and tries to rehabilitate them, give them help getting back on their feet."

"And how did you come to know this man?" Missy lifted a forkful of rare roast beef as she looked across the table at her daughter.

"He foiled one of my missions, almost two," Aurora stated with a nonchalant air that had her parents lifting their brows.

"Did he see you?"

She turned to her father. "Not enough to know who I am." She'd proven that to herself when she'd gone to visit him. "I think it's great what he's doing."

His hand paused as he cut into his beef. "Might I remind you that those are the exact sort of people you're in charge of bringing to Lucifer?"

She waved him off. "There's plenty to go around."

"Have you been practicing your meditation, dear?"

"Yes, mother." Rolling her eyes, Aurora sliced into a nice huge piece of roast beef. Her mother constantly asked her that same question.

"Meditation is a wonderful art, Aurora. It will help you to control your emotions, if practiced regularly."

"I do it. You can ask Unkie Hunter."

Again, Hunter growled.

Aurora chuckled and carried on. "Anyway, this place is huge, and there are doctors and nurses and counselors and Scott seemed so into it, passionate."

"You seem quite taken with this place," Her father spoke while cutting into his meat.

Aurora lifted one shoulder in a passive gesture and swallowed. "It interested me, so I went to see the owner."

"And who might this owner be?" her mother asked casually.

"Scott Monroe. He's very nice, or at least from what I could tell when he showed me around." She swirled her mashed potatoes, thinking dreamily about Scott. He looked so incredibly handsome, like those male models she'd seen on TV.

"Scott Monroe, from the Monroe Shelter?"

Aurora tilted her head, angling to meet her father's attention. "Yes, do you know him?"

Draco nodded as he sipped from his glass. "Who doesn't? He's been in the papers or on the news several times of late."

"Why would he be in the news?"

"They say he's aiding in the addictions, giving addicts a place to stay to get high, supplying them with clean needles and a place to shoot it into their systems. The city has tried several times, unsuccessfully, to have him shut down, but he's got some strong friends that help to keep it open."

Leaning her chin on her folded hands, her elbows resting on the table, Aurora listened to what her father said. "Friends, like who?"

"His father was a legendary rock star, Dustin Monroe. He founded the place after his own addiction nearly took him down. His band mates helped him out. The word spread amongst the rich and famous and others chipped in. When Dustin passed on a few years back, he not only left his son in charge, but also the billons he had tucked away in a Swiss bank account.

"Billions?" Scott had said he had money, but she had no idea how much. He certainly didn't show his wealth.

"Apparently. He bought out the other members of the band a short time ago. I actually had my eye on that property, so I had it researched, as well as the owners, and went to him with a generous offer."

"So that's how he knew you." She tapped her fingers on her

wine glass. "I'm glad you didn't buy it or I might never have met him." Smiling, she sipped her wine.

"You're not thinking of going to this place again, Aurora?" her mother asked with worry in her voice.

Aurora lifted her shoulders casually. "I might."

"He can't ever know who you are."

"Yes, Daddy, I think you've emphasized that point several times." It annoyed her being told time and time again of what she could and could not do.

"Would anyone care for more wine?"

"It's not your job to serve us any longer, Hunter. You're family."

Hunter nodded. "I wasn't going to serve, I simply asked."

Grinning, her father lifted his glass. "In that case, yes, I would love some more."

Aurora toyed with her glass, watching the blood-red liquid swirl in the crystal, her mood suddenly sour. She would never be allowed anything.

Chapter Seven

*H*er mood still a bit low, she pulled herself out of bed the next morning. Going about her usual routine, Aurora showered and brushed her hair. It was her pride, and she made sure to take perfect care of it. When she'd been younger, her mother had sat her on her lap and played with her hair before reading her a bedtime story. It had become a nightly ritual.

She missed those days. They were simpler days, so unlike now.

She lived on her own, a grown woman, yet still it seemed everyone around her ruled her life. Couldn't her father see that she wouldn't take risks, that she would be careful with her true identity? Couldn't he just let her have an ounce of a normal life? She sighed. When your father was a direct descendant of Satan himself, you weren't allowed normalcy.

From what she had learned of her father's past, he'd been born into evil and raised to obey it. Satan had taken him under his wing, so to speak, and guided him into the life that would provide him with plenty of souls.

Now she had the job of collecting souls for Lucifer and she hated every moment of it.

Aurora grew tired of having him in her head, grew tired of him telling her how to live, telling her what to do. She wanted her freedom, to explore new things, to learn and to experience. But mostly, to be free. She wanted so desperately to be normal.

Sitting at her dressing table, Aurora decided the time had come to take over her life. Dressing in a plain white cotton blouse and blue jeans, she wound her hair into a twist, clipping it.

Lifting off, she decided one more look couldn't hurt.

Cloaked in invisibility, she set herself down outside of the shelter. So what if her curiosity got the best of her, and yes, maybe she was a little infatuated with the gorgeous man, but she couldn't help it. At times, she cursed her ability to read people's auras, but not this time. Scott Monroe's aura was so pure, so clean, it shone bright around him. Oh he'd sinned—what person hadn't in their lifetime?—but nothing of great significance.

Watching the people as they went about their daily routine, she longed to be a part of it. Maybe she could portray a regular person, if only for a little while. On the outside, she looked perfectly normal. No one needed to see what lay beneath the beauty of a woman.

Making sure no one saw her, she reappeared and walked through the doors. And there he was.

When he spotted her, he politely lifted a hand to wave at her as he spoke to the woman he'd been standing with before heading her way. Aurora felt a ripple of desire zero in on her belly just from looking at him.

"Hi."

"Hi again."

She liked the way he dressed today. He wore a T-shirt that boasted *Life ain't so bad as long as the music is loud*. "I just thought I would come for a visit."

He tucked his hands in the pockets of his jeans and gave her a sour look. "I already told you, it's not for sale."

He had the sexiest voice she had ever heard. "I'm not here to convince you otherwise. I just came to hang out."

His brow curled. "Hang out here? I'm sure there are much better places for a young woman like yourself to hang out in."

She didn't particularly like the tone in his voice. "Naturally. I just meant this place fascinates me." And she'd almost said *he* fascinated her. "I'm interested in helping." Where that came from, she had no clue.

He stared at her as if she'd just spoken gibberish. "You? Want to help?"

She didn't like that tone, either. "Yes. Why is that so hard for you to believe?"

"It's just that, well, you're a little young."

"I am not young. I just turned twenty-one."

He let out a tiny snort of a chuckle. "Wow, twenty-one. You are ancient." His laughter and mocking attitude didn't impress her one bit. "You're still a baby."

"You don't even know me, Mr. Monroe. If you did you would know that I have experienced more in my twenty-one years than you ever have in your—what—forty-odd ones?" She aged him purposely, just for spite. From the look on his face, she'd succeeded.

"Thirty," he corrected. "All right, Miss Starr, you want to help, you can help, but I warn you, it gets ugly. This isn't a fancy hotel and we don't have doormen and maid service, like you're obviously accustomed to. It's down-and-dirty here. You'll see things you will wish you hadn't."

If he thought that would scare her away, he was sadly mistaken. Stepping closer, she jabbed him in the chest with a pointed finger. "First, I am not a spoiled rich brat as you implied, and second, I've seen things that would make your toes curl."

He stared at her for several moments before responding. "All right, Miss Starr. When would you like to start?"

"Now," she challenged, reminding herself to keep her rage buried.

"It's a little late. Aren't you expected home?"

He tried her patience, and she normally had an abundance of it. "No, I live on my own. No one is expecting me," she remarked snidely.

"All right, Miss Starr, let's get you started."

"Stop calling me Miss Starr. My name is Aurora." She saw the smirk he fought and slanted her eyes. "Is there a problem with my name?"

"Oh no. It's an interesting name, astronomically speaking."

She narrowed her eyes as she responded. "Are you making fun of my name, Scott?"

"Nope. Just find it interesting. Have you ever washed dishes, Aurora?"

"Yes, Scott, I have." She mimicked him with her own sarcastic tone. What was so wrong with her name?

Again, his brow rose. "I'm sure you've had to do so many dishes, with all those servants lounging about."

"Let's get something straight. I am not pampered. My mother taught me that a little work never hurt anyone. She cares for the house mostly herself, and I grew up helping her."

"If you say so." He led her into the kitchen with a shrug of his broad shoulders. "Let's get started." Pushing open the kitchen doors, the sound of hard rock blasted at them from the speakers. "I'll just turn this off."

"No leave it. I like it." She'd always been a fan of music, every kind, though she preferred the current pop and rock. "Your father was a singer. Do you sing?"

He turned the music down just enough so that they didn't have to shout when they spoke. "Only in the shower." He led her to the mess of dishes. "I'd planned to get some of the regulars to help with these, but, well, now you're here."

He gave her such a bright smile she wondered why he didn't smile like that more often.

"Don't you have an automated washer?"

"Afraid of a little dish-pan hands, *Aurora*?"

She whirled on him. If he didn't stop pissing her off he was going to be in for one hell of a shock. "Stop emphasizing my name like that. So what if my parents gave me a celestial name? I happen to like it. And as for your little comment there, no, I am not afraid of dishpan hands. I simply thought with a facility of this size the owner would be smart enough to equip the kitchen with an automated dishwasher rather than spend his time, which I am sure could be used elsewhere, on doing mounds of dishes." She crossed her arms over her chest and gave him a *take that, jerk* look.

He cleared his throat, and responded calmly. "Yes, I do. It's over there. I didn't mean to offend you. I just wanted to see if you understand how to wash a dish."

She grabbed the bottle of liquid dish soap and aimed hot eyes at him. "Fine, I will prove to you that I am not pampered, but you are going to help." Grabbing a dishcloth, she rammed it solidly into his chest. Firm, she thought with interest. "I'll wash, you dry."

"Look, I'm sorry if I offended you."

"Shut up and dry." She ran hot soapy water and began loading in dirty dishes.

He closed his mouth and did as she asked. After half the pile of dishes was washed, he finally spoke up. "I stand corrected, Blackie, you are a real pro. You're hired."

She turned at the nickname and tilted her head but didn't comment. "I'm hired?"

"Yes, as in a job. If you want it."

She dropped her cloth. Water sloshed everywhere, and she threw her arms around his neck to give him a wet hug. "Thank you! You won't regret this." She finally felt like someone, someone real.

He quickly pried her arms from his neck and took a step back. "Enthusiastic, aren't you?"

She felt the arousal, that ache deep in her gut, warm and liquid and definitely sexual and she wasn't too sure what to make of it. "I won't disappoint you, Scott."

"I'm sure you won't. Can you start tomorrow, say, noon?"

She turned back to her dishes. "I'll be here." Not only did she have a real job now, a job that she could talk about and enjoy, but she was developing a definite crush on her boss.

Life definitely wasn't so bad when the music was loud.

Chapter Eight

"*Y*ou *what?*"

"I got a job at the Monroe Shelter," Aurora repeated as she drank her glass of orange juice. She'd had a long night, between her job with the shelter and working with Satan, but she felt invigorated. What was the big deal if she had a job?

Hunter pulled up a chair beside her and leaned in with a wide-eyed look. "Aurora, you can't be serious?"

"I'm perfectly serious, Unkie Hunter." She patted his cheek with a smile.

He pushed her hand away. "Stop that. He is not going to like this." He shook his head. "Not going to like this at all."

"Oh for pity's sake. Do you have to continually run to my father with every detail of my life? I chipped a nail yesterday, did you tell him that?"

"I wasn't referring to your father, though I'm sure he won't be pleased either. I was referring to the Master."

She slammed her glass down on the table, orange juice slopping over the edge. "I am sick of hearing about him." She despised hearing him called Master.

Hunter shot out of his chair as if he'd just received a jolt of electricity. "Aurora, you need to watch what you say."

She pushed from the table hard enough to have her chair topple over. Snapping her fingers, she held a lit cigarette, and watched the shame-on-you attitude whip onto Hunter's face. "Oh get bent. I'll smoke if I damn well want to smoke and you can run and tell my father, I don't care. It's my life, damn it, and the last time I looked I was an adult."

Spinning around, smoke trailing behind her, she ran from the room, slamming the door as she left. Why couldn't anyone see? It was her life.

 C8

She needed to walk, as she did often when she was frustrated. She liked the feel of solid ground beneath her, liked knowing her steps would tarnish the pavement. She could fly anywhere to be alone, but she didn't want to fly. She wanted to walk. It made her feel human, and she so longed to be one.

Aurora stomped her way down the street, breathing in the air that was stale and humid but feeling as if it were her life. She heard footsteps behind her, and paid little attention to them until she felt the presence inch perilously closer. Spinning around, she was just fast enough to dodge the knife in his hand. She very nearly zapped him into a cryogenic state, until she saw Scott running toward her.

His left leg shot out, knocking the knife from the guy's hand. In a flash, Scott had him and was shoving him face-first into the building beside them. "Are you okay?" he asked Aurora as he held the guy in place.

Aurora swallowed the lump in her throat. "Yes." *Isn't he something?* she thought dreamily. Like a white knight sent to her rescue. And just as she thought that, the guy spun around, pushed Scott out of the way and ran off.

"Damn it!" He turned to her, his jaw clenched. "What the hell are you doing out this late, in this neighborhood?"

It was dark. If it hadn't been for the fact that he was nearly in her face, she wouldn't have seen the whip of temper cloud his beautiful blue eyes. "Taking a walk." She came back with her own temper. "And I'm fine, thank you."

"Taking a—at one in the morning? In an area like this one that is known for its seedier side? Are you stupid?"

She yanked her arm free, spewing nasty at him. "I can take care of myself, you jerk." She flipped her hair behind her shoulder, snapping her head with arrogance.

"Sure you can. That's why you nearly wore a knife in your back."

"Nearly, but I didn't." She spat the words at him.

"Because I saved you."

Her eyebrow shot up. A spurt of laughter slid from her lips. "Oh my hero, whatever would I have done without you?" She gave his chest a good hard shove, once again showing him only a hint of her strength. "You arrogant ass. *I* saved me!" She certainly didn't need a man's protection.

Scott took hold of her arm and shoved her into his car. Scurrying around, he joined her as he climbed into the driver's seat. "We can argue about this elsewhere."

"I don't much care for being manhandled."

"Lucky for you I was there to stop it."

"Stop it? I was talking about you manhandling me, you fool." She wanted to spit fire.

"I didn't manhandle you. Where do you live?"

Crossing her arms over her chest, she snarled. "I can find my own way home, thank you very much."

"You're welcome. Address?"

"Fine, be all macho." She recited her address.

He angled his head slightly so he could look at her. "You're kidding me, right?"

"Why would I kid you?" she spat at him.

"Come on, Aurora. I know you're mad at me, but I'm not falling for that. Where do you really live?"

Her hands balled at her sides, she slipped them into her pocket and conjured up a cigarette and lighter. "I've already told you where. If you don't believe me, that's your problem, not mine." Clicking on the lighter, she drew in as the tip glowed red.

"I hardly believe the daughter of the wealthy Draco Starr would live in such a seedy neighborhood, or that he would let you."

She blew a cloud of smoke forward to have it drift to him. "I live where I choose, and I happen to like where I live."

Turning to her, he snatched the cigarette from her lips and sent it flying out the window.

"Hey!"

"No smoking." He tapped the sign on the dash that clearly stated that.

Huffing, she crossed her arms over her chest. "What the hell is wrong with everyone? I can smoke if I want to."

"Not in my car you're not, and besides, it can kill you." He turned up a deserted road.

"Yeah," she snorted. "Right." He had no idea how untrue that statement was.

Shaking his head, he pulled up in front of her house, coming to a stop at the curb. "Everyone always says that, and when they start coughing up chunks of their polluted lungs they whine and cry about the cigarette companies' lies."

Aurora didn't much care for his preachy attitude. "I can't—" She halted her words. She couldn't exactly tell him her lungs didn't work like humans. "I don't smoke that many."

"Only a few will do it." He climbed from the car, swung around to open her door.

"I can manage from here, thank you," she snapped at him as she exited, deliberately not taking his hand.

He lifted a shoulder. "You're welcome. I don't mind walking you to your door."

Gritting her teeth, Aurora tried to ignore him as she walked up the narrow path to the white, two-story house her father had bought when she'd decided to move out. She was about to tell him where he could put his macho attitude when the door swung open.

"Where have you—" Hunter halted, seeing Scott beside her.

"See, I live here. Hunter, Scott. Scott, Hunter. Now you can let me go."

He nodded to Hunter before turning back to Aurora. "Do yourself a favor, Blackie. The next time you decide to wander the streets late at night, try a vehicle. Less dangerous."

She snarled, stomped inside, and slammed the door in his face. She yanked it open again just as Scott walked toward his car. "And you didn't save my life you jerk. I did!" She slammed the door again and leaned against it. "I don't need saving." But deep inside, she felt she did.

"What was that all about?"

Shooting a heated gaze at Hunter, letting the demon in her slip out, she yelled at him. "Nothing. None of your business. I'm going to bed." She spun around, her hair flying and headed up the stairs.

Chapter Nine

*W*hen she woke the next morning, Aurora's mood was still off. She'd barely finished dressing when her father appeared in her room. Ignoring him, she walked to her dressing table and sat to brush her hair.

Her father simply stared at her in silence.

"Are you just going to stand their glaring at me or are you going to speak?" Aurora said finally, when his stare began to grate on her.

"I wasn't glaring, I was watching." He walked to her, ran his hand down her hair. "You had us all worried last night."

"Hunter and his big mouth."

"He called to ask if you were with us. He was worried. We all were."

Her gaze met her father's in the mirror. "Why? Am I not allowed out of my own home, to come and go as I please?"

"Of course you are. It's just that Hunter said you were quite upset when you stormed out of the house."

She had been, and was quickly getting there again. "You know, I am damn tired of him running to you every time I so much as sneeze."

"We don't sneeze."

Whipping up from the chair, she lashed out as her demon form showed itself. Her face darkened to a bronze tint, her forehead became ribbed and protruded. Her eyes, now red, grew larger and more fierce. And her teeth, as she bared them, would be as sharp as knives. "I'm not joking, and you know what I meant," she tried to calm herself by deep breathing, as her mother had showed her. "I'm a grown woman. Stop treating me like a baby."

"You've been sheltered, little one, maybe too much—"

"Yes," she cut him off short. "No maybes about it."

"We did it for your own good."

"My own good, my ass." Her father's eyes narrowed. "I wasn't even allowed education at a normal school. What were you afraid of, that I would fry some poor student if they pissed me off?"

"In a sense, yes."

She sat on her bed to pull on her black leather boots. "You could have made it better. Cast a memory spell over them."

"How would you have learned if I'd cleaned up after you every time?"

"Bullseye, Daddy." She stood up, ready for a fight. "Yet isn't that what you're doing with me now? You agreed to let me move out, but you still keep tabs on me, my every move. Waiting to see if I slip up so you can leap in and fix whatever it was I might have done wrong." She jabbed a finger at him, saw his temper flash in his eyes. "I can fix my own problems."

"Aurora—"

"No, just listen." She drew in a deep, cleansing breath. "I love you dearly, but for pity's sake, I need to breathe." His watchfulness was going to suffocate her. *Was* suffocating her.

He ran his tongue over his teeth and looked at her as she looked up at him. "Does that breathing include being employed?"

She should have known Hunter would tell him. Walking back to her table, she grabbed an elastic band, and quickly began braiding her hair. "Yes, it does."

"How will you separate yourself? The souls he is trying to save are the very souls you are going to damn."

She drew in a deep breath, held it, let it out. "I just will. I'm not saying this will become my life's crusade, it's just an experience for me. I know you don't understand—"

"No, I think I do. All right, Aurora," He turned her to face him. "I'll back off and let you breathe a little, but Hunter stays."

She'd had a feeling he would say that. "No running to you with every detail of my life?"

"I will tell him to back off." He kissed her head. "Better?"

"Yes." She felt much better.

"If you need me—"

"I know where to find you." Lifting to her tiptoes, she kissed his cheek and smiled. "Now go away. I need to get to work."

ᙅᔆ

Aurora showed up at exactly noon. At least she was prompt, Scott thought as he watched her walk toward him. Her hair was once again braided, and made her already young face look even more innocent. She wore a pair of faded blue jeans that were tight enough to show off every curve of her body. And the T-shirt she wore didn't hide her womanhood one bit. He could still remember how she'd felt in his arms when she'd hugged him for giving her a job. How firm yet soft her breasts had been, how wonderfully intoxicating she'd smelled.

Berating himself—he shouldn't be thinking about wanting to have a nibble of her—Scott drew in a deep breath and checked his watch. "Right on time. Impressive."

"You doubted I would show up?"

"No, you're too determined to prove yourself."

"See, now you're getting to know me." She smiled with absolute sweetness.

She had a way of getting under his skin, deep inside, that left him so unbearably uncomfortable. "I just thought you'd still be mad at me."

She shrugged delicate shoulders. "Lucky for you I don't hold a grudge. What's that for?" She pointed to the mop he held in his hand.

He held it out to her with a sly grin. "The floors. And your first assignment." She took the mop, but not without giving him a heated glare. "Follow me, and I'll show you how it's done."

"I know how to use a mop, Scott," she snarled.

"You should have no problem with this task, then." He opened the door to the dining room. "One of our new-comers indulged in a bit too much at breakfast. As you can see, it didn't sit well." He turned to her, the stench making his stomach turn. Let's see what you're made of, Blackie. "Your job is to clean it up. That's if you can stomach it." He really shouldn't rib her like that, but he couldn't help himself.

"Oh, my." Turning away, she began gagging.

Putting his hand on her back, he rubbed it up and down. "Just let it pass. Breathe through your mouth and you'll be okay." He felt like a heel. He shouldn't have done this to her.

Looking over her shoulder, her eyes glittering with amusement, she smiled wickedly. "Gotcha."

"What the...."

"Sucker." She gave him a hardy shove. "I'm not the squeamish type, Scott. Nice try, but you'll have to do better next time."

He didn't know whether he should laugh or strangle her. He preferred a simple grin. "Okay, you win. I'm a moron."

She patted his shoulder condescendingly. "It's always good to admit your faults." Smiling, she dipped the mop in the bucket of hot, soapy water.

She was something, quite something. "You know what, Blackie? You might just amaze me yet." Shaking his head, he left her to clean up.

⚃

He kept calling her Blackie, and oddly, she rather liked it. Putting her elbow into it, she cleaned up the mess. She could easily wave her hands and the mess would be gone, but she had a point to make, not just to Scott, but to herself as well.

Twenty minutes later, having finished her job, she scouted around for Scott, and stumbled into an elderly man who smelled almost as bad as the vomit she'd just cleaned up. Grabbing him, helping to hold him up, she could tell he was drunk. "Do you need assistance, sir?"

He lifted his wobbly head to look around. "I...where am I?"

Oh yes, he was definitely drunk. "You're at the Monroe Shelter. Do you need help?"

He wobbled, and grabbed hold of her to steady himself. "I don't know. Should I be here?"

Aurora shifted him in her arms. He wasn't heavy, just awkward to hold up. She could feel his bones beneath the ratty shirt he wore and wondered when he'd last eaten. "Yes, I think you do." She looked around for Scott. "You wait here and I'll see if I can find help." But when she sat him on a chair, he pulled out a bottle of drain cleaner. She knocked it out of his hand before he put it to his lips. "What the hell do you think you're doing?"

He scrambled to the floor, licking up the liquid that seeped from the bottle.

"Stop that! You're going to kill yourself." With no effort at all, she lifted him up, one-handed, and set him on the chair. "Stop struggling with me."

"Is there a problem?" Scott inquired, coming up behind her.

"He's trying to drink household cleaner." She held him in place, firmly, with only one hand.

Grabbing hold of the drunk, Scott stepped in front of her. "I've got him now."

"I had him just fine." Seeing he wouldn't let go, she did, and snarled. Kneeling down, she picked up the nearly empty bottle. The drunk lunged for it, almost knocking Scott on his butt. She simply pushed him back. "What is wrong with him? Why would he drink this?"

"It's cheaper than booze. Anything for a buzz, but however diluted, it's still poison." He had to hold the man by both hands. "What's your name?"

The man lifted his heavy head, it wobbled. "I don't know. Can I have my drink back now?"

To remedy it, Aurora dumped the bottle in the trash. "He just stumbled in here. He seemed disoriented."

Scott signaled one of the guards. "Okay now, we'll get you some help." Handing him over to the guard, Scott turned to Aurora. "Are you okay? Did he hurt you?"

"Oh for pity's sake, I'm not frail. Where is he taking him?"

"To the hospital to get checked out. They'll take care of him. Tomorrow, when he's sobered up, I'll go and see him."

"Is that how you do it?"

"In some cases. Some I get off the streets before it gets that far." He touched her arm gently. "In the future, you should leave the tough stuff for me and the guards."

Infuriated, she stiffened her back and glared at him. "Careful, Scott, you're pissing me off."

"When someone high on whatever attacks you, they have the advantage and the strength. You should remember that and steer clear of them."

"I can manage, thank you."

"You're welcome, and I doubt that very much."

"Stop saying that," she growled. That was it. She'd had enough of his macho attitude, his treating her like some frail woman who batted her lashes and cowered in the face of danger. "You don't think I can handle myself? Well, let me show you."

"Come on, Blackie, there's no—" His words were cut off sharply when Aurora grabbed his arm, spun him around and slammed him face first into the wall.

"Take me, Scott. See if you can."

"Blackie, come on, don't be silly. Ouch!" He winced when she shoved his arm higher up his back. "Fine, you want me to show you what these people can do to you, I'll show you." Spinning, he had but a split second to see the grin on her face before she lifted him off his feet and dropped him hard on the ground. Flat on his back.

She climbed onto his chest, legs spread on each side as she held him down. "That, Mr. Smart Ass, is me taking care of myself." Flipping her braid behind her back, she stood up and walked off.

Chapter Ten

She'd had a wonderful day at work. Though most wouldn't consider what she did enjoyable, she did. A little blood and vomit didn't faze her. She was tougher than that. But as joyous as her day job was, her night job was not.

For weeks now she'd worked under the cover of darkness, collecting souls for Satan. She hated it, passionately. Though she hadn't been doing it that long, she'd already grown weary of it. She hated taking people's lives. Hated seeing the look in their eyes as their breath was stolen, as their hearts began to pound rapidly. And she hated having their deaths on her conscience. If only she could quit it, like a regular job. But she couldn't.

"I know," she huffed when the voice grew stronger inside her mind. "I'm going." Lifting off, she sent herself to the vacant lot at the edge of the city. Setting down, she saw the woman up ahead. Slowly, her feet not even touching the ground, she moved toward the woman, and saw with horror just what she was doing.

The knife in her hand shook. The full moon made it shimmer. Closing her eyes, the woman slid it along her wrist.

"No! You don't have to do this!"

The woman jumped. Lifting her head, she gasped. "What are you?"

Do it! the voice screamed inside Aurora's head.

Aurora didn't want to do it, but she was given no other choice.

"Death."

Holding her arms out, the woman wept. "Please take me."

Aurora hesitated as the blood trickled down the woman's arms. Suicide was not the answer. Aurora had had enough. "No, there's help for you. You don't have to end it like this."

Aurora cried out when the piercing pain shot like fire into her head.

Take her!

"But she's so young." The pain had her falling to her knees. Grabbing hold of her head, she pleaded. "Please." She begged for a woman she didn't even know. "Let her go." The slice shot into her, so intense she was sure her head had exploded. "Okay." She cried out, whimpering in pain. "Okay, I'll do it." The pain slipped away, leaving only the memory.

Catching her breath, Aurora stood and looked down at the horrified woman. "I'm sorry." Closing her eyes, because she couldn't watch, she split the artery the woman had begun to sever. Aurora cried as the woman screamed in pain, and as her life drained away, Aurora grieved.

"Why? Tell me why she had to go!"

It is not for you to question, but to deliver.

"But it's a shame to end someone's life so young." The woman couldn't have been much older than she was.

No more! You will do as I say.

Aurora stood up, enraged, her black hair flying out behind her as she stirred up the wind. "I will not do it anymore," she screamed into the darkness and had it echo back at her. It happened so quickly, she barely noticed herself being lifted off the ground. She did, however, notice when she was tossed up against a building with enough power to crack the foundation. She coughed, sputtered as she slid to the ground. But determination was pushing her.

Standing, she sucked in a deep breath, and let it fly. "Is that all you've got?"

The ball of fire, unseen by the naked eye, shot toward her. A demon certainly could see it, and Aurora had only a split second to brace herself before it hit. White-hot lightning slashed into her flesh, burning a jagged line across her torso. Slumping to the ground, she clutched her chest. She understood when she was beaten. "Okay, you win." Her body weak, she sent herself home.

Hunter was busy reading his book when Aurora set down on the floor in front of him. "Oh little one, you didn't...."

"He's wrong. They are worth saving." With that said, she collapsed.

Cʒ

Missy tended to her daughter's wounds while her husband attempted to speak with the Master. He'd been gone far too long and she feared he might never return. It had been their agreement, that if ever her daunting task became too much for their daughter, they would sacrifice their lives for her. Missy feared now her husband was bartering with his life.

"She's healing."

Missy nodded at Hunter and continued to stroke her daughter's face. "It's meant to heal slowly." A message—a strong one—that Satan was still in control.

When Draco finally appeared, Missy instantly ran to him, grateful to have him back. "You've been gone so long."

He cupped her chin in his hand. "You don't just pop in on Lucifer and expect him to see you." He turned his attention to Aurora. "How is she?"

"Resting. Healing. Oh Draco, what have we done?" Burying her face in her husband's chest, Missy wept silently. She never should have agreed to Satan's conditions, however, if she hadn't, she wouldn't have had her precious Aurora. There were no easy solutions.

He tipped her head up and sighed. "We did what we had to for love." He turned back to his daughter. "She's strong. She'll recover from this. There are no permanent scars." Sitting down, Draco stroked his sleeping daughter's hair. "Daddy tried, little one, but he won't budge. I'm sorry."

"He won't let up?"

Draco shook his head, continuing to stroke his daughter's hair. "She defied him. He doesn't take that lightly. She questioned his motives, challenged him. He wouldn't have stopped until she gave in. I'm grateful she did."

Resting her hand on Draco's shoulder, Missy looked down at Aurora. She'd always had spunk, attitude, but not with defiance. She had a free mind. Unfortunately she chose to exhibit it with the wrong being. "She is so much like us, and it's damning her."

"Perhaps this will shake her up, make her realize she isn't invulnerable." He leaned down to kiss his daughter's cheek. "We'll stay with her for a few days until she's stronger."

** og**

Aurora woke to the feeling of a lead weight on her chest and a deep burning sensation. Every breath hurt, every movement was labored. It was an effort to even think of changing position. She hurt. Bone-deep, she hurt. So this was what happened when you pissed off the mighty Lucifer.

Aurora looked down at the scar that ran a jagged line across her chest. It would heal. It would disappear, but not inside. He'd made his point quite painfully. Frowning, she pulled on the slate-grey robe hanging on her door, wincing as she moved. Taking a few deep breaths to ward off the dizziness she was beginning to feel, Aurora headed down stairs. She was very surprised to see her parents sitting at her kitchen table.

"Oh darling, you should have called for help." Up and at her daughter's side, her mother did a thorough search of Aurora's face. "How do you feel?"

"Like I've been steamrolled." She eased into the chair her father pulled out for her. "Why are you both here?"

"You need to question that?"

She turned to her father, her aches and pains putting her in a foul mood. "I just did, didn't I?"

"Honey." Sitting down, her mother tried to smooth her ruffled feathers. "We were just worried about you."

"I'm fine. I messed up, learned a valuable lesson, life goes on." Turning her head, she slanted her eyes at Hunter. "Fink." She should have known he would call them.

"Don't jump down his throat, Aurora. He only did what he thought was best. He called us because he was worried." Her father tilted her face and looked deep into her eyes. "We all were."

She softened as she usually did when her father looked at her as if she were his world. "I know, and I appreciate it. I'm just a little testy. Being tossed about by the big guy doesn't put a person in a cheery mood." She sighed, then turned to Hunter. "I'm starved."

"She's definitely on the mend." Smiling, her mother began to help Hunter with her breakfast.

"Aren't you going to ask me what I did to piss Satan off?" But the look she got told her they already knew. "Okay, what did he have to say?"

Her father sighed. "Just that you defied him and challenged him by refusing to send him a soul." He stroked his daughter's face gently. "Why would you do that, my sweet?"

She thanked her mother for the food she set before her. Taking a fork full of scrambled eggs, she chewed and swallowed before answering her father. "The woman was so young. It just seemed like a waste, an unnecessary waste to end her life."

"Sin has no age barrier, sweetie." He stroked her hair as Hunter went to answer the door.

"I know that, yet still—"

"No, sweetheart, there is no other way. Please, don't do this to yourself. It will only cause you more pain and suffering."

She nodded her head, but inside she still questioned it.

"There's a gentleman here to see you, Aurora. A Scott Monroe," Hunter announced as he entered the room.

She could practically feel her eyes light up. Though she tried to keep her voice even, she felt giddy. "Scott is here? Where is he?"

"Waiting Iin the living room. Shall I tell him you're not up for visitors?"

"No."

"Yes."

She rose carefully from her chair, sending her father a warning look. "I'll see him."

He narrowed his eyes and followed his daughter to the door.

"Scott, what are you doing here?"

"You missed work yesterday and the day before. I was worried."

She turned to her father and the robe she wore parted to reveal her bare legs. "Two days?"

"You slept most of it away." He told her without taking his eyes off Scott.

"Oh." She turned back to Scott. "I'll make up for it. Do you need me tonight?"

"You're not going anywhere. You still need to recover." Her father insisted.

"Recover?" Scott inquired.

"I was…sick," her voice mild, Aurora sent her father some very terse words using her mind. *Back off! I can handle myself.*

"Oh, I hope it wasn't anything too bad?"

"Just the flu. I'm feeling better now, though," she lied with complete sincerity, a smile on her face.

"No, you are not," her father emphasized through gritted teeth. *You need more rest,* he told her telepathically.

"I said I was fine," she snarled.

"Listen, Aurora, if you're not feeling well—"

"I'm fine." She turned to Scott with a bright smile.

"No, she isn't," Draco insisted, his voice low and dangerous.

Aurora sent a spark flying into her father's thoughts and had his eyes widening, not in pain, but surprise. To a demon, that spark was the equivalent of lashing out at her father with a foul tongue. "What is it with men? I said I was fine, and I meant it."

"Okay, obviously I've come at a bad time. I should go."

"No! Scott, wait." She hurried after him, her bare feet slapping on the cool hardwood floor.

"If you're feeling up to it, you can come in for a few hours tomorrow, but don't push yourself. There's plenty of help." Opening the door, he closed it before she could give a response.

Aurora spun on her father, the effort costing her a great deal of pain. "Don't ever do that to me again." Her temper lashing out, she tossed the contents of the room violently about. Letting out a huff, she stormed up to her room.

Chapter Eleven

*B*ecause she'd been summoned, and that was exactly what it was, Aurora couldn't wallow in her room the rest of the night. Satan was very demanding. Dressed in her usual black jeans, black turtleneck, and black boots, Aurora prepared to do her duty. Her body ached. She was beyond tired and her head throbbed. Unfortunately, when she was called she had to go. Taking a deep breath, Aurora stomped down the stairs. She was still fuming at her father and wasn't pleased to see him waiting by the door for her.

"Only children with ill tempers throw tantrums, Aurora."

She should have known he would be waiting. Shooting an intense, deadly look at her father, Aurora went to the kitchen for a glass of blood wine. If she spoke to him now she would only lose her cool.

"Another childish act. The silent treatment."

"Go away, Daddy, before I get mad."

"Haven't you already? And on that note, I've instructed Hunter not to clean up your mess. You will do it manually."

She slammed her glass on the table, making the crystal ring. "You're still dictating my life, treating me as if I were a child."

"If you want to be treated as a grownup, perhaps you should start acting like one," her father pointed out firmly.

"I'm trying to act like a grown up by actually working for a living, which isn't easy to do when you embarrass me in front of my boss."

"You already have a job. You don't need to work at the shelter."

"I want to work there."

"Enough," her mother demanded, appearing in the kitchen just in time. "Draco, go tend to some business." When he glared at her, she waved it off and sent him away. "As for you...." She turned to Aurora, face stern.

"Don't you start." Her eyes narrowed, Aurora lifted the glass and finished off the wine.

"Aurora, you need to settle down."

"Mamma—"

"Sweetheart...." She sighed as she ran her hair down the length of Aurora's hair. "I was young once, too. I know how you're feeling."

"Were your parents overbearing, too?" The instant the words were out, she regretted them. The hurt in her mother's eyes made her feel worse than anything Satan could've thrown at her. "I'm sorry, Mamma. Only Daddy's overbearing."

"My parents loved me dearly, as do yours."

Aurora reached out and touched her mother's arm. "I know you love me. But I'm a grown woman now, not that little girl you both chased around the house before bedtime. Couldn't you just make Daddy see that?"

"I'll see what I can do." She kissed her daughter's cheeks. "It might be best if I wait a bit. I imagine right now he is more than furious with me and I'll be in for a tongue-lashing for sure."

"He loves you." There couldn't be two people more in love than her parents.

Her mother smiled warmly. "I know, and he loves you, too. You mustn't be angry at him for that love."

Pursing her lips, Aurora felt bad for yelling at her father the way she had. "I know. I love him too. I need to get going." She set the glass down.

"Go? But you're still healing."

"Tell that to the big evil guy." She vanished into the night, wishing she could do anything but what she was about to do.

CS

It had begun to rain sometime that mid-afternoon and had yet to let up even though it was now late into evening. A slow, steady stream fell from the dark night sky. Now, at just past midnight, the rain had turned into something more vicious. Aurora wondered if Lucifer had a direct line to Mother Nature. The weather seemed fitting for what she had to do. Lightning flashed a jagged line across a turbulent night sky. Very apt, Aurora thought, as the thunder vibrated the ground on which she stood. Tonight there would be two kills instead of one, she'd been told, to redeem herself.

She had the strangest feeling inside of her that the two souls were only the tip of the iceberg. Satan had something else up his sleeve to show her he was boss. She could feel it. That feeling also told her she wasn't going to like it.

The lightning flashed a white-hot hue and illuminated the house she'd been sent to. Moving closer, Aurora looked though the window. She was cloaked in her invisibility and couldn't be seen.

Inside was a middle-aged man, a bottle of Scotch in one hand, who was yelling at the young boy before him. Slipping through the walls, Aurora stood in the center of the room, watching both father and son.

The father was so angry, telling his son how worthless he was, shouting about how humiliated he'd felt when the police had called him at his office to tell him his thirteen-year-old son had been arrested. In the instant it took Aurora to blink, the man's hand shot up and cracked against the young boy's face. The sound snapped into her. The boy staggered to the floor, blood trickling from his mouth. Then, very calmly, the father knelt beside him. Setting the bottle down, he grabbed the boy by the shirt. Curling his fist into a ball, he lifted it and began pounding it into the boy's

67

face.

Ready to intervene, Aurora moved to help, and felt the hot hand of Satan clamp down on her shoulder. She wanted to scream at the man to stop, but her voice had been taken. She was helpless but to watch the man beat his son.

Finally finished, the father got to his feet, wiped his bloodied fist on his pants, and grabbed his bottle. As he walked off, the young boy sat up. Woozy, he crawled to the couch and pulled himself to his feet. Blood dripped onto the cream-colored carpet, leaving a small pool of red at his feet. Swaying, he walked to the cabinet, opened the door, and grabbed a rifle and a handful of cartridges. His hand shaking, he pulled the bolt handle back, pressed the rounds down, then pushed the handle forward and locked it.

"Get the hell out of my gun case."

Turning the gun on his father, he pulled the trigger. The force of the recoil tossed him back against the case. The father jerked, stumbling back against the wall, as the bullet hit his gut. Clutching his belly, he looked up in shock. The boy staggered to his father and lifted up the rifle. He shot him between the eyes.

Aurora wanted to scream, but couldn't. She felt sick, but was forced to hold it in. Blood splattered across the walls, as if a paintbrush dipped in red paint had been flung there. Flesh, grey matter...the man's head was split open and in complete disorder. He fell to the floor with a huge thud. The boy lowered his gun, stood over his father and watched the blood pool around him.

Now! Take him now! the voice demanded, splitting into her mind.

No, not the boy, she cried back silently as the shadows carried the father away.

Now!

She felt the sharp vibrations from his angry voice reverberate throughout her body. With a hard push she was shoved toward the boy. It was obvious what she had to do and it sickened her. The words screamed inside her head, filling her mind. Knowing she had no choice, hating that she had no choice, she closed her eyes and slid her powers into the young boy's hand. He inserted another round and lifted the rifle to his head. She didn't want to see, but her eyes were forced open. Her body shaking, she watched helplessly as he inserted the barrel into his mouth.

The boy pulled the trigger.

For the first time in her life, she vomited.

It wasn't so much the brain matter that shot out like a missile, or the blood that came and coated the wall behind him, or even the skull that was split open, but the senselessness of it. Falling to her knees, she screamed, loud, feral and with so much pain. It shook the walls, cracked the foundation, and was not drowned out by the thunder overhead. "Damn you!" She had but a moment when she felt herself lifted off the floor and sent to another place.

The instant her feet hit solid ground, she drew in a deep breath of air. Even the rain that soaked her was welcomed. "He was only a child!"

He sinned. He is mine.

"He was being beaten and abused by a drunken father."

A sin is a sin.

She closed her hands over her ears, a useless attempt to block him. Satan couldn't be shut out. "I've done as you demanded. Now go away and leave me be."

There is more.

Her eyes opened, focusing on the dark alley and vacant buildings surrounding her. "What? No!" She saw him stagger into the alley, and recognized him instantly. It was the old man she'd helped in the shelter, the one who had been drinking cleaning liquid. "No, he was going to get help." The electricity from the hand that pushed her forward singed her skin. "Damn you!" The hand clasped hard on her shoulder, making the bones crack under its pressure. "All right, all right, damn it." Taking a few deep breaths, she walked to the staggering man and laid a hand on his bony shoulder. She didn't want to do this, hated having to do this.

He turned to her, blinking rapidly.

"I'm sorry." Closing her hand around his throat, she cut off the air he breathed. They would find him later, determine he had choked to death on his own vomit.

Aurora closed her eyes, unable to watch another human being die. When she felt it, felt his life force drain away, she laid him gently on the ground. She didn't stay, couldn't stay, while the shadows dragged him off. She'd had enough. She was spent, mind and soul.

It was too much. She couldn't do it anymore. Day after day she was forced to kill, forced to watch as people's lives were ended and their souls carted off. Her mind reeling, feeling dirty and low, Aurora set herself down inside a busy club. Wearing a short black leather skirt and a red tank top, she walked to the dance floor.

For now, she wanted simply to forget.

Chapter Twelve

Once a week, Scott liked to tour the clubs. He always picked a different one, a different day. He liked to get a feel of what was out there, know what he was up against so he was better prepared for it. It seemed more and more often, young people were lured in by wild promises of euphoria. And with every passing year, new drugs were making their way to the world with dire consequences. When would people learn nothing came free, and loading your body full of mind-altering drugs for a moment's pleasure would inevitably end in disaster?

He wandered the busy club, sweaty bodies gyrating to the heavy beat of music that played at near-deafening decibels. It made him smile, a memory so fond, it touched his heart. He could still hear his father saying to him, "Son, it's not music unless your ears hurt." His father had liked his music loud, and would have appreciated this club, with its heavy beat and raw style.

He scanned the crowds, keeping an eye out for the bouncers. Some were familiar with him, and weren't too keen with him trying to talk their clients out of a life of misery. So he stayed in the shadows.

He watched a child, much too young in his opinion, indulging in glass after glass of alcohol. She looked way past drunk, and was most certainly high on something. The glaze in her eyes was a dead giveaway. Though the clubs stated no drugs allowed, some always slipped by. Scott watched two young women as they left the washroom, their hands busy wiping the noses they had most likely just filled with cocaine.

So young and so utterly stupid.

About to approach them with his card and the usual speech, he spotted her. He wasn't sure how he'd known it was her when she didn't look anything like herself. Maybe it was the hair. Not many women wore it so long, long enough to graze her backside. It certainly wasn't the clothes she wore, or lack thereof. The skirt should probably be illegal. The top—he didn't want to even go there. It was her, there was no doubt. It was Aurora, and the way she moved to the beat of the music looked damn good.

Her body floated, rolling in such erotic moves it had him swallowing a hard lump in his throat. And apparently, he wasn't the only one affected. As she swayed on the dance floor seductively, men crowded around her.

It was time he put a stop to this.

He stepped into the crowd surrounding her and before he could take control of the situation, she leaned against his chest, wound her arms around his neck, and began gyrating. The curves of her ass, moving against his pelvis, urged his member to attention.

He probably should put an end to this, his mind was all but screaming it, but his body refused to listen. Putting his hands on her hips, he swayed to the beat with her.

Slowly, seductively, she turned, and her eyes widened with surprise. "Scott? Well, you certainly know how to move."

Gathering his thoughts, Scott grabbed her by the arm, and dragged her away.

"What the hell do you think you're doing?"

He didn't answer until they were outside the club and far enough away from the crowds. "Getting you out of there."

She jerked her arm free. "I wasn't ready to leave."

"Well, now you are." When she turned back to the noisy club, he grabbed her arm. Before she could protest, he slung her over his shoulder, getting a perfect view of those gorgeous, shapely legs. Sucking in his lust, he carried her to his car.

"Put me down!" She wiggled, kicking her legs, which he held down for his own safety. "I said put me down!"

He did, but not before he'd unlocked his car. Setting her in the passenger seat, he shut the door and engaged the locks with his key fob. He unlocked his door, climbed into the driver's seat, and was instantly bombarded by her attitude.

"What the hell do you think you're doing?"

He slammed the car into drive and sped off. "Taking you home." His body was throbbing as hard as the beat had been in the club. Good lord, the woman had a body.

"I don't want to go home." She reached for the door, yanked at it good and hard before turning back to him. "Open the damn door, Scott."

"Strong words for a little girl."

She slanted her eyes and hissed a response. "Fuck you. I am not a little girl."

No, he could clearly see she wasn't. The outfit she wore showed off more than was necessary and told volumes of what a woman she really was. Giving his face a mental slap, he ignored her verbal abuse and the attitude. "What the hell were you doing in that place, anyway?"

"Partying, having some fun. At least I was, until you came around."

He swerved around a corner, his temper simmering, his body still vibrating from her touch. "I thought you were sick." She certainly didn't look sick now.

Slipping her hand in her purse, she pulled out a cigarette and lighter. "I was, but as I told you earlier, I'm fine now." She lit the cigarette only to have him snatch it from her lips. "Hey!"

He lowered his window and tossed it outside. "No smoking. You looked like hell earlier and yet now, you look—" He stopped himself before saying what he was really thinking. *Hot.* "If you wanted a few days off, you should have just asked. Pretending to be sick is…childish."

She pulled out another cigarette. "I *was* sick and the only reason I looked like hell was that I had slept for two days without showering, and if you touch this cigarette I'll rip your arm off." Clicking the lighter, she sneered at him.

He had no doubt she would try, and since he didn't fancy getting into an accident, he gave in. "At least blow it out your window so you don't kill me in the process."

She pressed the button and had the window sliding down. "Happy?"

"I'd be happier if you put that thing out." Even with the window open, he could smell it.

Her eyes narrowed. She drew in a huge mouthful of smoke, and blew it directly at him.

Coughing, he reached over, grabbed the cigarette from her lips, and tossed it out the window. "Light up another, and I'll rip *your* arm off," he said with absolute ferocity. Coming to a sharp halt, he turned to her with a sneer. "Now, do I have to walk you to your house or can I trust that you'll go inside and not back to the party?"

"Get bent. Aaahh! I am so sick of people treating me like a baby. I'm a grown woman, for pity's sake."

"All I see is a little girl posing as a grown up." His eyes flicked from her ample bosom to her face and what he saw not only made him want to throw caution to the wind, but forget he was a gentleman as well.

"Is that so? Would you like me to show you just how much woman I am, Scott?"

"No, not—" He'd meant to say *particularly,* but she cut him off by slamming her mouth hard against his. The kiss was a bit sloppy, but it packed one hell of a punch. Her hands slid from his face to his head, digging her nails in and grabbing hold of his hair as she angled her head to take more of his mouth. A raw, nagging punch of desire slammed into him. Forgetting for just one moment what he was doing and whom he was doing it with, he grabbed hold of her waist and pulled her hard against him. He took the kiss deeper.

The faint moan drew him back and he realized what he was doing and with whom. Releasing her abruptly, Scott pushed her away, and gulped in a deep breath of air. The woman certainly knew how to hurt a man where it mattered, and he ached in all the right places. "Go inside, Blackie." *Before I beg you to stay.*

"I'm all woman, Scott. Remember that."

He watched as she slid from the car and swaggered to the house. Oh yeah, she was all woman all right. Unfortunately, she was nine years younger than him. But as he pulled away, he realized quite painfully that he wanted more, age be damned.

◌ß

Aurora opened the door to see a toe-tapping, stern-faced Hunter. He took one look at her attire and shook his head. "Is that the new look for damming souls?"

"I'm not in the mood, Hunter." Her night hadn't exactly been a pleasant one. And just when she thought she might have put it behind her, Scott had shown up. Now she not only was depressed because of the job she was born to do, she had to deal with the vibration of arousal that ached inside of her. Who would have guessed it could hurt so much yet feel so damn good?

"Where have you been?"

"Out!" On high heels that made her feet ache, she marched into the kitchen, Hunter right behind her. She didn't need a damn shadow nagging her.

"You couldn't think to let me know. I've been worried about you."

She spun on him with fierce demand. "You are not my keeper." Taking a deep breath, Aurora turned and yanked the bottle of wine from the fridge. She wished everyone would just let her be all ready.

"Perhaps we should go over the agreement you made when you asked to move out on your own? And don't drink from the bottle."

Giving him a contemptuous look, she tipped the bottle back

and drank. She slapped his hand away when he reached out to take it. "Do it and I'll twist the bones in your body to show you I mean business."

He lowered his hand to his side. "I was concerned, especially after the incident a few days ago."

Grabbing a glass from the cupboard, she poured some wine. "There's no need to worry about me, Hunter. It's not like I'll be mugged or stabbed in some dark alley." Not with her powers, her keen sense of hearing. Grabbing her wine, she waltzed off to the living room. Why couldn't everyone just trust her to do the right thing?

"That may be true, Aurora, but still—"

"Done listening now. Silence." With a wave of her hand, she sealed his lips shut.

He sat down on the sofa beside her, turned, and kept his eyes steady as he stared at her.

"That won't work this time, Hunter. I'm much too keyed up." Wishing him away, she sent him to his room and locked the door. She'd had enough for one day. No one realized just how hard it was for her to do her job, to take the lives of people she was directed to on Satan's word. It was a wonder she didn't go stark, raving mad. Now wouldn't that be a sight? A demon going mad and running rampant on the streets.

And if that wasn't bad enough, now she had jumpy hormones aching for release, all fighting inside of her.

Damn it! Why had she kissed Scott? Now she wanted more.

Chapter Thirteen

She hadn't been told to come in to work, yet she was there. Aurora was finding herself drawn to the place. It wasn't just the people that needed help, it was Scott. And after the previous night's kiss, it was Scott even more so.

She'd spent the night tossing and turning with thoughts of his lips on hers. They'd been so soft, despite the demand of the kiss. Though she'd never kissed a man before, he kissed magnificently. It was unfortunate for her that she also imagined what those lips would feel like sliding along her neck, down her shoulders, and further. She was well aware it was taboo to engage in a sexual relationship with a human. It was an offense punishable by something much worse than death. For that, she'd receive an eternity of life, no powers, nothing.

Yet she couldn't help but think that if a demon hadn't impregnated a human, her mother wouldn't have been born, nor she, for that matter. And although her mother was half demon, she and her father had been made to sign their only born child to Satan for retribution. Simply because part of her mother had been human.

Sighing, she pushed through the doors of the shelter, and saw Scott smiling as he spoke with a young boy. All the reasons why she shouldn't be with him vanished the moment he turned those dreamy blue eyes her way. Even her anger toward him vanished.

The way he was looking at her took her breath away. Her body felt alive. For the first time in her life, she felt alive, and all it had taken was one kiss. One mind-numbing kiss. Holding her breath, she walked to him. It was silly. She shouldn't be feeling nervous or jittery, yet she was. She was surprised the room didn't shake with her tensions. She felt as if she was on unstable ground and at any moment the floor would crack and she'd go tumbling into the darkness.

He stood and greeted her as the child ran off. "I don't recall asking you to come in today."

Stay calm. Breathe. "You didn't, exactly. You said I should come in when I was feeling better, and well, here I am."

"Yes, here you are." He took a deep breath and turned from her. "Let's get you busy."

Did he have any idea how much his voice affected her? It was so deep, so damn sexy and she could literally feel it echoing inside of her, setting off a dozen fires in her loins. She didn't say anything until they were far enough away from the crowds. "Scott, about last night."

"How are you with laundry?"

Okay, she'd let it go, for now. "Is that when you put soiled articles of clothing into a big tub that spills water over them?" When he turned to her, his face captured in utter shock, she burst out in laughter. "I'm joking. Boy, you sure are easy to tease. I know how to do laundry."

"Ha, ha. Joke's on me." He ran a hand through his hair making her body quiver just a bit more.

"Well, I figured since you seem to think I'm some idiotic rich girl who doesn't know anything, why not play the part?"

Scowling, he turned to the stairwell. "I'm beginning to understand that you don't much care for that stereotype."

"Now you're catching on." She followed behind him, watching him more than where she was going. He had a really nice butt, she decided, and felt her skin flush as she watched it move.

"Why is that, Blackie?" Clicking on the lights, he turned her to the left.

"Just because I came from money doesn't make me spoiled or incapable of doing everything everyone else does." She saw where they were going now. "Take you, for example. No one would guess you're worth billions."

He stopped, turned. "How do you know that?"

She lifted one shoulder, smiled slyly. "My father had you checked out."

"Does he have everyone you know checked out before he approves of them?"

"Nope, you're the first." Literally.

"Lucky me." Turning back, he moved them along. "Point taken." Pushing through a swinging door, he entered the laundry room. "You'll find everything you need here. The laundry comes out of that chute so I wouldn't stand directly under it. All you'll need is on that shelf there. Any questions before I leave you to work?"

"Yeah, what's down there?" She pointed to the hall they had just come through.

"My place."

She turned back to him, surprised. "You live here?"

"You seem shocked by that. Yes, I live here."

She shifted her feet, leaning on the wall. "Why?"

"So I can be on call if anyone needs me."

"Can I see it?"

He hesitated as if contemplating her question. "Fine." Pulling his keys from his jeans pocket, he led her back down the hall to his door. "No one is allowed here without my permission." He clicked on the light when he'd opened the door, and stepped inside.

"What's all this for?" A row of computers sat on a curved desk. All the monitors displayed what looked like the upper floor of the shelter.

"Precautionary measures. We had an incident last year that if I'd had the cameras installed, wouldn't have escalated to the degree it had."

She heard something in his voice. Something...sad. "What happened?"

"After lights out, three men, high on everything, cornered an eighteen-year-old girl by the washrooms. They pushed her inside, locked the door, and shoved a rag in her mouth. They took their turns with her, and held nothing back. They raped and sodomized her over and over again." He needed to pause a moment, and she understood his need for time. She could tell how hard it was from him to talk about the incident. It was hard just to listen to it. "If I'd had these, it wouldn't have happened."

"Is she okay now?"

He turned and walked to the adjacent door. "No, Aurora, she isn't fine. When they were done with her they smothered her to death." He unlocked the door and stepped inside.

"They killed her?"

"It's an ugly world out there, Blackie. The more you work here, the more you'll see for yourself."

She'd already seen plenty. The memory of the young boy she'd killed the night before made her stomach ache. "What happened to the men?"

"They got off. Not enough evidence to hold them. Last I heard, they were still free." He pushed the door open, stepped aside. "This is where I live."

He tried to sound callous, but she heard it in his voice. It had affected him deeply and he blamed himself. As she stepped into what appeared to be his living room, she was completely surprised.

The room was done in brown, cream, and taupe. A single sofa and chair sat angled so they could best see the TV that sat in the corner. Not a lot of personal items like pictures, except for the one on the TV. From what she could tell, it was a picture of Scott, his arms around two men. Another two stood behind him. One of them had sandy blond hair and she thought she saw a faint resemblance to Scott in him. "Who is that in that picture?"

"My father and his band. The kitchen is this way."

"What's behind here?" Before he could answer, she threw the door open and the light on. In the center of the room sat a huge bed draped in black silk. It was interesting, but it wasn't what captured her attention. On the walls were pictures of constellations, and to her amusement, a wonderful picture capturing the Aurora Borealis covering the dark night sky. She smiled as she turned to him, her eyes gleaming. "Seems we have something in common."

"The kitchen's this way."

"Why haven't you ever mentioned your love of stars?"

"It never came up. Can we move on? I need to get back upstairs."

He was embarrassed. How sweet. Now, she could play nice and let it go…or press it a little more. It was tempting, but she decided to let it go. "It's nice, very clean. Maid?"

"No, why would I have a maid?"

She ran her finger seductively along the counter that separated the kitchen from the living room. "I just figured, it being clean and all. Why don't you?"

"Why should I?"

"A man with your kind of money could easily afford one."

"Why waste money on the unnecessary?"

"So, despite the fact that you grew up with money, you chose to live like a regular person instead of showing off?"

"I wasn't raised pampered."

She leaned in nice and close, grabbing hold of his shirt, and looked him square in the eyes. "Here's news, Scott. Neither was I."

He took hold of her hands and carefully removed them from his shirt. "You had better get started on the laundry or you'll never be finished."

She'd affected him. She saw it in his eyes. "Don't you simply hate being wrong?" she teased as she turned to the door.

Chapter Fourteen

*A*urora kept herself busy while doing the laundry by reading a book. She pretended to pull it out of her purse when, in fact, she'd conjured one up. She didn't need the cameras picking it up. The story was an edge-of-your-seat thriller that would make the reader wish they hadn't read it, but compelled them to turn the page and read on. There wasn't much that scared Aurora, given who she was and what she did as a night job for Satan. But there were exceptions.

"Lunch break."

The book flew out of her hands as she let out a loud yelp. Now honestly, she was a demon. The last thing she should be is scared. Yet he had her heart jumping like a jackrabbit.

"Oh, God, I am so sorry! I didn't mean to scare you."

"I wasn't scared." One blond eyebrow shot up as Scott smirked at her. "Okay, maybe I was a little startled."

Shaking his head, Scott set the tray he'd carried down to her, on the table beside the washers. "You were scared, Blackie. Face up to it. What were you reading?"

She scooped the book up before he could read the title. "Just some silly horror." She tucked it behind her back. "You brought me food?"

"It's part of the package. You work for me, you get breaks to eat. Sit." He pulled out a chair for her.

Sitting, she lifted the lid on the plate and smiled. "Pizza?" Even a flesh-eating, blood-craving demon loved pizza.

He lifted one shoulder as he took a seat. "Once a week I make it. It seems to go over well."

She lifted the slice and took in the wonderful aroma. "It smells wonderful." She took a big bite and sighed. "You're a pretty good cook, Scott."

"I thank you. Are you nearly done here?"

She swallowed what was in her mouth, licking sauce from her lips. "Almost. Last load's in now."

"You'll be worshiped later when everyone has clean sheets and towels." He lifted one leg and rested his booted foot on his knee. "Tell me why you're doing this?"

"Because you asked me to." She took another bite.

He shook his head. "I meant working here. Why do you do it?"

She licked her fingers clean as she polished off the first slice. "I like my job here."

"But you could get any job you like at any one of the many places your father owns, or anywhere, in fact. Someplace a little more…hospitable."

"This place is hospitable, and I enjoy being here much more than I would some menial secretarial job at my father's offices." Not that he'd ever offered her a job, nor would she ever have taken one.

Scott tapped his fingers on his boot. "I got the impression he wasn't too keen on you working for me."

"He's just overly protective."

"I can see why. A place that deals with junkies and drunks on a daily basis probably doesn't score up there on his rating of what is good enough for his daughter."

"This place isn't as bad as you make it out to be." Sure there were drunks and junkies, but it was clean, quiet for the most part, and respectable.

"You haven't been here long enough to decide that, Blackie."

She angled her head, setting her juice on the tray. "Why do you call me that?"

He gave her long braid a tug. "It suits you."

"You know, the first time I saw you I thought you were an angel." He didn't have to know the first time had been in the alley, and not by his office.

He lifted an eyebrow and gave her an amused look. "An angel?"

"Yes. The blond hair, soft face, your gentleness. The epitome of angelic." She lifted her hands. It had seemed like a decent comparison in her head. Spoken aloud, though, she sounded like a fool.

"I've been called many things, but angel has never been one of them."

"To the people here, you are."

"I'm only a guide, someone to help them see there is a better way. I give them hope that there will be a better way."

"You do a lot more than that, Scott. Don't sell yourself short." The timer on the dryer dinged, she got up and began pulling warm, dry sheets out. Didn't he see how much people valued him, how dependable he was?

"You can go when that's done. Mark down your hours so I know how much to pay you."

"I don't expect payment." She gave the sheet a snap and began folding it, nice and neat.

He stood, gathered up the plates, and set them on the tray. "You work for me, you get paid."

"I'm volunteering." She didn't want his money. She had plenty of her own. Not that she needed much when all she had to do was snap her fingers and could have anything she wanted.

"You said you wanted a job here."

"I do, but not for pay. I want to contribute to helping these people because I think what you're trying to do is commendable, but I don't want payment for it." She pulled out another sheet, gave it another snap.

He shifted his feet, giving her a very interested look. "Volunteering?"

"Yes, is there a problem with that?"

He shook his head. "No, if that's what you want, that's what you get." He turned to leave. "Catch you later, Blackie."

She smiled as she folded the last of the laundry.

CB

Having finished the laundry, Aurora carried the full basket up the stairs. Though Scott hadn't said for her to do it, she wanted to. Heading up the stairs, she heard it. Whimpers, tears, people crying, crowding her mind before she even stepped foot in the lounge area. Setting the basket down, she walked toward the sounds.

"You don't need to do this, Ed. Just put the gun down and we can talk."

Standing with his back to her, his hands in the air, Scott spoke softly. As she moved to the side, she saw the man, dressed in grubby jeans and a weathered plaid jacket. In his hand, pointed directly at Scott, was a gun. To the side of the room, innocent people huddled together, trembling, crying as they watched the scene unfold before them.

"Not until I get what I want. I know you keep a stash here. If you want to live, you'll get it for me." His hand shook as he held the gun.

"You know I don't carry any drugs here, Ed," Scott responded calmly.

"Bullshit. You have some somewhere, for emergencies. Your old man had some around. I want it, now!" His hands shook as he held the gun aimed at Scott. "One quick fix and I'll get out of your hair."

"How long has it been, Ed?"

He wiped his shaking hand across his face. The other still held the gun out, aimed at Scott's chest. "Too long. Couple of days. I'm hurting, Scott. Just give me one, okay? Just one," his voice quivered.

"I can help you, Ed, but you need to put the gun down first."

"No way in hell, not until I get what I want."

Aurora stood and watched. She'd never seen an addict on the edge before. She could smell his fear, and the sweat that was beginning to soak through his shirt and pants. Dipping into his mind, she read his intentions clearly. He wasn't leaving without getting what he wanted, and he was more than ready to kill everyone for it. She had to do something to stop him.

She couldn't take his life, not without asking for permission first. She could sedate him, give him a heart attack, but would he still manage to get a shot off if she did? She had to try something. But when she tried to use her powers, she realized they were blocked. It didn't take her long to figure out who it was that held them back.

Let me end this before anyone gets hurt, she spoke inside her mind.

Leave it be! Lucifer ordered, still holding her back.

No, I can't. Too many innocent people will get hurt. I need to help them.

Why take one when there are so many more for the taking?

No, you can't do this. They're innocent people. Closing her eyes, drawing on all the strength she could find, she broke the hold. Opening her eyes, she focused on the man with the gun. She needed to make it quick before Satan took her over again. Centering her intent on Ed, she dipped into his mind and made him raise his weapon hand to his head. And made him pull the trigger.

Everything happened so fast.

"No!" Scott cried as he rushed to Ed's side.

Aurora stood back in tears as Scott stared down at the bloody lifeless body of a patient and friend. He couldn't know the shadows were coming to take the soul away. She wanted to go to him, comfort him, but before she could take one step, Aurora felt the slice of heat scorch her.

Dizzy, she fell to the floor, trying to breathe.

Never disobey me!

She lifted her head and found herself in a dark room. If she didn't know better, she could've sworn she was standing in the center of a large black void. "I couldn't let you take innocent lives." The flash of blinding white light shot out, piercing her vision. She could handle that. It was the zap of electricity that followed, spiking into her like a dozen sharp knives.

Crumbling, she felt the air clog in her lungs. Her chest felt heavy and on fire. Her head exploded with pain.

Never defy me again or you will pay in the worst way.

Before she could blink, she was shot back to her room, her equilibrium a mess. Gasping at the air that suddenly filled her lungs, she began to gag. Curled up on the floor, she waited out the pain. Satan might have the power, but she still had her mind, and what he'd wanted to have happen in that room tonight she would never agree with. And, she was proud to say, she had stopped it. Stopped *him*.

Closing her eyes, she slept the pain away.

Chapter Fifteen

*W*aking the next morning, Aurora could still feel the sting of Satan's fury. Aside from the fire in her chest, it felt as if she'd been sucker-punched by a wrecking ball. The pounding in her head had a damn good beat, if it wasn't so annoying.

It was a strong message. Satan certainly had a temper. Rubbing her chest, she decided today would be an exception. Today she would be demon. With merely a thought, she dressed herself in a pair of cream slacks and a coral blouse. A glance in the mirror told her it might be best to wear her hair down. Her face was a tad bit red, and looked as if she'd been in the sun a few hours too long. Another gift from Satan as a reminder not to piss him off. Frowning at her reflection, Aurora decided a light coat of make-up couldn't hurt, either.

It was a toss-up which to use, her feet, or just materialize where she wanted to go. She was much too exhausted to move and even the thought of walking tired her out. So she went with the latter and sent herself downstairs into the kitchen. Where she expected to find Hunter in his usual spot at the table, waiting for her to wake, she found only her mother.

"Mamma, what are you doing here?" Leaning down, she gave her cheek a tiny peck. She always smelled of the coconut lotion she wore. It was a comforting smell.

"I decided to do some baking." She stood and walked to the

oven to check on her cookies. "I thought I would bake enough for you to take to this shelter you seem so smitten with."

As far back as she could remember, her mother had baked for the needy. Cookies, cakes, meals, she did it all. It was her way of contributing to the life she'd once led. "That's very nice. I'm sure everyone will appreciate it." Stealing a gooey chocolate treat from the table, Aurora leaned against the counter. As usual, the cookies were incredible. Aurora wondered how many other demons sat around eating cookies, or other human foods.

"At least have some milk with it to make it somewhat of a balanced breakfast." She handed Aurora a chilled glass. "You look tired."

Aurora rubbed a finger under her eyes, frowning. "A little, maybe." She didn't need to know why.

"You're working too hard." Her mother turned at the sound of the oven timer and pulled her cookies from the heat to replace them with another tray.

"I'm fine. Where's Hunter?" Aurora had a feeling there was an ulterior motive for her being here, and was using baking as a ruse.

"I gave him the day off. You tend to be a bit of a handful to look after." She smiled at Aurora.

"I don't need anyone looking after me. I'm a grown woman, and if that's the only reason you're here—"

"Whoa, calm down." She laid a hand on Aurora's shoulder. "I came to spend time with my daughter. I miss you, miss having you at home. The place is too quiet with you gone."

Aurora sighed, dropping her shoulders. Boy did she feel like an idiot now. "I'm sorry. I miss you, too." She plunked down in a chair at the table, feeling awful for lashing out.

Missy sat beside her, resting her hand on Aurora's. "It's not easy for a mother to let her only child leave the house she thought would be her child's home for the rest of her life. I worry about you."

"I had to move out sometime, Mamma, and there's no need to worry, I'm doing just fine."

"You're too young to be on your own."

"You were younger than I was when you moved out of your parents' home."

"Yes, but I didn't move out on my own. I was married."

Aurora didn't know exactly what had happened to her mother's first husband, only that it ended badly and had caused her to sever ties with her family. "I'm not on my own. I have Hunter." She patted her mother's hand, seeing how the mention of her previous life upset her. "Do you ever think of your family, miss them? Regret what you did?" Aurora wouldn't admit it, but the idea of having relatives, aunts, uncles, cousins, out in the world, intrigued her.

"I miss them, sure, but I did what was necessary."

Aurora took a fresh, hot cookie from the sheet that had just been removed from the oven. "You don't even wish, even for one moment, that you had never found out who or what you really were, that you're a demon?"

She took her Aurora's face in her hands. "No, never. Do you wish not to be demon?"

She looked down at the cookie in her hands. How would it feel as a human, not to have to feed on raw meat and blood? Being normal. Yes, she wished exactly that. "Sometimes. There are times I wish I could be like all the other women in the world, able to love whom I choose." It was a depressing thought that the only man she could ever be with would have to be demon. She didn't want a loveless marriage. She wanted a marriage like her parents had.

Loving.

Her mother stood behind her, played with her long dark hair. "I once wished I wasn't a demon, but I soon learned how great it was."

Aurora rose to pour herself some more milk. "Would that be so bad, really, being with a human?" She remembered the way Scott had tasted, felt when they'd kissed. She would give up everything for that.

"Yes, darling, it would be. You would have no powers, yet never age. You would witness everyone you know die, see the world change, knowing that there would never be and end for you, walking the earth alone, going from place to place. It would not be a life I would want for you."

Why didn't anyone ever ask her what she wanted for her life? "But so much of that is how we live now."

"Yes, but we have powers."

"I don't see the difference."

Missy sighed. "There is a big difference."

Aurora pushed from the chair. "How? We still live for eternities, watch everyone we know die, the world changes, how is it different?" She didn't see it.

"You would be constantly reminded of what you once had, what you once could do, to fly at will, to snap your fingers and have anything you want. Without that you are half a person, at best."

"I would think, for love, it would be worth it." Not wanting to argue any more, she sent herself soaring.

Chapter Sixteen

*T*ime seemed to go a lot faster when you had something you enjoyed doing. For Aurora, the time since she'd begun working for Scott at the shelter had flown right by. The job was messy, sure: dirty dishes, dirty laundry, dirty floors. Dirty, dirty, dirty. But she enjoyed every moment of the filth she cleaned up.

It was what a normal human would do for a living, and she so longed for an ounce of normalcy. Since her discussion with her mother, Aurora gave serious thought to why she needed her powers. Most of the time she simply forgot they were there at her disposal. Instead of snapping her fingers and transporting herself to where she wanted, she walked or took a bus. Whether it was midnight or midday, she walked. She had no fear.

More and more she found herself forgetting to eat the usual ration of raw meat and blood her body required and had thrived on for twenty one years. Human food was much more interesting, and tasted a hell of a lot better.

Having finished a full eight hours of work at the shelter, Aurora felt tired but happy. She had five hours before her night job with Satan would begin. She hated the fact that she couldn't terminate that position, but after the last incident, she had no other choice. Satan played dirty, and he liked to win. So she reluctantly worked for him, resenting every moment of it.

She heard the car in the distance, but didn't pay much attention to it and continued walking. When it pulled up beside her and slowed down, she finally glanced over.

"What are you doing?"

Her face instantly lit up as she walked to Scott's car. "Walking home. What are you doing?"

"Looking at an obviously stupid woman. Get in."

Scrunching up her face, she opened the door and slid into the passenger seat. "I don't care for that crack. I am not stupid."

He shifted into gear and pulled away from the curb. "Any woman that walks alone on a dark, dangerous street after dusk is, in my opinion, stupid."

"Gee, Mr. Monroe, do you flatter all the ladies with such endearing words, or am I the first?"

He shot her a not so nice sneer. "Where is your car?"

"I don't have a car." She shifted in her seat, trying to get comfortable.

He glanced over briefly before turning back to the road. "Come again?"

She turned to Scott and spoke slowly, spacing each word she said. "I. Don't. Have. A. Car." She bit back the grin when she saw his knuckles strain on the steering wheel.

"I assumed you owned a car, smart-ass. How have you been getting home from work all these nights?" he turned up the street to her house.

"I walked."

His head jerked to her, his eyes wide. "Did I hear you correctly? You walk?"

She nodded. "Yes, Scott, you heard me correctly. Are you deaf or something? I walk. W-a-l-k." She spelled it out for him. Leaning in, she turned up the radio when a favorite song came on.

He leaned over and turned it down. "I hear just fine, at least I did until you turned that up."

"That wasn't loud. This is loud." Cranking up the volume, she had the bass booming and was amused at the startled jerk from Scott. Leaning over, she turned it back down while he scowled. "See the difference?"

"That was funny, real funny. You're quite something, Blackie."

"You don't know the half of it. Where are you going?" She recognized her street.

"I'm taking you home."

She frowned. She was enjoying his company. "Do you have to? We could go somewhere, say, for a coffee or something." She wasn't looking forward to going home to watch TV and eat whatever Hunter had cooked up for her, and wait for Satan to call her to duty.

He paused, and she thought he was about to say no when he spoke up. "Sure, why the hell not?" He turned up the next street and headed away from her house.

"See, there you go again with the sweet talk. Keep it up, Scott, and I'll be a puddle at your feet."

His laughter rumbled out, making her heart speed up just a bit more. "You are definitely something. I'm not too sure what to think of you, though."

The car came to a stop at a tiny roadside dinner. "Do you think of me often?" She thought of him, dreamed of him. Did he do the same?

"I try not to. It gives me a headache." He slid from the car and walked to the coffee shop doors.

She hurried to catch up with him. "Such a gentleman. Your charm is staggering."

Shrugging, he opened the door and slipped in before she could.

Smiling, she followed him. Okay, so he wasn't quite the white knight she'd once envisioned him being. But that didn't halt the feelings she was developing for him.

He chose a booth near the windows. She sat across from him. "Charm is overrated. He smiled at the waitress as she approached the table. "I'll have a cup of tea, plain." He turned to Aurora.

"Chocolate milkshake, extra chocolaty." She shrugged at Scott's lifted brow "What's the point of sinning if you don't do it to extremes?"

He rolled his neck, leaned back in his seat. "I suppose you're right."

He looked comfortable. She wanted him comfortable around her. "This is nice. We never just get to sit and talk."

He nodded with a shrug. "You're right, we don't."

She leaned back, like him, getting comfortable. "Tell me about yourself."

He toyed with the napkin. "You already know who I am."

"I know what you do. Who you are is a completely different story. Fill in the blanks for me."

He smiled again when the waitress brought their drinks. He dipped the tea bag into the steaming hot water in his cup as he spoke. "My father was a rock legend, which enabled me to travel a great deal. I think I've been practically everywhere. I grew up on the road, grew up with the music. I even began toying with a career as a drummer."

"Really? How fascinating. Why didn't you?"

He laid the used tea bag on a plate and stirred the tea. "I had other ideas."

She sucked the rich, dark chocolate through the straw, keeping her eyes on him with interest. "And what might those be?"

"A doctor."

Always the humanitarian, she thought sweetly. "Should I be calling you, Dr. Monroe?"

He shook his head as he sipped from his tea. "No, I prefer Scott. I couldn't finish my internship. My father grew ill and needed my help."

"Where was your mother?"

"She died when I was three. My father raised me."

"So you and your father must have been really close?"

He nodded as he lifted the cup. "Very close." He took a sip.

"So, you gave up your career to further your father's dream?"

He tilted his head. "Yes. Your turn. Who is Aurora Starr?"

You wouldn't believe me if I told you. "A woman." She smiled teasingly.

"That's obvious. Did you go to college?"

"Nope." She sucked up more shake, licking the chocolate from her lips.

"Why not?"

"I had no inclination to do so." She hated lying, was so desperately sick of lying. But she couldn't exactly tell him she'd been born a demon and was destined to work for Satan.

He leaned back, one arm draped over the seat. "So you were content to sit around and spend Daddy's money?"

Her back straightened her defenses coming up. "I didn't spend my daddy's money and I sure as hell didn't sit around. I helped my mother with a great many charity functions, volunteering to help feed the homeless, visiting the burn units to lift the spirits of the victims of the aftermath of a fire. Haven't you got it yet, Scott? I'm not a spoiled rich brat." She stuck the straw in between her lips and fumed, her eyes looking down to hide her hurt. She'd thought he knew her better by now.

"I'm sorry, Blackie. I didn't mean it like that. Maybe I should have spoken to you about setting up a function for the shelter before I hired the evil bitch monster."

"I've heard talk around the shelter about the ball. I take it things aren't going well?"

He set his cup down and frowned. "The planner tells me everything is going fine, then asks me for more of a budget so she can plan it properly. In her exact words, 'This isn't a rinky-dink party, Mr. Monroe. If you wanted simple, you shouldn't have hired me.'" He shook his head, closing his eyes on a sigh. "The woman is maddening."

Aurora laughed. She could picture Scott nodding patiently, all the while screaming at her in his mind. He was a cool one, but she had a feeling in private he let himself loose. "And yet you hired her."

"She's the best party planner in the city. She gives me a headache." He squeezed the bridge of his nose. "I hate these things, passionately."

"They're not that bad."

He snorted a laugh. "I can feel the wrinkles and gray hair taking over more and more every day I have to deal with it." He shook his head as he lifted his cup.

Smirking, she patted his hand. "They make hair dye and wrinkle cream for men, you know."

His blue eyes lifted and twinkled as a grin slowly formed across his mouth. "You're such a help. Will you be attending?"

She toyed with the straw in her shake. "I haven't received an invitation."

"I'm told they're being sent out this week. You and your parents are on the list." He took a sip from his cup. "You can bring a date if you like."

"If I had one, I would definitely bring him."

"Don't feel bad, I don't have one either."

She leaned her arms on the table and grinned slyly. "Want to go together?"

"A real modern woman. So rare to find these days. Okay, Blackie, why not? We can go together."

Shaking her head, she leaned back, smiling. "I'm telling you, Scott, you have to stop this flattery or I'll be a mess." She loved it when he smiled. It made his dimples even more prominent. "I'm amazed women aren't falling at your feet."

"Smart ass!" he laughed as he lifted his cup.

"Can I get the two of you anything else?"

Aurora scented it, like a hot meal arousing the hunger of a starving person. Her stomach clenched, her blood began to boil and she felt like a million ants had decided to picnic inside her body. Turning, she saw the bandage on the waitress's hand, with obvious signs of blood beneath it. She quivered, grabbed the woman's wrist and nearly put it to her lips, before she realized where she was. "You're bleeding."

The waitress yanked her hand free and glared down at Aurora as if she were insane. "Yeah, it happens when you cut yourself."

"We're fine, thanks." Scott waited for the waitress to leave before he leaned in to her. "Are you okay? Did the blood make you queasy?"

Anything but. Her body ached for the blood. She had to curb herself before she gave herself away. "Yes...no. No, I don't feel well." Lifting from her seat, she tore out of the coffee shop and vanished into the night.

Chapter Seventeen

Setting herself into her foyer, Aurora raced to the kitchen, nearly running Hunter down. Yanking the fridge door open, she grabbed the bottle of blood and gulped it down.

"Late-night munchies?" Hunter leaned against the counter, crossing his legs at the ankles. "Forget your manners, did you?" He handed her a glass.

She licked her lips. Dropping the bottle on the table, she let out a breath. "That was too damn close." She could feel her body leveling out. It felt good, and Aurora realized she'd starved herself for too long. Reality was a hard thing to deal with when she'd been so happy living in her fantasy world. There was no denying the fact. She was a demon.

Grabbing the cloth from the sink, Hunter mopped up the spill she'd managed when she slammed the bottle on the table. "What was close?"

"I haven't been eating properly lately. I simply forgot to. I very nearly devoured some poor waitress tonight because I haven't been taking care of myself." And she hated it! Hated the thought that she wanted to drink a human simply for the taste. She so desperately wanted to be human, it ached deep inside.

Hunters hand stilled mid wipe. He angled his head. "Tell me you didn't?"

"I said nearly. Weren't you listening?" What was with men?

Were their ears all plugged, or what?

"Yes, but did you show yourself to her?"

"Of course not, Hunter. I'm not that stupid. I can control myself." She turned at the sound of the doorbell. "I'll get it." Feeling better than one-hundred percent, Aurora bounced to the door. Her face lit with surprise when she opened it. "Scott?"

He grabbed her arms and pulled her to him, nearly lifting her off her feet. The look in his eyes was so intensely concerned it astounded her. "Are you okay?"

"Yes."

"Oh, thank God." He released her and began rubbing his hands up and down her arms in a slow, soothing motion that did little to soothe and everything to arouse. "I got so worried when you disappeared."

"What?"

"At the coffee shop, you ran out so fast I couldn't catch up. How did you get home so fast, though?"

"I...uh caught a cab. One was waiting outside when I got there." She swallowed the lie.

"Oh, well." He released her, took a step back. "Are you feeling better, then?"

Aurora didn't want him to let her go. She wanted him to hold her forever. "Yes, thank you." *No, I'm all tied up inside and only you can release the knot.* "You didn't have to come all the way over here to ask me that. You could've called."

"I needed to see you—I mean, I wanted to see you in person, to make sure you were all right."

"That was nice." Leaning in, she nipped at his lips before he had time to realize what she was doing. She felt warm all over from that simple little kiss. When she pulled away, he grabbed her arms roughly and yanked her back so fast, the air burst out from her lungs in a gasp. She felt a fire burning so deep she couldn't douse it even if she tried. His lips caressed, searched, nibbled, and she gave. Her hands slid from his arms up to his face before cruising through his hair. She'd never felt anything so intense before, not even the hunger for blood was this strong. She could drown in him for a lifetime.

When he suddenly stepped back, she was left with an emptiness so great it made her knees weak.

"Oh, God! I'm sorry."

"Why on earth would you be sorry? That was the most incredible thing I have ever experienced." How could he be sorry for igniting the passion that had been buried deep for so long?

He took another step back, bumped into the wall. "It shouldn't have happened."

"Why not?"

"It just shouldn't have. I'd better go." He turned to leave.

"Scott, wait!" Hunter cleared his throat startling her. Spinning around, she saw the narrowed eyes, the lift of his brow, his disapproving face. "Don't start."

"You know that is forbidden."

"Shut up." She didn't want to hear it. She only wanted to enjoy the moment.

"Aurora, this can't go on."

She waved her hand and turned him into a braying donkey. "Let's see you run to Daddy now." Leaving Hunter stomping his hooves, she hurried up to her room.

Closing her door, she leaned against it and drew in a breath, long and slow. She felt giddy and her body was quivering. She wanted to jump up and scream and laugh. She'd had moments of attraction to the usual actors and singers on TV, but it was nothing compared to what she felt now. How was she supposed to function when he was floating in her veins, pounding in her heart, echoing in her head? She could taste him, feel him, smell him.

His hands had held her so tightly, pressing her to his chest and aroused her beyond comprehension. His lips hadn't been easy, smooth, or sensitive this time. They had devoured, taken, plundered. Why did he have to stop? She wanted him so badly now that if she didn't have him, she would explode. One time wouldn't hurt. Would it?

She nearly screamed when the voice echoed in her mind.

It is time.

"No, no. Not now."

NOW!

She closed her eyes, willed her system to level off, and sighed. "All right. Where to tonight?" As she was lifted and taken to her destination, she wondered what Scott would say if she showed up in his bed.

She set down in a dark alley, tall buildings beside her. She saw the young man leaning against the wall, smoking a cigarette. Boy, she wanted one of those now. "Why him?"

The vision speared into her with intensity that rocked her soul.

"You tell anyone what happened here, and I'll cut your dick off."

On the bed, a boy of about ten years old lay naked and shivering.

"What an added bonus. I get paid for this." The young man patted the boy's leg. "If your parents only knew they paid me to fuck their precious little boy while I babysat him." Laughing, he exited the room, leaving the boy crying.

She wanted to vomit. Whisked back to the present, Aurora swallowed the bile in her throat. Staring at the smug young man as he puffed on his cigarette, counting his money, she felt sick. Aurora hated that there was so much horror in the world.

Stepping closer, her long black hair flapping in the wind, she transformed into her beast form. As she neared him, she watched him get to his feet, an obvious gleam in his eyes. He wanted more, she could feel it vibrate off of him, and he intended to get it. He would be sadly mistaken.

"Well now, hello, pretty lady." He sauntered toward her, dropping the cigarette at his feet. "This must be fate, you showing up all alone like this." Grabbing her arm, he jerked her closer, making her long, black hair hide her face. "Let's play."

She let him think he was about to have his way, let him push her up against the wall, his hands gripping onto her arms. The wind stirred up at her will and parted the hair from her face.

He jumped back, shocked at what he saw.

"What's the matter, Danny? Don't you want to play?" She

clutched his arms and held him in place.

He tried to break free of her hold but she was much stronger than he. "Oh now, don't be that way. I only want to play with you." She lifted him off his feet, his eyes wide and frantic. Releasing her hold, she left him dangling in mid air. "You like forcing yourself on little boys, do you? You make me sick."

"Please, don't hurt me."

"Why should I give you mercy when you gave none to that little boy you robbed of his innocence?"

"What the hell are you?"

"Your worst nightmare."

She stepped back and, while she held him captive with her stare, she clamped on to his heart using only her mind. He let out a strained cry, gasped as he clutched his chest. Aurora felt it as it happened, his heart, his body, as it was taxed beyond its means. Just before his life ended, she smiled, and set him on the ground. "Die."

She stepped back as the shadows of death fell. She watched as they dragged his soul away.

You truly are great, my child. In no time you will be my best.

The voice inside her head rumbled with pride. Looking down at the lifeless body, she suddenly realized what she had done. And the joy she had felt doing it.

"No! No! No!" she cried as she sent herself soaring.

Chapter Eighteen

*S*leep had not come easily for her. Her mind had played the scene from the night before, over and over again. And the pride she'd felt from Satan sickened her to the point that she felt nauseous. She was not proud of what she'd done, despite the vile action the young man had taken upon the innocent child. Feeling less than jovial, Aurora slunk downstairs to grab something to eat.

Stopping short when she got to the living room, she nearly burst out in laughter. There was Hunter, glaring at her through donkey's eyes. He didn't look amused at all. Despite his discomfort and utter rage, she felt the simple action lifting her spirits.

"Oops."

Chuckling, she cast a spell to remove the curse of the donkey and make Hunter human once more. She'd simply forgotten about him. She'd been too busy hating herself for her actions. "Before you start jumping all over me, let me say—"

"You"—he literally vibrated with anger—"don't get a say." He drew in a deep breath. "You are just damn lucky you are too old to be put over my knee." He gave his black jacket a sturdy tug.

She wanted to grin, but bit her tongue to prevent it. "You've never once raised a hand to me, Unckie Hunter." Oh, the rage that filled his eyes at the cute nickname she'd given him would be enough to make anyone cower. Aurora simply stood her ground.

"There is always a first time for everything."

Seeing he was truly miffed at her, Aurora decided to smooth his ruffled feathers and walked to him. She leaned in and gave his cheek a peck. "You love me too much to hurt me."

"Don't ever, ever do that again," he warned her, giving her bottom a sharp slap with enough of a message to make her eyes widen. When she glared at him, he smiled, the lines on his face spreading. "Don't be angry. I did it with love."

Smarting, she rubbed her backside. "Yeah, I can feel how much you love me." It didn't hurt as much as surprised her. She was a grown woman receiving a spanking, however gentle it was, from the man that had helped raise her. She was mortified.

He gave his jacket another tug. "Hungry?"

She frowned at him. "I am sorry, you know. I just simply forgot about changing you back."

"But not for making me an ass in the first place, and before you come up with some smart remark to what I just said, might I remind you of the slap I gave you moments ago and how there's plenty more where that came from."

She narrowed her eyes at him. "Spoilsport." Huffing, she walked to the kitchen. "Was it so bad, really?" The look he gave her could have leveled a building. "Okay, geez. I was just asking." She took a seat at the table.

Hunter began preparing her breakfast. "Despite my risking being turned into another four-legged animal, might I ask what you intend to do about that young man you were lip-locked with last night?"

She rested her feet on the chair beside her and got comfortable. "I have no idea what you're talking about."

"Aurora." The authority Hunter used had always snapped her into shape. He had an uncanny way of using his voice to mean business. "I saw the kiss."

She fumed at his back. "Of course you did, because you're a nosy old man."

"Being nasty won't distract me from my mission, young lady." He turned, giving her a stern look.

"All right. Man, you're persistent. I kissed him. Big deal." And what a kiss it was. She could still feel it, taste it and wanted it more and more.

"It is a big deal, Aurora, you—"

"Hey, if I wanted a lecture I would go see my father." She narrowed her eyes at him. "Is breakfast ready or do I have to whip something up myself?"

He slammed the plate down in front of her. "It's ready. Just how you like them, runny."

She looked down at the half-cooked eggs and grinned. "Yummy."

"We're not done with this conversation."

She waved her hand at him as she swallowed her eggs. "Don't make me turn you into something worse than an ass, Hunter."

Throwing his hands in the air, he stormed off.

As she ate her eggs, Aurora wondered how long it would take for her father to show up.

ଔ

The moment Aurora stepped into the shelter she heard the commotion. Drawing closer to the activity, her ears perked up.

"I'm telling you. She wasn't no human."

Betty, one of the women who was a regular to the shelter rolled her eyes and went on knitting without looking up at him. "Oh, Gus, you were just drunk."

"I wasn't so drunk I couldn't see, and I tell you, I saw plenty." He had dozens of questions thrown at him all at once. "She had wings, big black wings that flapped behind her. Her hair was so long it dragged on the ground. When she spoke it was like she was growling. Her face was funny, animal-like, and she shot lasers with her red eyes."

Betty let out a hoot of laughter that had everyone turning. "Oh come on, Gus, lasers?"

"She had great powers, unbelievable powers."

"What did she do?" Someone asked from the crowd.

107

"She lifted that boy right off his feet like he was a tissue. She let him go, but he still hung in the air. His feet were well above the ground, just hanging there on his own."

Aurora stood in shock as she listened to Gus explain what he'd seen. She had no idea someone had been watching her, but the detail—aside from the wings and laser eyes—were too accurate to have been made up.

"Oh, Gus. What an imagination you have."

He scowled at Betty. "You got nothing better to do, old woman?"

"Nope." She continued to knit while everyone focused on Gus.

He turned back to the crowd. "I couldn't see what exactly she was doing to him, but he was screaming like she was torturing him. Cops say he died of a heart attack."

"Big deal."

"He was eighteen and never had heart trouble a day in his life."

"You were friends then?"

He snarled once more at Betty. "No, it said so in the papers." He turned back to the crowd. "Looks like the Dark Angel strikes again."

Aurora left them to their discussion. She saw no harm in it. They didn't know it was her. She felt a bit of amusement in the way he had described her. She was no angel. Thinking again about the young man, she sighed.

"Feeling better?"

Startled, she turned to see Scott behind her. "Much," she lied.

"Made it through the wall of gossipers, I see."

"Barely. Interesting tales, though."

Scott nodded as he turned to the kitchen. Opening a cupboard door, he held up a cup to her and when she shook her head, he filled it for himself. "Gus claims to have seen her and of course he's soaking up the fascination and attention from everyone. I just wish it would all die down. Dark Angel." He shook his head.

"You don't believe she exists?" Leaning against the counter, she watched his expressions change. He was so handsome it took

108

her breath away.

"The dark plays tricks on your eyes, makes people think they see something that isn't really there."

"Like a mirage in the desert?"

"Exactly, and given the fact that most of the people that have seen her have been either drunk or stoned, it doesn't say much for their story."

How wrong you are. "So, what's on the agenda for today, boss?"

He sipped from his cup. "Hmm, I don't really know. I was up most of the night working on details the maniac of a party planner left on my desk. I haven't even had time to check the place. Guess I'm a little disorganized."

She moved in closer to him, smiling with ease. "You look pretty good for someone who's been up all night." She ran her fingers along the lapel of his dark green suit jacket. He looked incredible in it, a contrast against the blond hair and blue eyes. Her body was edgy being near him. Smelling the sharpness of his cologne, she felt the same sexual pull she had the night before. She was playing with fire, but to hell with getting burned. "Kiss me again, Scott, like you did last night."

He scooted out of her way, setting the cup down on the table. "I'm late for a meeting, and last night never should have happened."

"So you said last night." She reached out to touch his cheek. "The question is, why not?"

He took hold of her hand. "You're too young."

"I'm twenty-one."

Released it. "Too young," he responded firmly.

"Says who?" she asked seductively as she ran her hand along his jacket. His blue eyes grew darker when he was aroused, she noticed, and she could tell he was aroused by the bulge in his pants.

He slapped her hand away and backed off. "Says me."

"Don't I have a say in it?"

"No." He stepped away when she moved in closer. "Stop it,

now."

Huffing, she gritted her teeth. "You kiss me with obvious passion and intent, get me boiling, make me believe you want me, and tell me it shouldn't have happened. You ass!"

He nodded in full agreement. "Yep, that's me, an ass. Gotta run now."

"We're not through here, Scott," she yelled as he fled the room. Aurora turned to the sink full of dishes, picked up a plate, and threw it at the door. "Jackass!" He was lucky, damn lucky, she wasn't allowed to change him into one.

Chapter Nineteen

Home sweet home.

As Scott stood before the house that had been his home, off and on, throughout his lifetime, he wondered if he was doing the right thing. So many memories—some good, some bad—were contained in that tall Victorian-style house with its white shutters and big windows. Yet letting it sit empty all this time seemed a waste. He'd chosen not to live there simply because it was too large for one person and…he couldn't handle being alone with all the memories floating around him. The house deserved to have a family live in it, with children who could enjoy the space, the yard, and the warmth of their surroundings.

Pulling the keys from his pocket, he entered the house.

He could still smell him here, that dark, woodsy smell of his father's cologne mixed with the scent of tobacco. He drew it in deep, let it linger.

Before him stood the long staircase he'd run on and slid down so many times in his lifetime. The wood was scarred, aged, and needed repair. It showed plenty of use. He took most of the credit for that. Smiling, he traced the scars in the wood with his fingers.

To the left was the living room, to the right, the kitchen. Either way you went, you circled around, going through the dining room, and ended back at the door. He chose the path to the left.

The huge brick fireplace was a little dusty, but the stone was still shining, and if he closed his eyes, he could smell the cedar they used to burn on cold winter nights. In the corner, by the window, and just short of the fireplace sat his father's favorite easy chair, now looking faded and sad where once it had looked new and inviting. It just needed a good cleaning. He could remember all the times his father had sat there, smoking his cigarettes and reading over contracts while Scott sat at his feet doing his homework.

The dining room hadn't been used much when they lived here, only when his father entertained. In the later years, those times were far and few between. The huge oak table with its high-backed wooden chairs was covered in dust, and sat as a lonely beacon in the large room.

He carried on to the kitchen.

He could still smell the meals his father had concocted. They weren't always edible, but at least he had tried. When they weren't on the road, his father liked to pretend he was a great chef. There had been plenty of times Scott had swallowed down a meal that tasted a great deal like burnt rubber.

The small table for four still sat by the huge bay window. Many a meal had been spent there, especially later on when his father grew too weak to tour. They'd shared horrible food and plenty of food fights. He'd give anything to have a chunk of sticky pasta thrown at him now.

Turning left, he took the stairs to the basement, to where his father had set up his own recording studio.

All the equipment was still here, though the pieces had been silenced by their master's death. Nothing had been played since his father's death and it was much too quiet.

Sitting down behind the drums, Scott felt a familiar tug as he began to play. It had been years since he'd beaten on the drums, since he'd wanted to. It was like riding a bike; he hadn't forgotten any of it. "Still got it." Laughing to himself, he climbed out from behind the kit.

In the later years, his father's band, *Metal Death*, had recorded many an album here. And Scott had sat behind the glass in the booth, watching as they played. Was it any wonder they held the status of number one so many years running? They had an uncanny knack for belting out one hit after another. Even when his father grew too weak to record for long periods at a time, they still reached number one. With his father gone—the lead singer—the band wasn't doing so great. They still played, but not like they used to, and the last time he'd talked with the men he considered uncles, they hadn't wanted to carry on with the band. It wasn't the same without Dustin Monroe as their lead.

Leaving the room, Scott felt the ghosts of the past surround him.

He took the stairs up, through the kitchen and to the door. Standing, he looked up at the second level, where he and his father had once slept. He slid his hand along the wood as he slowly made his way up the stairs. He smiled, turned, and thought, what the hell. Once for old time's sake. If it broke, he would repair it. Climbing on, the banister between his legs, Scott let himself go. He slid all the way to the bottom, laughing. It was childish, immature, and he hadn't had this much fun in a very long time.

How could he do it? How could he get rid of a place that had meant so much to both of them? A place he'd cherished, a place filled with happiness and fond memories. Despite the one horrible nightmare that was his father's death, there were far more happy memories in the house.

When the doorbell rang—more than likely the real estate agent—Scott turned to the living room and his father's chair. He could almost see him sitting there wagging a finger.

"Son, why would you want to get rid of this place? Do I need to give you a shake?" Scott laughed. It would be exactly what his father would say.

Still, it would hurt too much to live there alone, and silly to keep it for a family of one.

Turning to the door, he let the real estate agent into the house.

☙

Aurora had her hands full of soapy bubbles, scrubbing soiled dishes, when Gus strolled in. She didn't pay much attention to him. People were always coming and going through the kitchen, grabbing coffee or a drink of whatever was in the fridge. She put the pot in the double sink, and turned to grab a towel.

He gasped. "It's you." He nearly dropped the cup as he stared at Aurora with bewilderment. "You're…the Dark Angel."

"Don't be silly, Gus. I work here. My name is Aurora." She needed to calm him down, make him believe he was wrong.

He shook his head so hard coffee sloshed over the rim of his cup and onto his hand. "No, no, you're her. You're the Dark Angel. Oh God, are you gonna take me now?"

She heard people outside the swinging doors and worried that others were going to come in. She couldn't have Gus telling them who she really was. She needed to take control. Controlling him, freezing him to his spot, she moved toward him.

"Close your eyes. This won't hurt." She slid her hand over his eyes and erased his memory of her, of what he'd seen that night in the alley, of what had happened here. "You'll be just fine now." She stroked his face, held him while he rested silently in her arms.

When the doors opened, she looked up at the bewildered face of one of the women who'd come in the night before.

"What's going on?"

"He just blacked out. Call an ambulance." She stroked his face as the women rushed for help. "I'm sorry," she whispered as she held him in her arms.

☙

Scott showed up just as the ambulance pulled away. Baffled, he rushed inside to find one of the guards standing by the door. "What happened?"

Mark lit up a cigarette, drawing in heavily before responding. "Gus blacked out. He should be fine. He was stable when they loaded him up."

Loosening the tie at his neck, Scott watched the ambulance pull away. "I'll want all the details."

"I filed a report on what I handled, but you'll have to ask Aurora for the details of what happened. She was with him." He drew on the cigarette, letting it rest in his mouth and lungs before he blew it out.

"I thought you quit."

"I did. You didn't just see that." Smiling, Mark tapped it out in the can filled with sand set out for the smokers, then headed inside.

Loosening the top button of his shirt, Scott entered the facility to search for Aurora.

He found her comforting one of the patrons, stroking the woman's hand gently. He removed his jacket, flipped it over a chair, and walked toward her.

"Everyone okay?"

She nodded, than patted Molly's hand once more before she stood to lead Scott out of the crowd. "Everyone's a little upset, but I think I've calmed them down. They were just worried. When Gus strolls back in here, looking as good as new, they'll all be fine."

He nodded, undid yet another button. He really hated the restriction of button-up shirts and ties. Thank God he didn't have to wear them often. "What happened? Mark said to ask you."

"I was doing the dishes when Gus strolled in for a cup of coffee. I heard him pouring it and a second later, it crashed to the floor. I turned, saw him lying on the floor, and went to him instantly. One of the ladies came in and I asked her to call for help."

He drew in a deep breath. "I'll check on him later." He looked up at her and despite her beauty, he saw the fatigue. "You look beat. Why don't you call it a day?"

She shook her head, caressed his cheek. "I'm fine, but you don't look so good. Tough day?"

Her touch was soft and gentle, and he remembered how soft her lips had been, how perfect she'd felt in his arms. He reminded himself of how wrong it would be to give in to her. She was still so young, and he wasn't. "Tough meeting." He pulled away, walked to the kitchen for some coffee.

"It often helps to talk about it." She took him by the hand and dragged him to a chair. "I happen to be a good listener and, as an added bonus, I'm a terrific masseuse."

She came up behind him and began massaging his stiff neck. He shouldn't be letting her touch him, but it felt so good. "I'm selling my father's house."

"Why?"

He closed his eyes and let her ease the stiffness from his muscles. "Several reasons, really. It's silly letting it sit there empty."

"Why don't you stay there?" She pushed his shirt aside and ran her hands over his shoulders, along his neck.

"The ghosts of the past are too difficult to live with alone." He felt his muscles relaxing, and what a glorious feeling that was. He'd been so tense lately, so much to worry about.

She circled around before stopping directly in front of him. "I can imagine how hard that must be for you."

He looked up, regretting that she'd stopped massaging him, and saw the beauty in front of him. Her face was so delicate, and her eyes, that golden brown, were so big and innocent. He wanted her more than he wanted to breathe.

She straddled him and before he could protest. She dove in, grabbing his head in her hands and stealing his breath.

His mind was numbed by her. The seductive way she took his lips, angled this way, then that, as her tongue slipped out to tease his. He could feel the heat radiate from her, scorching him, begging him to douse it. Gripping her hips, his fingers digging in, he pulled her closer. When her hands slid to his chest, he deepened the kiss.

Somewhere at the back of his mind he heard himself say *this can't go on.* Yet he wanted her so badly. He couldn't think, he could only feel, and what he felt was pure lust. He wanted, oh Lord, how he wanted. He could take, and he desperately wanted to take.

A crash in the dining room brought him back to reality.

Appalled, he pushed her off his lap. "Stop it." He couldn't seem to breathe.

"Why?" She tried to straddle him again, but he stood.

"We can't do this." He noticed his shirt was nearly undone, wondered when that had happened, and quickly began to do up the buttons.

"Why not? You seemed to be enjoying yourself. So was I. What's the problem?"

He noticed the bulge in his pants and decided tucking his shirt back into his pants was a bad idea. "The age difference, for one." He took in slow, even breaths trying to get himself back to normal. Would he ever be?

"Age is irrelevant when two people want each other as much as we want each other. My parents are years apart, and they managed to come together despite the difference in their ages."

His head jerked to the door and the ruckus behind it. "I need to check out what that crash was." He left her standing alone in the kitchen, his body aching, his mind reeling. She felt so good, yet she was so young. What was wrong with him, wanting her so badly when she was barely out of her teens? Shaking his head, he went to check out the noise.

⚃

Unable to resist, Aurora sent herself to Scott's house. It was wrong to slip into his mind, but he'd looked so sad at the fact that he needed to sell his house. The instant she set herself down inside, she felt the love, the warmth. There was pain as well, and she wondered what had happened that caused so much darkness.

Moving about, she took in the beauty that surrounded her. The woodwork was lovely, and well kept. The flooring, a little worn in places, looked clean. She loved the fireplace, with its black-and-white contrasting design. She imagined lying in front of a roaring fire, Scott holding her in his arms.

The kitchen was modern and looked as though the appliances had been replaced not too long ago. The view out the window was breathtaking. Trees surrounded the property, which boasted a lovely green lawn and flowerbeds on either side.

There was no way she could let him sell this place and that was when the idea hit her.

She had the perfect person in mind to help her out.

Chapter Twenty

*H*er father was in the middle of pruning his bonsai trees when Aurora appeared. Anyone who knew him knew better than to disturb him while he was working on his precious little bushes. It had been a hobby he'd taken up years before as a means of relaxing. Aurora could only imagine how much stress he was under. She imagined it took a lot to run a huge corporation.

"This better be an emergency, little one."

She stepped a little closer, marveling in the beauty he'd created in the tiny tree. "It is."

Setting his clippers down, he turned to her. "You don't look hurt, and I see no stress in your eyes, your mind is at ease. How big of an emergency could this be?"

"I want you to buy me a house."

Growling, he lifted the clippers in his hand and turned his back to her. "You have a house. Now go away while Daddy works."

She could wait him out. She'd done so plenty of times before. She watched as he cut and tied, meticulously. For a big man, well over six feet, he had the most delicate touch. She remembered fondly how he used to tickle her with those big hands, tickled her until she cried out for mercy. Or when he would tuck her in bed, stroking a hand along her face, when he would grab her around the waist and hang her upside down so that her long black hair would sweep the floor. He always threatened to turn her into a dust mop, but he never had. He was an incredible man, and an even more incredible father.

But if he thought she would go away quietly, he didn't know his daughter very well. After several moments of watching him work, of seeing him fighting to ignore her, she decided to play dirty. Lifting her hand, she blew a tiny cloud, white and fluffy, toward him. It hovered over his precious tree.

"Aurora," he growled in a deep voice.

"I want a new house, Daddy."

"Well, we can't always have what we want."

"It's a special house, Daddy."

He turned to her, letting out a long breath. "All right, since you won't leaving me be. Go ahead and tell me why this house is so special, that way Daddy can tell you no and go about his business."

She batted her long lashes innocently and was determined to win. "Have I told you how much I love you?"

His eyes narrowed. He took her by the shoulders. "You've disturbed my calm, Aurora. A tiny gesture meant to butter me up won't work. What makes this house so special?" he repeated.

She frowned and plucked at the tiny bush her father had been working on. When he growled at her, slapping her hand away, she jumped. "Sorry, geez. Territorial." She rubbed her hand.

"The house, Aurora," he demanded, sternly, his eyes warning her he was losing his patience.

She huffed, deciding now wasn't a good time to ask him for a favor.

"Too late, my love. You've already pissed me off. You might as well just ask me."

She hated when her father read her mind. "It's not nice to invade my mind, you know."

"One."

"Okay! Boy, you are testy today." When he started counting there would be hell to pay if she didn't do as she was told. "The house belongs to Scott Monroe. It has too many unsettling memories for him, so he's decided to sell it."

"And this is my problem because…?"

He was being unusually ornery today. She couldn't help but wonder why. "It's not your problem. It's not a problem at all. I just wanted you to purchase it so he knows it went to someone who would appreciate it."

He crossed his arms over his chest and focused deeply penetrating eyes on her. He said nothing.

She ran her hand over the cool blue polo shirt he wore. "I really like that color on you. It brightens your face." It was rare to see her father in anything but a suit.

He let out a long breath and the ground shook beneath her.

"Okay, man. I was just commenting." She sulked. "I want the house, Daddy."

He lifted his brow, but his expression never wavered. "As I said, we can't always have what we want now, can we, love?"

"*We* can," she corrected, sober-faced.

He narrowed his eyes. "We don't obtain properties with our powers."

"You did, once, to get your business started." Aurora saw the flash of lightning come into his eyes. Way to bring up his past.

He stood, towering over her, a dark cloud with an imminent storm brewing. "That was centuries ago, young lady. I have changed. It wouldn't be wise to piss me off further, small one."

She nodded, undaunted by his stormy temper. "Couldn't you, just this once, bend the rules just a little bit?" She held up her index finger and thumb, spaced only a fraction apart. In a flash, she found herself standing in her old room.

Scowling, she yanked open the door. "Crabby old man." She stomped down the stairs, her heels snapping like a whip, to search for her mother. She found her mother in the place she so often went for solitude—the library.

It was huge, with wall-to-wall shelves of books. Her parents had eclectic tastes, ranging anywhere from fiction, non-fiction, self-help books, romance, mystery, suspense, and several very old mystical books her father kept at the top of the shelves. She was never allowed to touch them, and had often sneaked away to try to see what all the hubbub was about. Unfortunately, she could never read them. Whatever language they were in, she hadn't been schooled in it.

"Are you busy?" she asked her mother with a bit of a huff.

Her mother lowered the book she was reading and slowly lifted her head. "Not any longer. What's up?"

Aurora took a lounge chair and sat, sulking. "Daddy's in a crabby mood."

Missy smiled as she set her book on the wrought iron table beside her chair. "Lack of cigarettes is making him a little edgy, I'm afraid."

"Well, I wish he would have one already. His mood is unbearable." She dusted her pants, though nothing clouded them.

"You didn't disturb him while he was working on his trees, did you?"

"Yes. But—"

"Oh darling, you know better."

"It was important I see him."

Missy shook her head. "Unless it's death or mayhem, it's not important enough to disturb him. Now why don't you tell me what was so important that you would risk serious harm to yourself?"

Aurora lifted her mother's glass of wine and had a sip. "I want him to buy me a house."

"Oh darling, you are lucky he didn't crush you." Shaking her head, Missy lifted her book.

"He dropped me in my room, hard."

Her mother snickered as she lowered the book once more. "You got off lucky. What house do you want him to purchase?"

"Scott's house. He needs to sell it, but doesn't want to. It's has sentimental value while at the same time the memories are too hard for him to deal with. I thought if Daddy bought it for me, I could live there, and he would see that someone who loved it was living there and would take care of it. It's a beautiful house."

Her mother sat straight up in her chair. "You've been inside his home?"

"Yes, I was curious, so I went to see it."

"Did anyone see you?"

"No, I used my cloak of invisibility." Taking her mother's glass in hand, Aurora gulped down the remainder of the wine.

"Why is this so important to you, sweetheart?"

Aurora set the empty glass down. "It just is." She couldn't tell her mother the real reason: because she'd fallen in love with him. A mortal. A human. Taboo.

"Please tell me you're not smitten with this young man?"

Aurora sighed, leaned back, and looked up at the ceiling. "A little crush, maybe."

"You need to stop this now, Aurora. Stop seeing him. Do you hear me?"

Aurora pushed from the chair. "I can see whom I please."

"Not when he's a human and you are not."

"I'm part human," she reminded her mother sternly.

She stood so she was eye level with Aurora. "Only a quarter."

"So what's the big deal? You're part human—half—Daddy's not, yet you got married."

"Yes, but I did have some demon blood. Scott does not. Oh honey, I know it's hard for you—"

"No, you don't!" Aurora blasted the words at her mother. No one did.

"You will only hurt yourself if you pursue this, my sweet."

Arguing with her mother would do her no good, so she relented. "Fine, but I still want the house. It's beautiful." It really was, and she felt at home in it, more than she did in her own house.

"Are you still at it?" Grumbling, her father clomped into the room.

"It's important to me." She squared her shoulders, ready this time for a fight.

"Aurora, this isn't the time," her mother murmured.

"Oh, have a damn smoke already and save us all the grief." Waving her hand, she produced a lit cigarette between her father's lips.

Angered, he whisked it out of his mouth and made it disappear. She watched as his eyes went deadly sharp. "Do you wish punishment?"

"You're punishing me already by not giving me what I want," she shot out at him with raised temper that very much matched her father's.

"If I were to have given you everything you wanted in your life, you would be a spoiled brat, and I would be broke."

"Draco," her mother warned him.

Aurora narrowed deadly eyes at her father and spit fire with her words, aiming to hurt. "As far as I see it, you owe me. If it wasn't for you, I wouldn't have to work for Satan, taking innocent people's lives." She vanished in her rage before either her father or her mother could retaliate. What she'd said was hurtful, but she was tired of keeping her anger inside.

As she sat down on the bed, the tears began to fall. She'd been so cruel with her statement, and after all, if it hadn't been for her parents, she wouldn't be here now. Despite the deal they'd had to make to conceived her. If anyone deserved her rage, it was Satan for forcing her parents to deal for her life.

Dashing her tears aside, Aurora wished she could end her ties with Satan once and for all.

Chapter Twenty-One

*A*pproaching the door, dressed in a black tux and feeling completely restricted by it, Scott rang the bell. He doubted Aurora would be ready. Women were always late. He should have known better than to show up on time. The door swung open and he lost all the air from his lungs.

She was a goddess in white shimmering lace. The bodice was snug, strapless, coming to a V, dipping down to reveal plenty of cleavage. If he didn't know better, he would swear the diamonds on the bodice were real. The skirt billowed out, pure lace, and it shimmered as she walked. Her hair was caught up in dozens of curls at the top of her head, and falling down to her shoulders. She wore diamonds in her ears, around her neck, and on her wrists. One look at her would have any man drooling.

She truly looked like a princess ready for the ball.

Then there was the face. She had painted her eyes with pale blue that seemed to shimmer in the light as well. Her dark lashes were enhanced, making her eyes look as if tiny caterpillars were resting comfortably, protecting eyes of gold. Her lips were painted a ruby red, and she smiled as she moved toward him. He put his hand to his chest to make sure his heart was still beating. One look at her, and he was sure it had stopped.

"With a look like that, I don't need to ask if you approve."

He caught his breath, but just couldn't seem to take his eyes off of her. "Oh, I very much approve." She certainly didn't look like a little girl now.

Her face lit up with a brilliant smile. "I approve as well." She ran her fingers along the silky lapel of his tux, lifting her dreamy eyes. "You are very handsome, Scott."

He cleared his throat, knowing if he stood here any longer, he would make a fool of himself. "We should go before we're more than fashionably late." He held his hand out for her to exit first.

Her eyes went wide. "A limo?"

He put his hand on the curve of her back and felt just how soft her skin was, as the back of her dress dipped to her waist. Pushing his lust aside, he led her to the long, white car. "You didn't honestly think I would pick you up in my car?"

"I never gave it much thought." She held her hand out when the driver opened the door. "This is incredible. I feel like Cinderella, the modern version." She laughed as she slid along the bench seat.

He was sure she'd been in many limos before, but right now, she was in his and she was looking like a dream. Sitting beside her, he lifted the two flutes of champagne he'd set out before going to her door. "In celebration." He held a glass out to her. "Here's hoping I can make others understand the importance of what I do."

Smiling, she sipped the bubbly. "Mmm, very nice. You certainly know how to show a girl a good time."

"I think I've made a horrible mistake, inviting you."

Her face sank. "Oh?"

He smiled as he lifted the glass of champagne to his lips. "I'll never be able to look at anyone else." And that was as truthful with her as he wanted to get for now.

"Now see, that's flattery." She touched his hand with hers.

༚

The turnout was incredible. The ballroom was filled to its capacity with people dressed in formal wear and beautiful gowns. Everyone from rock stars to businessmen attended. Even the mayor and police commissioner had shown up.

As arranged, there was a section in the entryway that showcased what the shelter did for the people that came to it for help. It gave names of dozens of people that had been saved, all because they had a place to go for help. Some of the names were of well-known celebrities, including his father's at the top of the list. Scott hoped that in time, others would see his facility for what it was. It wasn't just a place to go if you needed a refuge, and it was there when you wanted solitude and time to heal. He always made sure those who came to him got the privacy they deserved while they were healing. Most of the time, no one knew they were there until well after they had left.

He hoped the city would now see that his shelter was a place that helped people fight their addictions, and learn how to live a normal life.

Scott milled about, greeting people, smiling, chatting, and having long, meaningful conversations about his shelter. But all the while he was chatting, socializing, his eyes scanned for Aurora. He had been correct in telling her he wouldn't be able to look at anyone else. His eyes seemed compelled to look at her. As he spotted her at the far end of the room, he watched as her father approached her.

❧

"Is your dance card filled?"

Aurora turned and her heart simply ached. "Not yet." Twin pangs of happiness and shame fought for dominance within her.

"May I?" Her father held his hand out to her.

She took his hand and instantly felt at home.

"You are absolutely radiant, my sweet." He held her in his arms like he had so many other times before. "You have grown into a beautiful young woman, not the same little girl I used to carry on my shoulders."

He always said just the right things to get to her, and he always smelled so good, as he did now. She lifted her head, looking up at her father. "I may be all grown up, Daddy, but I will always be your little girl." She reached up on her tiptoes, but when she still couldn't reach him, she pulled him down to her and kissed his cheek. "I'm sorry, Daddy."

"As am I, little one."

"I was being hateful. I didn't mean what I said."

He lifted her chin, looked down with softness in his eyes. "I have regrets, love, of agreeing to have you work for the Master, but never of wanting you more than air. Your mother and I dearly love you."

She refused to ruin her makeup with tears. "Oh Daddy, I love you both so much." She hugged his chest, feeling comforted by his big, strong arms.

"I bought the damn house."

She lifted her head as her lips curved up into a bright smile. "You did?"

"I could never resist you." He kissed the top of her head once more. "Don't tell your mother just yet. She loves to rub my spinelessness in my face."

Laughing, Aurora hugged him once more. She should have known her father would come through. He wasn't a spiteful man. She felt the shame trickle in once more at her behavior.

"Can I have everyone's attention please? Thank you."

Aurora turned her attention to a dapper older gentleman as he stood atop the huge stage. "For those that don't know me, I'm Terry Ledger, lead guitarist and vocalist for the band Metal Death. Scott asked us to perform tonight. Though it's been forever since we've played the clubs, I think we're managing quite well."

The crowd clapped, cheering them on. "As most of you know, Scott's father, Dustin, was our lead singer for many years. He started the band, kept us going right up until his end. Unfortunately, years of drugs abuse took him too soon. But there was one thing he was determined to do before he died, and that was get his shelter up and running and help people in need." He turned his attention to Scott. "He would be damn proud of his son if he were here now, for keeping up the dream. But, there was another dream Dustin had, one that never came to fruition. Though Dustin was determined to let his son take his own path in life, choose what he wanted to do, he had a secret dream that his son would follow in his footsteps. Now, anyone that has heard Scott sing will know when I say, we thank *God* he never did."

The crowd roared with laughter. Scott simply nodded and didn't blush.

"But there was one thing Scott did incredibly well, and that was play the drums. So, the band and I would like to ask Scott to come up here, and show everyone what he's got."

Aurora noticed Scott's reluctance as he was shoved toward the stage. He walked up and behind the massive set of drums, positioning himself as if it were second nature.

"This one's an oldie, but a goodie. Had to say it." Tapping the drumsticks together, Scott got them started.

Aurora, standing beside her father, listened in awe as Scott played. He was good, better than good. He was fantastic. Her eyes focused in on him. At that moment, no one else existed in the room.

Minutes passed, while Aurora, trancelike, kept her eyes on Scott. When the music stopped, he laughed over something one of the band members said, and shook their hands before leaving them standing on the stage. Releasing her father's hand, Aurora took slow steps, at first, until she was nearly running toward him.

"You were absolutely fabulous, Scott." She took his hand, her eyes lighting up with her smile. "You should play professionally."

"It's only a hobby. Dance with me, Blackie."

She went with him eagerly and leaned into him when he pulled her closer. She remembered quite well how he felt against her, and like before, her body warmed to his touch.

He rested his cheek on her hair, holding one of her hands while the other rested lightly at her back.

"It's a wonderful party."

"Yes, it is."

"I wish I could stay like this forever."

"For now, pretend we can."

 Cʒ

"I don't like this."

Draco turned to his wife and saw the face she was making. "You're not enjoying yourself, my love?"

"It's a lovely party," she stated gruffly, her eyes glued to her daughter.

Confused, Draco followed where her gaze focused with such intensity. And he saw his daughter in Scott's arms, dancing to a very slow song. "Ah, I see."

"No, you don't," Missy corrected. "She's in love with him."

"Don't be ridiculous, Missy." He took a glass of champagne from the waiter as one wandered past him.

"I am being perfectly serious, Draco, and if we don't stop it soon, it will be too late."

Draco heard the desperation in his wife's voice and decided maybe he needed to have a closer look. Knowing it wasn't right didn't matter; he needed to know. Slipping into Scott's mind, Draco frowned deeply.

"It's not just her we need to worry about. The boy's in love as well."

The champagne flute snapped in half from the force of his grip.

Chapter Twenty-Two

Sitting alone in a chair, Aurora rubbed her aching feet. She'd had a glorious time, but wasn't used to wearing heels for more than two hours.

"You look tired, dear. Let's get you home."

Looking up at her mother, she smiled as she slipped back into her shoes. "Scott's taking me home."

"I think it would be best if we took you home." Her father took her hand and lifted her to her feet.

"I don't want to leave yet."

"Well, that's just too bad."

"What's gotten into you, Daddy?"

"We need to talk to you, privately," her mother stated. "It's important."

"Okay, we can talk outside." Before her parents could reply, Aurora headed to the terrace doors.

"I want you to quit working at the shelter."

Her jaw dropped as she stared at her father. "I beg your pardon?"

"You will give your notice tomorrow."

She stared up at him in disbelief. "I will not." How dare he try to rule her life?

"Aurora, honey, we're just concerned for you." In a calming motion, her mother stroked her hand up and down Aurora's arm.

"You're getting much too close to Scott."

"So what?"

"So what?" her father snapped. "Need I remind you of the consequences of becoming involved romantically with a human?"

"No, you don't. I've heard it my entire life and I'm tired of hearing it." She pushed her father's hand away when he reached for her arm. "And, I'm very much done with this conversation." Making sure no one was around, she sent her parents home. She was sure she would pay for that later, but for now, she didn't care.

"Is everything all right?"

She whirled around to see Scott standing in the terrace doors. Had he seen what she'd just done? "I'm fine." He walked up to her, and she kept her fingers crossed he hadn't seen. "Shouldn't you be entertaining your guests?"

"There are no more guests to entertain."

"Where did everyone go?"

"Home, at last. It's after three in the morning."

"Is it? I had no idea it was that late." She saw the fatigue on his face, and touched his cheek with her hand. "You're exhausted."

"Only extremely." He smiled a little more, his blue eyes dancing. "Are you ready to leave?"

"I thought you would never ask." Letting him take her hand, she walked out with him. There, waiting for them, was the limo. "Did you have him wait the whole time?"

"No, I called half an hour ago." She slid into the seat. He followed, obviously glad to be off his feet. "Did your parents leave?"

"Yes." She didn't want to ruin her newfound calm by thinking of her parents.

He took her face in his palm. "How is it you've managed to look even more beautiful than I saw you last?"

Her heart took one long trip and she fell head over heels in love. "You're going to make me cry." No one had ever looked at her with as much love as he did. She wanted to tell him she loved him, wanted to ask him to take her home, but all her words were snatched away when he pulled her closer and kissed her with such softness, she melted.

Her heart hammered in her chest, her stomach knotted. She felt giddy and nervous all at once. When his hand slid from her waist up, slowly, until it cupped her breast, she moaned. She finally understood what it was like to have a man touch her, to feel her, to arouse her. And, she realized, she wanted it all. "Take me now, Scott."

She moaned as he released her and sat back in his seat. "No. This isn't the place, or the time."

Her body felt as a taut as a wire. "But I need you."

He took her hands in his, kissed them, before laying them to his cheek. "You deserve better than a quick romp in the back seat of a car, Blackie. Especially not from a man who's had too much to drink."

She shook her head, her long, dark curls bouncing wildly. "I don't care where we are. I want you." She pulled him to her. "I want you to be my first."

His eyes nearly bugged out of his face. "Your…first?"

She undid his jacket, smiling at his shock. "Yes, my first, Scott. The only one to have me."

He took her hands in his, stopping her before she went too far, and held them tight. "Aurora, are you telling me you are still a virgin?"

She scrunched up her face. "I hate that term. Is that a problem?"

He released her quickly and slid away. "God, yes!" He drew in a deep breath, running his hand over his hair.

She was offended by his comment. "Why?"

He looked at her, his eyes wide. "I was about to take you, here, in the back seat of a limo. What the hell kind of initiation is that?"

"A pleasant one if it's wanted, and I want it." She touched his arm and felt him flinch. "You don't want me now that you know?"

"God, Blackie, I want you so much it hurts. But not like this."

The car came to a stop. She was home. "Come inside with me." She saw him hesitate. "It's what I want, Scott. I want you, I need you."

The door flung open and she gasped when her father poked his head inside.

"You are needed inside."

"I thought I sent you home." She gritted her teeth.

"You thought wrong. Now, Aurora."

"You'd better go." Scott touched her arm lightly. "I'll talk to you tomorrow."

Her father would only persist if she didn't do as he demanded and she didn't want Scott involved. Sliding from the car, she was about to thank Scott for a wonderful evening when her father slammed the door shut.

"That was incredibly rude." She stormed off to the house. She wasn't a teenager, but her father certainly made her feel that way. "I hate you for that."

"As you wish, but I would rather you hate me then ruin your life."

"I am not ruining my life." She slammed the door as she entered, rattling the walls. "And it's my damn life to ruin if I choose."

"The hell it is. You are my child, and I will not sit by while you throw it all away for one human."

"I'm getting damn tired of you running my life."

"Aurora, I only want what is best for you."

"No you don't because what I want best isn't what you want for me."

"Aurora—"

"What if I said to hell with it, threw everything aside and took a human as my mate? What if I said I didn't care if I lost my powers as long as I had someone who loved me? If that's what makes me happy, Daddy, could you live with it?" She saw the answer in the way his eyes grew even more dark and fierce. "I didn't think so. Don't tell me you only want what is best for me. For the first time in my life, I feel whole. I have a job I enjoy, I'm with people who need me, and I make a difference to them." And she was in love, but she left that unsaid.

"How will you separate the two, Aurora? Saving by day,

damning by night?"

"I'm managing." She said the words, but each day it was becoming tougher to do exactly that.

"Yes, now, but what about when it all begins to unravel?"

She didn't want to think of it that way. "I will deal with it."

"Aurora, think about what you are doing."

"I am, Daddy, and I know what I want."

He drew in a deep breath. "Scott?"

"Yes."

He took a step back. "Will you tell him who you are, that you are a demon? He might, just might be able to accept that. But will he be able to accept that the people he is trying to save are the very people you are sending to hell?"

His words cut deep. "I'm tired now."

"Aurora, I don't want to lose you."

She turned as her father spoke then sniffled back her tears as she ran up the stairs. Why did everything have to be so difficult?

Chapter Twenty-Three

Stumbling from his bed, Scott trudged to the pounding on his door. Shielding his burning eyes from the bright sunlight streaming through the windows, he opened the door. "Mr. Starr?"

"We need to talk." Not bothering with formalities or an invitation, he pushed his way past Scott and inside.

Please, come in, Scott thought dryly as he closed the door. "I've had two hours sleep. I can't guarantee I'll be at my best. Let me guess. You're here about Aurora?"

"You guess correctly. I don't want you seeing her anymore."

He needed coffee, good strong coffee if he was going to be able to function and hold his own against this dark, dangerous looking man. "I see." He rubbed a hand across his face as he walked to the kitchen. "Any reason why?" He set the coffee pot in motion. He wished now he'd programmed it so it had been ready when he woke.

"You are much too old for her."

Scott didn't care for the way Mr. Starr put that. It made him sound ancient. Though he hated to admit it, be damned if he would admit that now to her father, he felt the same. But that didn't mean he was giving in to the guy. "She doesn't seem to have a problem with our age difference."

"Her mind is clouded with desire. You need to set her straight."

The scent of the coffee was helping, only minimally, to clear his head, but not enough. "Coffee?"

"No, thank you."

Grabbing a cup, Scott didn't wait and slid his cup underneath the stream. "Set her straight about what?" He added just a drop of milk, cradling the cup in his hands as he turned to Starr. The guy certainly looked intimidating. It was a good thing he was still half-asleep, Scott thought, or he might be afraid.

"Tell her there can be nothing between the two of you."

Sliding up on a stool by the breakfast nook, Scott took a good long sip of his coffee before he answered. "Maybe it's time you took a step back and realized your daughter is a grown woman able to make her own choices and decisions." The flash of heat in the other man's eyes could scare the life out of anyone, as it did for him right now.

"I could make your life miserable if you don't do as I say."

Who did this guy think he was? He had some nerve, threatening him. Scott's back straightened in defense. The caffeine was beginning to kick in and his senses were at full alert. "The last time I looked, Mr. Starr, I was a grown man, and you are not my parent. You might be able to command your daughter, but you can't do it to me. I don't take threats lightly."

"And I don't give them lightly. I could stop the check on the purchase of your house."

Scott tilted his head in confusion. "What does my house have to do with this?"

"I've purchased it, at my daughter's insistence, but I may very well cancel it if you don't agree to stop seeing my daughter."

Boy, this guy was certainly something. Who did he think he was, God? And how petty was he that he would threaten to remove his money? Scott didn't want or need his money. His temper flared. He did little to hide it as he stood and squared his shoulders. "You arrogant ass! Do you think your threats scare me? Go ahead and pull your money, stop purchase on my house. I don't want you owning it anyway." Scott moved to the door, fury riding high in the red of his face. "Now, I'll ask you to leave, nicely, before I get really mad."

He yanked the door open and was surprised to see Aurora on the other side.

"Good morning, Scott. I thought I would surprise you with breakfast—Daddy? What are you doing here?" she asked her father through gritted teeth.

"He was just leaving." Scott shot fierce eyes Starr's way, determined to stand strong. He doubted that he could physically throw the man out, but there were other ways of getting him to leave. Calling the cops was one.

Mr. Starr turned from Scott to his daughter. "I want to talk to you, Aurora."

"Not now, Daddy. I'm all talked out."

Growling under his breath, Mr. Starr spun around and stormed out.

"What did he want?"

Getting to his feet, Scott went for his coffee. Now that his legs had stopped shaking, he could manage the walk. "To tell me to stop seeing you." He turned to Aurora, coffee pot in one hand and his cup in the other. "You asked him to buy my house?" He hadn't had time to let that piece of news sink in before. It was now.

"Yes, but I was going to surprise you with it." She pouted.

Maybe if he'd had a full night's sleep and was at his best, he could get upset about that. He just couldn't see why now. "Why did you want him to buy it?"

"Plate?"

He pulled one out of his cupboard and handed it off to her.

"Because I saw how much it hurt you to give it up, to have to sell it." She dumped the bag onto the plate, letting the assorted bagels fall in a clump. Tossing the bag in the trash, she grabbed a cup from the mug tree and helped herself to coffee. With the steaming brew in hand, she slid up beside him.

He could smell her fragrance over the coffee and it made his stomach tighten. He could still feel the way she'd moved under him the night before, when he'd nearly taken her in the car. He just couldn't be angry at her for wanting to buy his house. "Well, I wouldn't count on moving in any time soon. Your father's going to pull out of the deal." He drank more coffee, willing himself to stop thinking of how smooth her skin had felt against his.

"He what? No. No, he won't, I'll see to it that he doesn't back out."

He didn't care for the anger in her words. "Aurora, I don't want to come between you and your father."

She set her cup down and turned to him. "You're not."

He slid from the stool to pace, mostly, but also to get further away from her. He didn't like what she was stirring up inside of him. He felt much too vulnerable, with the lack of sleep, to use his better judgment and hold her off. "It's obvious that I am. He doesn't want you anywhere near me." He'd made that bitterly clear.

She got up to move to him. "He doesn't run my life, Scott." She touched his arm. "I want you, I need you. He can't dictate my feelings."

Scott pulled away, the further away the better. "He has a point, though. I am much older than you."

"Oh, so we're back to that again. For pity's sake, Scott." She moved closer to him, her eyes filled with desire.

"Aurora, stop."

She did, her gaze furious. "Oh, please tell me you're not giving in to his bully tactics, because that will really piss me off."

"Nine years is a lot of difference, Blackie. You would be better off with someone your own age."

"It's my damn life. I'll have whoever I please, and what pleases me is you."

He didn't like how she worded that one bit, and narrowed his eyes. "I am not an object for the taking."

She took a step back. "That wasn't what I meant."

"Sure sounded that way to me." He turned to refill his coffee cup.

"I simply meant I am free to choose who I want to spend time with and who I want to be intimate with."

Was this why she'd never had a man in her bed before, why

she'd never been with a man before? Did her father chase them all away? "This may be bold of me, and you don't have to answer it, but may I ask why you've never slept with a man before? You're a very attractive woman. I can't see you being short of dates."

"Thank you." She cleared her throat. "No one has ever appealed to me before."

He drank a bit of coffee and decided, since he was digging deep, he might as well go all the way. "So what is it about me that appeals to you?"

"Come on, are you serious?" He nodded; she continued. "Okay, aside from the fact that you're a babe—and I love when you blush—I also enjoy being with you. You're easy to talk to, and you have a very generous heart."

She was making him feel incredibly uncomfortable. Yes, he'd been told he was attractive before, but no woman had ever described him so sweetly. He didn't know how to respond to that. "If…if we pursue this, how will it affect your relationship with your father?"

She took the cup from his hands and set it down. "Let me worry about my father. I know just how to handle him." She wrapped her arms around his neck, lifting to her tiptoes, and held her mouth only a breath away from his. "You look incredibly sexy when you're half asleep, Scott. Your eyes are so dreamy and blue."

Sighing, he rested his head on hers. "How is it you look so fresh at nine in the morning, when I'm sure you couldn't have slept any more than I did?"

"I thrive off of little to no sleep." She inched in even closer, her eyes twinkling with seduction. "Are you going to talk all morning, or are you going to kiss me?"

"Maybe." Smiling, he lifted her off her feet and sank into those plump, satiny lips he couldn't seem to get enough of. He only meant to make it a short kiss, but when she changed the angle and took him down a long dark tunnel of desire, he was lost. She had a way of clogging his mind to anything but her.

Her hand slid down his back, her nails scraping as she lifted his T-shirt, and it didn't take a genius to figure out what her intentions had been in bringing him breakfast. And, like the night before in the limo, this wasn't the time or place. "In time, Blackie." He held her, but kept his lips far enough away that she couldn't seduce him into giving in.

"Time is overrated. We have now." She began to unbutton her blouse.

He took her hands, stopping her before she went any further. "Not now, not when I'm half asleep." He kissed her fingers. "When I take you to my bed, I want to be fully alert so that I can do everything I've imagined doing to you. Now go, so I can catch a few more hours sleep. Unlike you, I need my sleep."

A sharp, seductive gleam entered her golden eyes as she smiled wickedly. "I could put you to sleep."

Still holding her hands, he gave them a squeeze before he released her to step away. *Much too tempting.* "I doubt sleep is anywhere in your mind." He turned her and gave her a gentle shove. "Leave, now."

She giggled and angled her head over her shoulder, her long hair feathering over her golden skin. "Fine, I'll go, if you agree to have dinner with me tomorrow night."

He let out a long sigh. "Sure, where do you want to go?"

She opened the door, giving him with a sultry look, and smiled. "A little place you call home. I believe you know the address." Kissing her palm, she blew it at him as she walked away.

Was he crazy, letting her go, when she so obviously had come to seduce him? Rubbing his eyes, he turned back to his bed. Maybe it was a mistake to want her, to have her, but at this moment, he was willing to step over that line.

And there was no way he was giving in to the powerful Draco Starr. He wanted Aurora, couldn't deny feeling for her. It was time he gave himself the pleasure he—and she—so desired. If it was wrong, so be it. He would deal with the consequences later.

Crawling into bed, he set his alarm clock for another two hours, and fell asleep the second he hit the pillow.

αβ

Aurora wanted everything perfect. The ambiance had to show what she intended. Because she didn't have a lot of time, she decided to use her powers. She'd need candles, wine, flowers—uh, maybe not, considering they were an aphrodisiac to demons. However, if her inhibitions were gone, she might not be as frightened as she was now. After all, she'd never seduced a man before.

Standing in the living room, she waved her hand, and cursed when nothing happened. She was about to try it again, when it hit her. "Daddy!" she yelled, her teeth gritted.

He appeared beside her, looking completely innocent. "You bellowed, my sweet?"

She was too furious to see the charm in his smile. "I want them back, now."

"You want what back, baby?" He played coy, looking at his nails as he spoke.

"My powers. Give them back." At times like this, she hated that her mother was part witch and that her father was able to use potions and spells.

"Your powers, oh, right. No," he stated firmly.

She narrowed her eyes. "If you think you can coerce me to stop seeing Scott by taking away my powers, you are sadly mistaken."

"We'll see."

"Daddy—" He vanished before she could finish her sentence. Stomping one foot, she yelled out. "Daddy, it won't work." When he didn't reply, she let out a scream that shook the ground.

Chapter Twenty-Four

*H*er father thought he was so smart by taking away her powers. But she still had fingers to dial with. So what if she couldn't whip up an elegant romantic meal in the blink of an eye, that didn't mean she was beaten. That's what caterers were for.

Lifting the telephone, she'd dialed one of the top restaurants in the city and ordered the works, including candles. As she set it up, she took a long look around. Romantic, elegant, perfect for what she had in mind. Was she crazy for doing this? Maybe. Should she be doing this? Probably not. Was that going to stop her? No.

Rules be damned, she was going to take what she wanted for once in her life. When the doorbell rang, she felt her heart leap into her throat. Checking her watch, she saw he was right on time. She walked to the door, feeling as giddy as a teenager on her first date. Essentially, she was.

Aurora opened the door and smoothed out the long, silk nightgown and robe she wore. "You didn't have to ring the bell. This is your house."

He stared at her for several moments before speaking. "No, it's your house now, Blackie. I got the papers this afternoon. Wow, you look…" She saw him swallow hard. "Something smells good."

"I ordered in." She led him to the living room.

"Oh…candles, too. Nice…um…I can help you get rid of all this furniture if you like."

She shook her head. She was making him nervous and it dispelled her own jitters. Taking his hand, Aurora led him to the roaring fireplace. Though it was beyond hot outside, she had the fire burning. It seemed more romantic.

"But this is my father's stuff."

She smiled as she pulled him down to the blanket she had laid out by the fire. "Yep." She handed him a glass of wine. "I like it."

He looked at her, his head tilted. "Why do you want to keep it?"

"Everything just seems to belong here, so why get rid of it?" She lifted the glass of wine to her lips, watching his face light with amazement. "How long did you live here?"

He took a deep breath. "Most of my life. This was our safety zone. No paparazzi, no phone calls. Just quiet."

"Must have been hard, growing up with a rock star." She caressed his arm, sensing his arousal, and let it warm her heart.

"It had its moments." He took hold of her hands, drew them to his chest. "I've never wanted someone so much that I lost all thought."

"Don't think, Scott, just take me." She set her glass down, took his, and set it beside hers.

"I don't know if this is right."

"I do."

"If at any time you want to stop, just say so."

She touched a hand to his face, tilted her head, and smiled. "I won't. Kiss me, Scott. I need to feel your lips."

He obliged her, but took her lips slowly, lingering, building a fire that would burn white-hot inside of her. While soft music played around them, he held her lips captive as his hands rested on her hips.

She met his fever with her own, as though they'd come together like this a hundred times before. When his hands skimmed up and down her back, touching bare flesh, she quivered.

Releasing her mouth, he slid his lips over her chin, caressed the nape of her neck. She tipped her head back, and moaned. With one finger, he carefully slid the strap down her shoulder, and replaced it with his lips. As he traced the line down to her chest, she let out a tiny whimper. He pulled away. "If you want me to stop—"

"No." She put a finger to his lips, and smiled. "I don't want you to stop."

"I won't hurt you, Blackie."

"I know." With shaky hands, she unbuttoned the green dress shirt he wore. "I'm not sure what to do."

"Let me." Taking her hands in his, he kissed her knuckles. "I want this moment to forever be remembered." Releasing her hands, he eased the other strap off her shoulder. Using his mouth, he placed tiny kisses to her skin. While his hands slid the silk from her arms, he took her mouth in a seductive kiss.

Un-belting her robe, she let both garments drop to the floor. She was so nervous, baring all for him to see, but when he pulled away, the look in his eyes said everything.

"You are incredible, Blackie. Absolutely incredible."

She held her hands out to him in invitation. She wouldn't be afraid to join with him, because it felt was right. As he came to her, held her, she knew nothing would ever feel more right.

He laid her on the blanket while the fire snapped and glowed. Lying beside her, seducing her mouth, he explored her body.

She moved to his touch, her body reacting perfectly. She felt on fire, a deep burning down in the pit of her belly, sinking lower, achingly lower. When he caressed her breast, she moaned against his lips and encouraged him to take more. He lowered his mouth, taking one taut nipple between his lips, she cried out as her body shivered. But that sensation was nothing compared to what his hands were making her feel.

He suckled her gently with his mouth. Her stomach quivered as he slid his hand down, past her belly button, to the heat that radiated from her.

The instant he touched her, she felt a sense of belonging. She parted her legs, giving him easier access, and as his fingers touched, stroked, she moved to his rhythm. She felt on fire, her belly ached. Her body tensed; something deep inside of her begged for more. Waves, contractions filled her body, making her convulse and shudder. "Now, Scott, now."

He removed his clothing, all the while looking down at her with those gorgeous blue eyes, drinking her in. She felt beautiful, inside and out, from that gaze alone.

When he stood to strip off his pants, she swallowed her embarrassment. She felt her cheeks flush as he lowered them past his hips. She'd never seen a naked man before—well, not in person. She'd seen diagrams in books and occasionally a naked butt in the movies. Lying on the blanket, with only the glow of the candles and fireplace, she scanned his body.

He was hard. The swell of his penis jutted out from his body. The thought of that rod penetrating her took her breath away. He slipped something from his pants, a tiny package she assumed was a condom. He tore it open and as he slid the latex along his shaft, gulped.

"Too much?"

"Yes. No! It's just…I've never…oh, this is embarrassing." She wanted to curl into a ball and die.

Lying down beside her, he took her face in his hands. "Shh. Nothing to be embarrassed about. We'll take it slow."

"I want you. I can feel it deep inside, the need, the ache—"

"But you're scared."

"A little."

"Want to stop?"

She shook her head "No."

"Are you sure?"

"Shut up and kiss me, Scott." Pulling him to her, she felt his bare chest touch hers, and dove into his lips. His hands touched her belly and she longed to have them all over her body. Yes, she was nervous—hell, scared—of what was to come, but her need was so great she found herself moving toward him.

"I think this might help you relax."

When his hands slid down past her belly to rest between her legs, she moaned.

"Just let yourself feel, Blackie."

He kissed her face as his fingers stroked below. His mouth was hot and oh-so-skilled as it skimmed down to her breast. He flicked the tip with his tongue, and she gasped with delight. His fingers continued to seek out pleasure, and she began to moisten. Reacting to the pleasure cascading throughout her core, she moved to the motion. When his finger slipped inside, her eyes flew open. As he slowly pumped that finger in and out, the heat began to rise from her belly all the way up to her chest.

She felt wild, crazy, and bucked against his hand. The sensation that hit her next took her breath away.

She panted as her body convulsed, cried out as the orgasm flooded her. When his fingers slowed and he slid up to take her mouth, she eagerly gave herself to him.

"Spread for me," he whispered against her mouth.

In a daze, she did as he asked and when he slid in between her legs, the nervousness set in again. She wanted to ask him if it would hurt, but was too embarrassed.

As if he read her mind, he said, "I'll take it slow. And any time you need me to stop, just say so."

She shook her head and kissed him deeply.

He pressed his engorged member against her, parting her lips to make way for his penetration. She told herself to relax, to stay calm, but as he pressed inside, she tensed up. He nibbled on her lips, slid his mouth along her neck, down to her breast. He took her nipple in his mouth, suckling as he pressed a tiny bit further inside. She felt herself being stretched, pried open, as he moved between her legs. It burned as he stretched her. Digging her nails into his back, she breathed through the pain. And when he began moving in and out, she felt herself easing open, relaxing to the movements.

He took her mouth as he began to move faster. She began to feel it, that deep arousal, that inner burn of desire. Clasping her arms around him, she met him thrust for thrust.

"Oh my God, Blackie!"

He thrust once, deep inside of her, and she felt his member pulsate. As it twitched inside of her, she cried out with her release.

What power she'd ever felt as a demon was nothing compared

to how she felt now. It surged through her like electricity, giving her energy she never knew existed. She lay on the floor, still quivering, the fire scorching her nudity. Scott rested over her. She giggled.

He looked down at her, lifted an eyebrow. "Something funny?"

"I feel incredible."

"I'm glad, but for future reference, it's not good to laugh after sex. It doesn't do much for a man's ego."

"Okay." She smiled up at him. "You were terrific, Scott. No—better than terrific. As soon as I think of a better word, I'll let you know."

"Are you okay? Really okay?"

He was so sweet in the way he asked her that. "A little sore, but other than that I feel incredible. I never expected it would be so good."

Again his brow came up. "Another *faux pas* after sex."

She bit her lip. "You know what I meant."

"I do. Just thought I would give you a heads-up for the future romantic partners."

She had no intention of having any other man.

"Come, lie down on my chest. I want to feel you against me." He held his arm out and when she snuggled in, he kissed her head. "Now that's perfect."

She had to agree. Lying in his arms after making love felt incredible. She wanted nothing more than to stay like this, with him, forever.

He stroked her hair, the strands slipping through his fingers to fall down onto her naked body. "You've created this entire romantic atmosphere, soft candle light, wine, great food and it's all nice, but one thing stands out above all else." He tipped her chin up with his fingers. "You gave yourself to me. I couldn't have received a more precious gift." His mouth came down to hers with a soft, gentle kiss.

He made her toes curl. "Scott Monroe, you are the sweetest man. I've waited a long time to feel this good, to feel...like a real woman. Thank you for giving that to me." She nuzzled into his chest, listening to his heartbeat. That steady rhythmic thumps lulled her as she let herself drift.

Then she heard Scott's stomach growl. "Sorry."

"We should eat…except the food's gone cold. I can reheat it." She hoped, anyway.

"That would involve moving. I'm happy where I am."

So was she, but when his stomach gurgled again, she sat up, laughing. "Here." She handed him a roll, which had been steaming hot not so long ago.

"Thanks." He dug in as if he were starved.

"I want to do that again in bed, all night long, and again in the morning."

He nearly choked on his bite. "I admire a woman who knows what she wants," he intoned with a wicked smile. "I guess we'd better fuel up."

CB

Two hours later, they tumbled into bed, clawing at each other as if they hadn't been sated before. Slick, damp bodies joining, sliding over, under, and together. Tongues probing, searching, tasting. Mouths ravenous to feed. They tumbled in the sheets, tangling limbs, fighting to break free so they could join once more. Aurora was alive, energetic, and on fire. She pulled at Scott, urging him to give her more, to show her everything, and more. When he grew fatigued, she rolled with him and took up the pace. She had never in her life felt so invigorated.

"I'll never be able to keep up with you." Drenched in sweat, Scott pulled the condom off his moist penis. "Crap."

"What?"

"It broke."

She took it from him, and leaning over the bed, tossed it in the trash. "It probably broke when you took it off." Taking him down with her as she lay against the soft, cotton sheets, she lifted his arm and snuggled in, just as before. "This is perfect."

As Aurora lay in her lover's arms, she desperately hoped Satan wouldn't call and disturb this, her very first taste of peace.

Chapter Twenty-Five

*S*cott woke to soft, sweet lips caressing his neck and chest. "Mmm, nothing better than waking to a beautiful woman." He pulled her up so they were eye to eye. The dreamy look in her golden eyes made him smile. "Good morning, Blackie."

"Good morning to you."

"How did you sleep?"

"Wonderfully. I like waking to you beside me."

Cupping her face in the palm of his hands, her hair falling to his chest, he kissed her softly, slowly. "Coffee?" he asked after he broke the embrace.

"Maybe later." She rested back against his chest. "Why did you pick this room?"

"Old habit. This used to be my bedroom." And nothing had changed since the last time he'd spent there.

"I like it. The other room was your father's?"

"Yeah." Memories of his father lying in his bed, sweating from withdrawal, came spiraling back.

He'd been meaning to pack up his father's things, but it just never seemed the right time, and he never seemed able to make himself do it. He would have to when the house sold, but he hadn't expected it would sell so quickly, or to Aurora for that matter. "I'll clear some things out for you." He'd been putting it off.

"What for?" She sat up, not even bothering to cover up with

the sheet crumpled at the foot of the bed.

"It's your house now. I'm sure you'll want to bring your own stuff here."

"I can still do that. I don't have that much, really, but you can leave your stuff here. It's still your home."

He turned to her. She looked like a mermaid, he thought, with her hair hanging down to her waist, covering but not concealing her body, her eyes glittering, and he felt his heart tug. "It hasn't been my home in a very long time."

"Why didn't you live here, instead of at the shelter?"

"I couldn't, not after my father died. Too many memories."

She stroked his chest and again, he melted. "Were they bad memories?"

"It had its moments." He teased his fingers through her hair. "He suffered his last days, but he refused being stuck in a hospital where he was just some person they looked after. He preferred being at home, where he was comfortable, in his own bed."

"How long did you live here?"

"He bought this house when I was born. When my mother died, he took me out on the road, said there was no way in hell some nanny was raising his only child. We came here occasionally over the years, when he would take breaks from touring. Summers off, Christmases, that sort of thing. When I decided to attend college, I came here to live." He played with her long, elegant fingers. "He came home one summer and stayed. He didn't say why, and it wasn't until a year later that he finally told me what had happened. He had nearly died of a drug overdose."

"How horrible. You didn't know he was using drugs?"

He shook his head. "I was blind, I suppose, plus I didn't see him much once I started college. Heroin and crack were his drugs of choice. He said he simply needed the edge. It wasn't long before he was hooked. While he stayed in the detox center, he got the idea for the shelter. He said the place he stayed at was so stiff, so formal. He wanted someplace a person could go to get better, and still feel at home."

"I think he definitely accomplished that." She stroked his

cheek lovingly. "Did he stay clean after that?"

"Yes, but his body had suffered terribly. I didn't find out until six months before his death that he'd contracted the HIV virus from dirty needles, but by the time he got help, it was too late. AIDS had set in with a vengeance." He could still remember the agony his father had endured, the pain, the delirium at times.

She sat up and looked down at him with sorrow. "How horrible for you, to have to sit by and watch your father die and know you couldn't do anything to stop it."

"It was hard, but even harder to find my father crumpled on the band room floor, an empty pill bottle in his hand, and a note beside him." He hadn't shared that with anyone in a very long time. It felt good to talk about it, to let it out.

"Oh, Scott, I am so sorry." Taking his face in her hands, she kissed him with such passion he felt it slide into his heart and ease aside the pain.

"The note he left explained simply that he couldn't sit by and watch me suffer for him. It was time I got on with my life. With the help of his doctor and the crew, we hid the real cause of death and gave the press the statement that he had simply died in his sleep."

She pulled him down and rested his head on her breast while she stroked his hair. "But you didn't get on with your life, did you, Scott? You put everything you had into the shelter."

He sat up, ran a finger along the line of her face. "I followed his dream. He'd worked too hard to make it a success for me to let it go. And I wanted to give other people the chance to survive. I wanted to help those in need as well." Because I wasn't able to help my father, he thought.

"You're doing a wonderful job with the shelter. Your father would be proud."

He hoped so. "Well, now that I've spilled my guts...." He leaned over and slid into a kiss that was so natural, as if he'd done it a million times before with her. "I need to get to work."

"Do you feel better having let that go?" she asked sincerely, stroking his face with her hands.

"Much. You amaze me, Blackie. You constantly amaze me."

She smiled, her amber eyes glittering. "Come back to bed with me, and I'll show you just how amazing I can be."

He moved just in time, one second slower and she would have snagged his arm. "You are a dangerous woman and, as tempted as I am to dive into bed with you, I need to go." He walked to the door and paused. Turning to the dresser, he picked up the gold watch that lay there, forgotten about for too long.

"What's that?"

He smiled. At one time, it had been too painful to look at, let alone wear. "The last thing my father ever gave me." He turned and lifted up the watch, slid it on his wrist. It wasn't as difficult now as it had been once. "If you hurry and get out of bed, Blackie, I'll treat you to breakfast."

ﭼ

"She didn't come home last night," Hunter informed Draco over coffee. "She called to say she would be staying at the new house, and I was not to disturb her."

Draco's hand tensed on the cup he held in his hands. He didn't like how that sounded, either. "I blocked her powers. She should come crying to me any time now." He was counting on it.

"What about her duties?"

Draco nodded when Hunter offered more coffee. "I've taken care of that." It had taken some convincing, but he had finally swayed Satan. It had been years, too many to count, since he'd done the duty for Satan. He couldn't say he missed watching a person die, or having their soul ripped away from an unwilling body, but he reminded himself it was what his daughter was made to do day after day. He shuddered with that knowledge.

"Do you honestly believe that by taking her powers away she'll see what she is doing is wrong?"

Draco sighed, flicked his wrist and held a cigarette and a gold lighter. "I'm counting on it." Clicking the lighter, he slid the cigarette between his lips and touched the tip to flame.

Hunter's brow creased. "I thought you quit."

Draco shrugged, one large shoulder lifting and falling casually. "I was told to start again or suffer horribly. Apparently, I was driving my wife crazy."

Hunter smirked as he lowered the cup to the table. "I can see why you would opt to start up again, considering she can kick your ass a dozen times over."

Draco blew smoke above his head, shrugging carelessly. "I like to amuse her by letting her believe she can."

Hunter let out a not-so-dignified snorting laugh. "You keep believing that, sir, but those of us in the real world know she can take you on, beat you down, and not even end up winded, or so much as chip a nail."

Draco narrowed his dark eyes. "You don't value your life much, do you, Hunter?"

Hunter shrugged, lifted the cup in his hands, and gave Draco a bland look. "You don't frighten me, Draco, not after living with your daughter for the past four months. Unfortunately, she inherited both yours and your wife's worst qualities."

Flicking his wrist, Draco had a glass ashtray floating over Hunter's head to land on the table. "Still sore she left you transformed into an ass all night?" Draco couldn't help but find that amusing and was damned proud of his daughter.

Hunter winced. "I prefer the term donkey."

Draco waved his cigarette in an erratic motion. "An ass is an ass." Laughing at Hunter's terse look, Draco slapped him on the back. "Thanks for the coffee, and the chat, old friend. Call me if you hear from her."

Chapter Twenty-Six

Three days went by without a call from Satan and Aurora couldn't have been happier. She was clueless as to why, but wasn't about to question it. She didn't miss it, nor did she miss having her powers. She spent her nights either in Scott's bed at the shelter, or in hers at the house. During the day, she worked hard, side by side with Scott.

When they tumbled into bed at night, Scott exhausted, Aurora took over. She gave him passion, showed him delights, and drove him up time and time again to the peak of all passion. She couldn't get enough of him, but she sensed he was getting worn down, and finally decided to give him a break.

As she sifted through her wardrobe at her new home, she realized she had yet to bring her stuff over from the old house. So when there was a lull in activity, and they could be spared, she and Scott headed to her old house to gather her things.

"My room's the third door to your right. Why don't you go get started? I need to see Hunter for a bit." Lifting to her toes, she kissed Scott slowly, sighing as their lips met. "You always taste so good."

"Packing, Aurora, nothing more, remember that." He tapped his finger on her nose.

"Are you worried I'll attack you in my room, Scott?"

"The thought occurred. Behave, or I won't help you." Kissing her quickly, he started up the stairs.

With a bounce in her step, she went looking for Hunter. "Oh, there you are." She found him sitting in the kitchen, busy working on a puzzle.

"Where else would I be?" he grumbled, not even lifting his head to look at her.

Taking a piece of the puzzle, she slipped it into the spot and pulled her hand back quickly when Hunter shot her a nasty look. "Sorry." She plucked it back out and laid it on the table. My, he seemed grouchy today. "I've come by to gather the rest of my stuff."

"Would I be part of that stuff?" Hunter snarled, slapping the piece back into place.

Oh yes, definitely grumpy. "You've always been invaluable, Hunter. You've been with my family for many years. But maybe it's time to retire." She walked to the refrigerator for a drink.

"Is your young man replacing me?"

She turned to him, surprised. "I'm not even going to dignify that with an answer."

"Are you sleeping with him?"

Her jaw tensed. "Nor will I dignify that one, either."

"Do you realize what you are doing?"

She poured a glass of chilled blood, cautioning herself to keep her temper in check. "I know perfectly well what I am doing and for the first time in my life, I am truly happy. Scott makes me happy." She gulped down the contents of her glass, poured another.

Hunter nodded, lifted a hand and jabbed a finger at her glass. "And what will you tell your young man if he sees you drinking that?"

She snarled. "He won't. He's in my room gathering my stuff."

"Now, but what about later, when you're together, at your new home? How will you hide the food you must eat, or the blood you need to survive, or the fact that you work for Satan gathering souls?"

"I may not have to tell him anything about my night job. I

haven't been called upon for days."

Hunter pushed from the table to rinse her glass and set it in the dishwasher. "No, you wouldn't be called because your father is doing the job for you."

Her body froze. Her eyes wide. She took Hunter by the arm. "My father is working for Satan?"

Hunter took her hand from his arm. "Yes, since the night he blocked your powers. Did you honestly think Satan would just let you go, give up his quest?"

"Why is he doing this?"

Hunter waved a hand in the air. "He has some silly notion that by taking away your powers you will see the error of your ways, see how much you need to have them and can't live without them. Without your powers, you can't do your job, so he took over."

She couldn't explain the amount of rage she felt inside. If he thought by taking away her powers she would come cowering to him, begging to have them returned, he was wrong. She didn't even miss them. She could easily go an eternity or more without them, and she was fully prepared to do so. "Well, it won't work. I don't need them, nor do I miss them. In fact, I had completely forgotten all about them. So you can tell Daddy when you check in, as I suspect you will the moment I leave here, tell him it won't work. And," she jabbed a finger at Hunter, "you can tell the Master that I refuse to resume my duties."

Hunter's face went absolutely white. "Aurora, you don't mean that. Think about the consequences. Think what will happen if you refuse Satan's calling."

She waved her hand at him. "He makes these threats in vain. He won't take my parents' lives. They're too valuable to him."

Hunter braced himself on the chair, looking as if he might fall over. "Listen to what you're saying, Aurora. If you believe that, little girl, you don't have a clue who you're messing with. To Lucifer, no one is too valuable to take back."

"Well, maybe, for the first time, someone is willing to challenge him. I'm more than ready to do so." She held her hand up to stop Hunter's rebuttal. "I have more important things to do."

Aurora walked the stairs to her room, and took a long breath before she entered. She found Scott shaking his head as he laid a stack of clothing on her bed. She had no doubt what she wanted, and what she was willing to sacrifice. There was only once in your life you felt so all-encompassed by one person. She would be a damn fool to throw that away just because Satan was a despicable being who held other people's lives in his hands. She wasn't his to toy with. She was her own person. It was time she started living like one. She stepped into the room, her heart an open book.

"What is it with you, woman, and clothes?" Scott grabbed another handful from her closet. "I swear, you have an entire department store in this closet alone."

She put her arms around him and leaned her cheek on his shoulder. "I love you." She felt him tense the instant the words left her lips. "No, don't say anything." She lifted her head and saw the raw shock on his face. "I just wanted to say that. I needed to say that." She released him to gather up her make-up and accessories.

"Aurora." He took her hand and led her to the bed. "You're not in love with me."

"I'm not? Then how do you explain how I feel when I'm with you?"

"Infatuation, maybe." He let out a long sigh. "I'm the first man you've ever been with."

She didn't like where this was heading. "First, second, tenth, however many it might have been, Scott, it doesn't change the fact that I want you to be the only. I know what I feel, and it isn't infatuation. I love you, deep in my heart. Achingly in love."

"You may think you are now, but someday some other man will come along and sweep you off your feet and show you what real love is."

He was beginning to piss her off. "No, Scott, there will be no other man, or men, because you are all I'll ever want." She was as sure of that as she was of living.

"You say that now, but someday, someday you'll realize you want more. You're still young—"

"Oh, cram it!" She stood from the bed, her steps angry as she moved. "I am sick and tired of people telling me I'm young. I'm sick of people telling me what I should or shouldn't feel, what I should do and shouldn't do, tired of people planning my future. It's my life—mine—and it's my heart. I know my heart, Scott, and I know that you are all I'll ever want, ever need." She was willing to sacrifice everything for him. Letting out a deep breath, she took his hands in hers. "Now, let's get this stuff packed up and moved out of here so I can cook you the most marvelous dinner you've ever had."

He pulled his hands free. "No, Aurora, you won't be cooking me dinner, not tonight, not ever again. I think it's time we ended this. B-best if we didn't see each other anymore."

Her eyes went wide with shock. Her heart felt as if it would burst. "You can't mean that, Scott."

He nodded, took a few steps back. "Yes, I do. It's for your own good." Turning, he walked out the door.

Listening to his footsteps fade along the carpeted hallway, Aurora sat on her bed, tears streaming down her face. She loved him, needed him, was willing to give up everything for him. Why couldn't he see that? Lifting her head, she cried out to Lucifer with rage. "I'm done, do you hear me? I'm done with you. I will not be your toy any longer. This is my life! Mine! And I want it back." Wiping a hand across her face, she stood, back straight. "I'm done being your slave." The wind stirred in her room, her hair flew out wildly. She took a seat on her bed and ignored it.

※

Holding Missy's hand in his, Draco strolled along one of the many gardens on his property. Though flowers were an aphrodisiac to demons, he insisted on growing several varieties.

"How long do you think she'll hold out?"

Draco snapped off a white daisy and tucked it in Missy's hair, behind her ear. "Not long. She'll come to her senses soon." He was counting on it.

"She's a stubborn woman," Missy said with pride.

"I'm used to dealing with stubborn women." Stopping their stroll, he turned his wife into his arms. "I've had years of practice with you, my love."

Her hand lifted to his face as she smiled up at him. "And you've loved every—" Her face froze. Her hand slid from his face. "Draco..." was all she managed as she slid lifelessly into his arms.

"Missy! Missy!" Scooping her into his arms, feeling the dead weight, he sent them to their room. "Oh, my love, wake up." Laying her on the bed, he began to stroke her face with long, slow, gentle strokes. What was going on? Why couldn't he feel her breathing? "My love!"

An icy wind churned in the room, cutting into him like sharp, jagged knives. As he held his wife in his arms, the message came through loud and clear.

"She has chosen. One must go."

༃

Determined she was not going to let Scott push her away, Aurora went to him. She found him huddled in his office, mulling over bills.

"You are a coward, Scott Monroe."

He lifted his head, let out a long breath. "What?"

She stomped into his office, fired up and ready. "A coward. A woman tells you she's in love with you and you run away with your tail between your legs. Well, guess what, Scott? I refuse to let you do this." The telephone rang, interrupting her. Just as she was about to tell him to leave it, he scooped it up.

"Monroe's Shelter, Scott Monroe here. How may I help you?" His eyes lifted to Aurora. "Yes, she's here. Just a moment." He held the phone out to her. "It's for you."

Baffled, she took the telephone and put it to her ear. "Hello? Hunter—"

"It's your mother, Aurora. You need to come home now."

"What's wrong?"

"There isn't much time. Your powers have been restored.

164

Hurry."

She dropped the phone and stared down.

"Blackie, what's wrong?"

"My mother. I…I need to go." She ran from the room and vanished without checking if anyone saw her.

Chapter Twenty-Seven

She had no idea what to expect when she set herself down in her parents' home. The bustle in the house, the worry on everyone's face, told her it was bad. Instructed to go to her parents' room, Aurora hurried up to see what had happened.

"Daddy." Her legs shaking, she walked to the bed where her father sat, holding his wife's hand. "What's going on?" Why was her mother lying on the bed, sleeping?

He turned to her, his eyes red and swollen, standing very slowly. "He has her, Aurora, he's taken her." He took her hands in his. "What have you done?"

"I didn't...I—" She clamped her mouth shut, realizing.

"I need to know what you said to him, Aurora."

She had never seen her father so frantic before, and he'd been crying. Her father never cried. "I...I told him I was done. Oh, Daddy, I didn't think he would—"

He squeezed her hands, pleading with his eyes. "You need to take it back, tell him you were wrong, make it better."

"No, no, this wasn't supposed to happen." What had she done? Oh, what had she done?

He gave her hands one hard jerk bringing her attention back to him. "Listen to me now, Aurora. He won't take me in her place, Aurora. I've tried. You have to stop this, please. I can't lose her. I just can't."

Tears fell like hot rain, sliding down her cheeks as she looked up at her father's pleading eyes. "I don't want to lose her, either." But to give in now would mean the end for her. She feared desperately that it would. Pulling from her father, Aurora ran to her mother.

She was so still, her chest flat, no air lifting it, and she was brutally cold.

"Mamma, Mamma, I'm sorry." She stroked her mother's sweet, gentle face. "I'm sorry, but I love him so." She leaned down, resting her face on her mother's chest. "I didn't think he would do this. Oh, I am so sorry."

"He doesn't say things he doesn't mean, Aurora." Her father rested a hand on her head.

Aurora lifted her head, her heart breaking. It was obvious what she needed to do. "I guess he's left me no choice." Kissing her mother's cheek, she vanished.

⌃

Aurora set herself down in her living room. Lifting her hands high above her head, she called out. "It's not fair, damn you! It's not fair." In an instant, she was transported to the dark void, her body quivering with fear.

You chose your destiny.

The icy wind whooshed in her ears, surrounded her, tossing her long hair in her face. "I didn't want this. I just wanted my life back."

You chose.

"No, damn you, no! Why can't I have both?" She turned in circles, hoping against hope to catch even the smallest glimpse of him. Though she'd been in communication with him, she'd never seen him.

There is only one way.

"Your way!" Her voice rang out in the darkness.

Yes.

"Well, I'm tired of your way. I'm tired of you." With the words barely out of her mouth, she was tossed around, her body slamming against things that were not there but injured with the sharpness of objects that were. The darkness around her began to suffocate her.

There is no other way. The choice was made.

"I didn't make the choice, the original choice. I'm innocent in all of this." She stood on shaky legs, straightening her back. "You can't do this to me."

YOU CHOSE!

Her head exploded in pain with his bellowing, deep gut-wrenching voice. Clasping her hands over her head, she fell to her knees. There was no solid ground below her yet she didn't fall through. "I chose because I'm in love. I shouldn't be punished for that." The pain sliced into her chest, as if someone had jabbed a knife deep, then slid it all the way down, tearing flesh as it cut. She wanted to cry out, but that would only fuel his anger more.

You cannot love a human.

"I love my mother." She gasped as the pain threatened to take her under its dark veil.

She is demon.

"She is also part human," she reminded him, her breath raspy, every word causing immense pain.

You chose.

"Answer me. Why is it different if I love a human when my father was granted the love for his?" She felt herself being spun wildly until her head fell and the dizziness swamped her.

Your love is pure human. His is not.

Though her breath was labored, Aurora refused to give in, and stood strong. "And what if I don't obey? What if I chose my lover over my mother?" The flash of light was so sharp, so bright, it stung her eyes and penetrated her brain. When the blur cleared, she found herself standing in her father's office. "Daddy?"

"Sir."

"Leave me." Draco waved his free hand, the other clutching a crystal glass filled with Scotch.

"You can't lock yourself away, Draco."

"I said leave!" His voice boomed out, shaking the foundation.

Hunter stood his ground. "It is tragic. We all miss her—" He was tossed across the room and landing with a violent thud.

"No, no one misses her as I do." He gulped down his booze, filled the glass once more.

Hunter stood, dusted off his jacket. "Yes, sir, that is true, but you can't let yourself go. You need to go on, for your daughter's sake."

His head lifted, his eyes bloodshot and swollen from tears he'd shed endlessly since his wife was taken from him. "She has what she wanted. I am of no use to her now."

"Draco—"

"Leave!"

Sending Hunter away, Draco gulped down the contents of the glass before throwing it across the room. It crashed against the wall, into a dozen pieces as it tumbled to the floor.

Aurora jumped, but before she could run to her father, to tell him she still needed him, he was gone. "No, no bring him back."

You have chosen, and sealed your fate as well as your father's.

"No," she wept. "No, don't do this, please."

You did this, not me.

She wiped her face but the tears still fell. "Okay, okay, you win." She gave in. "Bring her back."

Have you chosen differently?

"Yes," She would sacrifice her love, her need for Scott and the pleasure he gave her not just in body but soul, for that of her parents. "I'll do whatever you want, just bring her back."

As you wish.

He sent her back to her mother.

"Sir." Hunter patted Draco's back, his head still resting on his wife's chest.

He lifted his head, and watched his wife's eyes flutter open. "Oh, my love." Cupping her face in his hands, he smothered her with kisses.

She smiled turning warm eyes to her daughter. "Aurora."

Stiffening her back, Aurora walked to her mother. "I'm here,

Mamma."

"I am so sorry."

Fighting the tears, Aurora nodded, and vanished. She couldn't let her mother see the amount of pain she was in.

CR

Sitting alone in her house, the house that had once belonged to the man she loved, Aurora wept. She could never have him. Because of a decision made twenty-two years ago, she would never be allowed to love.

The cigarette smoldered in her hand, a stream of smoke drifting up, up and was gone, swallowed by the darkness. She felt swallowed by the darkness. She'd been granted a life, but not the opportunity to live it. She was doomed to be alone, lonely, for the rest of her long, agonizing life. She could never again have Scott, never feel him in her arms, never wake with him beside her, never have a life with him. Satan had made that brutally clear. If she chose her heart over her family, she would lose, her father would lose. Either way, she would lose. She didn't want to be with a demon. Perhaps it was the rebellious side of her, wanting something different, something more.

When the voice boomed in her head, she closed her eyes and wept. Her destiny was calling and she would give anything if it would only just disappear. Waving the cigarette away, she stood, sucked back her tears. With a thought, only a single thought, she transformed into the Angel of Death—her long black hair falling to her knees, the black clothes, her trademark, and the boots that walked silently to her master. Taking one long breath, she shifted into the beast she'd been at birth. Her face darkened, her teeth grew sharper, her mouth wider. Her forehead spread, became ribbed, her eyes, set and dark. She was now, and always would be, Satan's tool.

"I am yours." She closed her eyes, and let him guide her to her destination.

The smell of death was prominent, even before she opened her eyes. Daring to look, she saw the lifeless bodies spread out before her. So much death. So much senseless violence. That was life, in all its glory. Was it any wonder people grew depressed?

As a tall man dressed in blue jeans and a blue jean jacket entered the room, stuffing bills in his pants pockets. She prepared to do her duty. He had murdered his last victim, robbed his last shop. It was his time to pay.

A smile on his face, he stopped short when he saw the dark figure before him. "What the hell?"

"Exactly where you'll be going."

"You first." Lifting his gun, he aimed it at Aurora's head, and squeezed the trigger.

She stopped the bullet a fraction of an inch before her face. Though her hand never moved, the bullet turned, aimed at him. As it hung in mid air. She looked up and saw the wide-eyed amazement he wore on his scarred, rugged face. "No, you first." Releasing her mind control on the bullet, she sent it speeding toward him. "Say goodbye." The bullet crashed into his head. It went through tissue, breaking, smashing everything in its path. She watched it fly out the back of his skull, pulling matter with it.

As he fell to the floor, his eyes wide, she stepped back. She watched the blood seep out of a nasty wound to puddle beneath him. Despite the horror he'd caused, knowing his soul was black, she hated that it had been she who'd taken his life. Stepping back, she watched the shadows come. The body jerked, as the soul was torn from its host.

She turned to the innocent lives he'd taken, and a single tear slid from her eye. They'd been gone long before they realized what had happened. Turning, she felt herself lift off, taken to her next destination. She stood, ready to prey on her next victim, understood this was her punishment. This was now her life. By the end of the night, by the time the sun began to rise and light the sky a brilliant orange, she had ended six lives.

Exhausted, she fell into bed, and drifted off. Tomorrow, she had no doubt, would be much the same.

CঙB

Scott sat in his office as the sun rose, lighting the sky with a beautiful array of colors. *She loves me.* And God help him, he was in love with her. Where it had come from, when had it happened? He didn't know, but it had slammed into him when she had said the words to him. He hadn't believed her, couldn't, yet it would tear him to pieces to lose her, and he would, eventually, when she finally realized all she felt for him was infatuation. He wiped a hand across his face. He was bone-tired, yet he hadn't been able to close his eyes and sleep.

She'd been there every damn time he'd closed his eyes. She'd been there to taunt him, her long, dark, silky hair fanning over him while she held herself up over him. Those golden eyes filled with desire, seduction, luring him into her web. And that body, a body that fit his so perfectly, it felt as if they'd been molded for each other. That soft, purring voice, whispering to him to take her, to make her his. God, he was a doomed man.

He couldn't stand being without her.

He didn't have time in his life for a relationship. He was busy enough trying to keep the shelter his father had held dear from being shut down. Crumbling. And now, here he was at dawn, the revelation that he was head-over-heels in love with a woman he barely knew, wanting what he was sure he could never have. She had never been with a man before him. She was young; he wasn't. He'd had his share of women. She was in love with him. He was in love with her. Only he was sure his was the kind of love that would endure, that would last, that would never die.

Would hers?

Rubbing a hand across his face, he wished he had the answers.

Chapter Twenty-Eight

*F*or three days she'd done what was asked of her, taken life after life in an endless wave of ruthlessness. And after each night, she went to her room, and hid. She took no calls. Though the phone rang almost incessantly, she ignored it. She put a block on her bedroom door, an impenetrable wall that not even her parents could remove. And they had tried. She cast a spell of isolation, for that was exactly how she felt. She lay on her bed, hour after hour, watching the shadows fall as the sun shifted, as the earth moved, as time drifted endlessly on. Shadows, always shadows. Her life consisted of them.

Her mother was well, and back to normal. She'd traveled in her mind to see for herself. And she understood that her parents worried for her, but she simply couldn't bear to see anyone just yet. So she remained in her room, day after day, watching the time drift slowly, torturously slow.

She heard the doorbell ring. She rolled onto her side and ignored it. When it persisted, she clamped her hands over her ears and wished whoever it was would just leave her be. Finally, it stopped. A single tear slid from her eyes. She was alone, always alone. She jumped as the door slammed shut. She heard the tapping of shoes on the stairs. Bolting up, she stared at the door.

"Aurora, where are you?"

Scott! *No, not Scott*! He burst into her room. She was

dumbfounded as to how he had managed to break her spell.

"Oh thank God, there you are. Why didn't you answer the door, or the phone for that matter? I've been calling you for days. Are you all right?"

"How did you get in?"

He angled his head, lifted the keys in his hand. "My keys. I never got around to giving them to you. I suppose I should have, but now I'm glad I didn't." He sat on the bed. "Are you sick?"

She hadn't meant the front door. She'd meant the seal she had placed on her bedroom door, but he wouldn't know that, couldn't know that. "Yes." It seemed the easiest thing to say.

"Is it your mother? Did something happen?"

Aurora shook her head, biting back her tears. "She's fine now, better."

"What happened?"

As if I could tell you the truth. "Her heart," she lied. It was all she could think to say in response to his question.

"But she's better now?"

She nodded her head, her hair sliding from her shoulder to fall over her chest.

"But you're not?" He reached out only to have her flinch. "Is there anything I can do?"

She wanted so desperately to fall into his arms and weep, to have him hold her, but she couldn't. "No, but thank you for asking." It was his kind heart that had drawn her to him and now it was killing her.

"Aurora, I think—"

"I would like you to leave now." She pulled from the bed, terrified that if he touched her, grabbed for her, she would fall helplessly into his arms.

"Not until we talk."

She shook her head, picking up the brush on her nightstand and began stroking it through her hair. "There's no need to talk. You were right. I was foolish to tell you I loved you. I've come to realize I only thought I did." It stung her like a flame to her throat to have to say that. "I also think it would be best if I didn't continue working at the shelter."

"Aurora—"

"Don't try to make this better, Scott. You can't. Believe me, you never could." She stiffened her lip and turned to him, her eyes determined. "Now, if you wouldn't mind leaving, I need my rest."

He stood, stared at her with somber blue eyes. "You're doing this to hurt me. I know that, and I deserve it after the way I treated you, but—"

"No, no please, Scott, don't so this." She couldn't hold the tears. They stung her eyes like fire.

He walked a little closer, testing her. "I've also come to realize something these past few days, Blackie." He gripped her chin in his hand and held her face firmly. "And that is that I am in love with you. And I think I know why you're doing this now."

The tears slid from her eyes to wash over her cheeks. "No, Scott, you don't." How could he? He didn't even know the real her.

He closed his mouth over hers, solid, firmly; he made her head swim with the kiss. Releasing her, he strode confidently from the room.

"Scott." But by the time she went after him, he was gone. Spinning around, she ran to the door. Slamming it, she fell face first onto the bed. Why was she being punished for loving? Why, oh why, had she been born to such misery?

೮ઙ

Scott had never been to the great Starr mansion, but he had seen it from the outside many times, and he had heard a great deal about it from others who had been inside. They spoke of its magnificent beauty, of its huge rooms, of its elegance, and, they spoke of the strange activity that seemed to go on behind the doors as well. Only rumors, speculation, but Scott didn't take it seriously. If there were ghosts inside this home, they had better cut a path for him because he was a man enraged.

Lifting the elegant gold-encrusted, star-shaped doorknocker, he rapped it good and hard. He wasn't leaving until he got to the truth. When the door opened, he was more than surprised to see Hunter. "Are you everywhere?"

Hunter kept his face blank. "May I help you?"

"Nope, only one person can help me. Is he in?" Pushing arrogantly past Hunter , he entered the grand foyer and gazed up at the huge crystal chandelier overhead. "Wow, must be hell cleaning that thing."

"May I ask what you are doing here?"

Scott turned to Hunter, who looked as if he wanted to fillet him alive. "I'm here to see Mr. Starr. Get him."

Hunter's eyes went wide. "I beg your pardon?"

"You heard me. I want to see him. Go tell him I'm here and that I have no intention of leaving until he sees me." When all Hunter did was stare at him, Scott waved his hand. "Shoo, now."

With a loud grunt, Hunter spun around and stomped off.

This house wasn't so bad. It certainly didn't have the creepy feeling people said it did. If anything, he felt love, comfort, and happiness. This was the home Aurora had grown up in, yet she chose to live in the meager house *he* had grown up in. The woman constantly amazed him.

"He will see you now."

Nodding, Scott stuffed his hands in his jeans pockets and followed Hunter. Why did he suddenly feel as if he were walking the plank?

Pushing the tall oak doors open, Hunter showed Scott into Mr. Starr's office. Behind the huge cherry wood desk, he sat, regal as ever. This was a man of great wealth, a man who owned more than any given person should be allowed to own, but aside from that, he was a father. Scott had to remind himself of that. And he was sure the man loved his daughter dearly, despite trying to run her life.

Standing, Mr. Starr held his gaze firm. His dark eyes pierced Scott's very core.

"Mr. Monroe."

Scott felt licks of ice slide into him. "Mr. Starr." He didn't hold out his hand because he was sure it wouldn't be accepted, nor did Mr. Starr hold out his, apparently for the same reason.

"You demanded to see me?"

Scott nodded. He could tell the guy was less than impressed. And if he believed a person could kill with eyes alone, he'd be a dead man. "More or less. I'm here about Aurora."

"Have a seat."

Scott sat in the small-yet-comfortable wooden chair while Starr took his. One really couldn't call it a chair when it looked more like a throne. Boy, did this guy have an ego. "I was just with her, and she looks terrible."

Starr nearly jumped from his seat. "You've seen her? How? When?"

Baffled, Scott shifted in his seat. "I went over to see her. I used my key and walked in. She was in her room." Shaking his head at Starr's look of unease, he continued. "What did you say to her?"

"Did she invite you into her room?"

Was he not listening to him? "No, I walked in."

"Look, if you're going to flip out, don't bother. I still had a key from when I lived there. She didn't give me one. I simply forgot to give mine back. I'll ask again, what did you do to her?"

"I have no idea what you are talking about."

"You had to have said something to her to make her push me away."

Starr lifted cool eyes, pulled a cigarette from the gold case in his breast pocket. "I said nothing. If she pushed you away, it was on her own accord." Clicking the matching gold lighter, Starr drew on the cigarette.

Scott thought about what he'd said to her, how he'd insisted she wasn't in love with him but instead, infatuated. "I admit we had a spat. I said something that might have pushed her away, but there was something more. When she left my office, she was determined we could make it work, yet when I saw her today, she pushed me away."

"Young women tend to be fickle with their emotions, forever changing their minds."

Scott shook his head, leaning forward. "She is anything but fickle. If anything, she's an incredibly determined woman. Something or someone convinced her to change her mind." Scott narrowed his eyes. "I believe that someone is you."

Starr flicked the ashes from his cigarette in the glass ashtray on his desk and spoke dismissively. "I said nothing to her. If she's recanted her affections for you, it was by her choice and hers alone."

"See, that's the thing. I don't believe it was her choice." He kept his eyes firm. "I know you dislike me, disapprove of her seeing me, prefer I not see her. But I'm here to tell you that won't happen. I'm in love with her, and I'll do whatever it takes to get her back."

Starr set the cigarette in the ashtray and stood, planting both hands, palms flat, on the desk as he leaned over it. "You won't have her, Scott. You will never have her."

He could have sworn he saw red in the darkness of his eyes. Trick of the light, he decided. Standing, Scott matched Starr's determination. "Watch me." As he turned to leave, he could have sworn he felt electricity snapping in the room.

03

She stood in the darkness of the night, blending in but not so much that she couldn't be seen. Before her was a man who had beaten countless women, for sheer pleasure. He was bad, but she just didn't have the strength she once had to make him suffer.

Lifting her hand, she punched a hole in his chest, and clutched hard on his heart. He didn't have time to gasp, or even come to terms with what was happening to him. He simply died. As the man fell lifelessly to her feet, she stepped back and cried.

"No! Stop!"

She spun around, shielded her eyes from the piercing light of a flashlight.

"Blackie?"

Chapter Twenty-Nine

*I*n an instant, she felt as if time had stopped. She looked at Scott, who stood gaping at her. It seemed as if the air stilled, the earth paused, and time had stopped. Though it was only a few seconds of silence, it seemed like an eternity. In one quick snap, time seemed to rush back in and left her nearly breathless.

"What...what are you?"

"It's a long story, Scott. I need to explain." But when she took a step toward him, he backed off. Her heart sank.

"It's been you. This whole time, it was you. You're the Dark Angel."

"Yes. Scott. You need to listen to me."

"No, no, I need to go." But as he turned, she held him to his spot. "What the hell?"

"I did it, Scott. I'm sorry, but I need to keep you here so I can explain." She regretted deeply using her powers on him, but she couldn't let him go for so many reasons.

He looked down at his feet, grunted as if he was trying to move. "How...how the hell did you do that?"

She came up beside him silently, and her lips trembled when he flinched. "I'll explain it all to you, but not here." Taking his hand, hurting when he tensed, she sent them both to her new home.

"Did we just....?"

"Yes. It's going to hit you in a few seconds, so I suggest you sit down."

"I'm fine, thank you." He swallowed, looking around with bewilderment.

"Trust me, Scott, you will need to sit." She had no more than gotten the last word out when she saw the color drain from his face. "I warned you, just remember that." Grabbing him as his knees buckled, she sat him in the reclining chair by the fireplace. "Just breathe."

"Can't." He gasped for air, clutching his throat.

"Yes, you can." She stroked his back, encouraging him to breathe. "Relax, don't push it. It will come. This is only temporary." She stroked his face while the sweat clung to his forehead. "Here it comes now, take it slow." But he didn't listen, and gulped in greedily. "Relax." She stroked his face a little more, hoping he wouldn't hyperventilate on her.

He choked, gasped, coughed. "What the hell just happened?"

She patted his hand as he rested his head on the chair. "It takes a while for the human body to grow accustomed to being transported from one plane to the next. Picture the molecules in your body like water and oil in a bottle. If you shake them up, they try to blend as one, but when you set it down, they begin to separate and return to normal." She wasn't sure he was following her, or that his mind was grasping what was truly happening.

"Your head should start hurting soon and your body will ache. It'll probably feel like you've gone a few rounds in the boxing ring, and you'll feel nauseous. But it will pass."

He lifted his head, stared at her with wide eyes. "What is going on? You were a...your face was all... Are you for real?"

She wanted to stroke his cheekbone, but now that he was looking at her as if she were something he feared, she wasn't sure he would allow the contact. "I'm very real, and I'm still your Blackie."

"No, not quite. Oh fuck." Grabbing his head, he fell back against the chair, groaning while his eyes began to water. "Jesus Christ! You made it sound like a little headache. An axe to the head isn't a little headache. Oh God, I think I'm going to hurl. Isn't this just the perfect goddamn day?"

She stroked his hand, soothing him as much as she could. There was really nothing she could do to stop the process in his body. It took time for it to settle back to normal. "I've never had it happen to me, so I don't know."

"Well, the next time you try this on someone, don't." He rubbed his head, looking at her with narrowed eyes. "What are you?"

She sat back on the coffee table and began to explain. "My father is the direct descendant of Satan. He was born full demon. My mother was conceived by a demon and a witch. She is also part human. I'm a little of both."

"Oh yeah, yeah, I see it now." He laughed, uncontrollably.

"Oops, I forgot to tell you about the euphoria. You'll feel a little high for a bit. Ever smoked weed?"

"No, no I haven't, but I might consider it after this." Bent over at the waist, he couldn't stop laughing.

"No, you won't. See, it's almost over. I like your laugh, by the way. Very sexy."

"This is crazy." Pulling himself from the chair, he stood. His knees wobbled and he fell back down.

"Careful, you don't have your sea legs yet."

He ran a hand over his face. "I'm dreaming, hallucinating. None of this is real. It's some insane nightmare or illusion."

"I'm real, Scott. You aren't dreaming, or hallucinating, and I am no illusion." Taking his hand in hers, she pulled him closer and sank her lips into his. She took the kiss slow, making sure he could feel her, taste her, and know she wasn't a figment of his imagination. "See, real."

He leaned back, licked his lips. "How is this possible?"

She needed a smoke, desperately, and since she didn't have any on her, her only recourse was to conjure one up. "Sorry, but I need this." Snapping her fingers, the cigarette appeared in her fingers, smoldering.

"Oh Jesus, Jesus." He laid his head on the back of the chair and closed his eyes.

"I'm sorry, really I am. Let me try to answer your question." She stood, because walking helped her concentrate, helped with the nervousness she was feeling. "There are all manner of things that people choose not to believe. That they ignore. Witches, demons, vampires—all walk the earth."

"I'm trying to picture Glinda the Good Witch, but I keep seeing the bad one, you know, the Wicked Witch of the East, or was it West?" He shook his head. "Okay, let's see, witches, demons, and vampires. Are we talking vampires as in *I want to suck your blood*?"

She smiled as she blew a cloud of smoke in the air. He did a great Slavic impression of Count Dracula. "Yes, well, not in the way people have portrayed them, but close enough. You would be surprised how many walk amongst us, holding down normal jobs, living normal lives."

"Oh yeah, sure. The woman at the grocery store, she's got these fangs. I should have guessed." He snickered lightly, shaking his head. "Is that what you are?"

He wasn't really grasping it all, but she kept going on the off chance it would register soon. "No, though we do need blood to survive, as well as some raw meat. It's been a long time since my kind has preyed on innocent humans for food."

His eyes went wide. All the blood in his body seemed to drain from his face. "Oh God, do you have any idea how that sounds?"

"Sorry, I know it's hard for you to grasp all of this and try to understand it all."

"No, no, you don't. You have no idea."

She waved her smoke away. "I think I do, somewhat. See, I didn't learn what I really was until I was six," she began. "As a child, I was secluded from everyone, everything on the outside world, and kept in my home. My parents were afraid they would take me out and I would do something to give them away. You know, conjure up a toy they wouldn't buy me, make someone do something, change things, cause a minor storm with my tantrums, and so on. When I turned six, and I made Hunter disappear, they sat me down and explained what was happening to me."

She could still remember it all, the terror the disbelief. "They explained to me that because I was demon, I couldn't attend normal schools, I couldn't go out, and I couldn't have friends unless they were people that knew of our kind. The older I got, the harder it was for me to keep to myself, but that's neither here nor there. I'm veering off the topic."

She took a deep breath. "The fact is when my parents first told me what I was, it terrified me. I couldn't look in a mirror for fear of what I might see. And I didn't believe them, not completely, until I experimented. It hit me like a brick to the stomach. Once I got over my terror, I learned to accept it." *And detest it with every breath.*

He rubbed his fingers along his temples. "Okay, okay, tell me again. What are you, and your parents?"

She sighed. "Demons. My father was born in Hell. He is the great-great-grandson of Satan. My mother is part witch: half demon, half human."

He ran a hand through his hair, staring at her. "Satan, as in the big ugly red guy with horns and a tail?"

She nearly laughed. He had no idea how wrong he was. "That's only a depiction of what people have decided he looks like. Believe me when I say they are so far off. He isn't red, and he doesn't have horns and a tail. He is so much worse."

"Okay, let me see if I'm getting this." He stood now, his legs a little more stable. "Your father is a demon, a descendant of Satan, the big bad?"

"Yes."

"Your mother is a witch? Part demon, part human?"

"Yes, she didn't learn what she was until she was my age. It's a long story. I won't get into that right now."

"Thank you. I'm not sure how much data this fuzzy brain can handle right now. Okay, dad's full-fledged demon, mom is demon-witch-human, and that would make you...?" He turned to her, his blue eyes a little glassy.

"Three-quarters demon, one-quarter human/witch." She saw

his mind working. "I wanted to tell you, Scott, but it was forbidden. Us being together is forbidden. That was why I had to stop seeing you. It's forbidden for a demon to mate with a human."

He stopped, looked down at her. "Yet your mother was conceived, you were conceived from a human?"

She nodded her head, waved her cigarette away. "Yes, but it's complicated."

"Hey, my head's already spinning. Go for it. Explain how that can be."

She let out a long breath. "Okay, yes, my mother was conceived by a human, but her father is full-demon. Satan punished him mercilessly for mating with her and conceiving a child, tormenting him before he was stripped of his powers."

"Powers?"

She snapped her fingers, producing a glass of wine in his hands. His eyes bugged out, but it was the easiest way to show him. "Powers."

He stared at the glass, his mouth dropping. "Go on."

She set the glass beside her on the table. "My parents wanted a life together. They married, bending all the rules, and when they wanted to conceive, they had to go to Lucifer to beg for permission. See, Satan has no control of humans. My parents' punishment for having me was…let's just say they sold my soul to have me."

"Uh huh, go on."

Was he following her? "They understood they weren't allowed to conceive because my mother is part human, but they wanted a family, so, what else could they do but barter with Satan. Lucifer finally gave in, after years of being badgered by my parents, and granted them a child, with conditions."

"And those conditions were?"

"They would have their child, but when that child—me—turned twenty-one, I was to work for Satan, gathering souls."

Light came into his eyes as it dawned. "The Dark Angel." He grabbed the glass and downed the contents. "Can I have another? I think I need it." She snapped her fingers and the glass was full.

"Incredible." He gulped it down, as he looked up at Aurora. "So, you work for the Devil?"

"He really hates being called that, but yes. I go out at night, he guides me to the soul he wants, the ones that are tarnished, the lost, the evil, and I…do what it takes to send them to him." She couldn't say kill, but that was exactly what she did.

He shook his glass, indicating he needed it refilled, and smiled when more wine appeared. "Well, I guess that would make us rivals, wouldn't it? You take the people I'm trying to save." He gulped down the rest of the wine, and blinked his eyes rapidly. "I'm getting drunk. How is that possible after three glasses of wine? I think I need to lie down."

"It's all part of being transported and your body being out of whack. I'll help you to your room." She stood, reaching out her hand.

He eyed her hand, pulling his behind his back. "Uh, no offense, but do you think we could walk this time? With the booze in my system, I don't think scrambled molecules would go over well. I hate to vomit."

She smiled. Though he was drunk, his humor was welcome. "How about I carry you?"

His eyebrow shot up, his lips curved up. "Sure, I'd like to see you try."

"You're kind of cute when you're drunk. Okay, up we go, big boy." Scooping him up, lifting him in her arms, she didn't even break a sweat or grunt at his weight.

He looked up at her, down at the ground. "Hmm, guess you can." He squeezed her arm. "My, my, what strong arms you've got. All the better to carry you with, my dear. Oh yeah, drunk. Very very drunk."

She shook her head and smiled. "Close your eyes, Scotty." She carried him to her bed, laid him down, and covered him with the blankets. He was out cold in seconds. She placed a tiny kiss to his forehead, hoping that when he woke up, everything was clear to him, and he didn't hate her. Sighing, she left him to sleep.

Coming down the stairs, she found her parents waiting for her in the living room.

Chapter Thirty

She could tell the instant she saw them that they knew.

"We waited until you'd taken him from the room." Her mother informed her, holding her hand out to her daughter. "He knows."

She took her mother's hand, held her for the longest moment. "It's good to see you up and about."

"I have you to thank for that." She kissed Aurora's forehead.

"What will you do with him now that he knows?" her father asked as he leaned one arm on her stone fireplace.

Aurora could tell he wasn't impressed. "That will be his decision to make."

"How so?" Her mother asked, drawing her daughter down to the sofa beside her.

"If he can handle what I've told him, who I am and keep it a secret, I see no reason not to just let it go."

"If he can't?"

She looked up at her father, who now held a long, thin cigarette between his fingers. "I'll decide that if the time comes."

"It would be best just to erase his memory and send him to his own bed."

She lifted cool eyes to her father and spoke in slow, even tones. "He *is* in his bed."

"Aurora—"

She held up her hand to stop him. "It's my decision, Daddy.

I'll deal with him how I please." She turned to her mother, ignoring the growl from her father. "How are you feeling?"

Aurora felt comforted when her mother took hold of her hand.

"Better. Oh, darling, I am so sorry for what this has caused you. We never wanted this for you."

There had never been any doubt that her parents loved her. "You and Daddy wanted a child to complete your family. I understand that."

"There was no other way." Her mother sniffled back her tears.

"I know."

"You love him very much?"

Aurora hesitated, sighed. "Yes, yes, I do."

"Oh love, this must be tearing you apart inside."

She stood now, no longer able to look her mother in the eye. "I never thought I'd feel so much pain. Not even the pain Satan has inflicted on me can compare, but I know we can't be together. A cruel twist of fate."

"You will have to let him go."

She turned to her father, fighting her tears. "I know." It was painfully obvious.

"Will you be able to?"

Now she turned to her mother. "I don't have a choice."

"Oh darling, if there were some other way."

Her mother meant it. "I won't lie and say I'll get over it, get over him, because I never will. But I will go on." Day by day, night after night, alone, and lonely. This was now her life. She looked over t her father. "Will he?"

His face was so stern. "He'll have to."

"Come home with us, dear."

She smiled at her mother, but shook her head. "I can't. I belong here now. This is my home. I can't hide from my problems all my life. I'll be fine, Mamma, I promise." She wouldn't ever be fine again.

Her mother stood, taking Aurora's hands in hers. "You will hurt, you will cry, but yes, you will go on." She kissed her cheeks. "You know where we are if you need us."

Aurora nodded, squeezed her mother's hands. "I love you both." She turned to her father. "Always."

"We love you too, sweetie."

What her father said was true. Still….

Her parents vanished and Aurora walked back to the window, looking out into the night. She hated her life. Destined to be alone, tied to a contract that had been made long before her birth and there was nothing she could do about it. Sliding to the floor, Aurora wept tears she'd fought back since she'd first seen Scott standing in the alley. Why, why did life have to be so cruel?

And when Satan called upon her to finish her job, she went, sobbing the entire time.

Ɒ

Scott dreamt of witches, vampires, and demons chasing after him. And in the midst of all the fear, all the chaos was Aurora. A light in the darkness, a candle in the storm. She'd held her hand out to him, and he had walked to her willingly. As she drew him into her arms, he felt her change. Lifting his head, he saw what she was, and screamed when she sank her teeth into his flesh. As she pulled him down, took what was his, he felt himself giving, willingly, giving his life to her.

He woke in a sweat-drenched haze, his mind reeling. What the hell was that? Wiping his eyes, he focused on the room. His room. He was home. It had all been a dream. His father hadn't died, he wasn't in charge of the shelter and he hadn't met an incredible woman and fallen in love with a demon. But when he saw her robe, saw her perfume and her makeup, it became obvious just how real it all was.

Climbing out of bed, his body aching, every muscle sore and rebelling his movements, Scott went to shower. If he was going to face off with a demon, the woman he loved or not, he wanted to be fully alert. Scott turned the taps on, setting the water at a near-blistering temperature, and entered the shower. Stepping under the spraying water, he washed away his fatigue. He couldn't wrap his mind around everything he'd been told, and really, would any sane human being be able to? Demons, witches, vampires and…Satan.

Drying off, he had no choice but to put his sweaty clothes back on. Drawing in a deep breath, he walked down the stairs.

It felt as if he'd drunk the contents of an entire bar. His mouth was sandpapery and he was so thirsty he could probably drink an ocean of water. But when he stepped into the kitchen and saw her sitting at the table, her long black hair fanning her body, he forgot his thirst.

She looked up at him, concern in her eyes. "Hi. Did you sleep well?"

"No," he stated sharply as he headed to the fridge. His thirst returning, he pulled out a jug.

"Uh, Scott, you don't want to drink that."

He looked down, his eyes focused, and he saw the contents. "Blood?" He was holding a container of blood.

"Yes." She took it from him and set it back in the fridge. "Why don't I make you some coffee?"

"Good idea. Coffee would be good." He touched her arm. She felt warm, and he remembered how she felt in his arms, against him, sliding with him in ecstasy as their bodies joined. "You're real."

"We established that last night." He released her. She proceeded to make him coffee, reaching for the paper filters and then the grounds. "Or can't you remember what we talked about?"

"No, no, I remember." It was painfully clear in his throbbing head. "You're a demon and you drink blood, obviously, chilled." He shook his head.

"You should sit down, Scott."

"I'm fine. So…." He looked up at her. "Now what?"

"I'm not sure I know what you mean."

Why did coffee always take so long to drip? Grabbing a cup, he noticed all of his father's dishes were still in the same place he'd left them. He held a cup under the slow-dripping coffee. "What will you do to me now that I know what you are? Will you hand me over to Satan?"

"No. Never. What I do depends on you, and if you can accept what I am, who I am, and keep it secret."

"That's a relief, but I'm not sure about the accept part." With his cup perched under the trickle of brew, Scott glanced over at Aurora. She looked somber, and if he didn't look away soon, he'd cave. "Just yet."

"I understand that, but I need to know you won't give me away, or my family."

"Who would believe me? I'm not sure I believe it myself. Damn, this is taking forever."

She snapped her fingers and his cup was full.

He nearly dropped the cup. "Shit, that's just too weird." Sniffing, he decided it smelled as good as coffee. *Might as well try it.* "It's good. How about a Danish? I'm a little hungry." In his free hand a lemon Danish appeared. "Mmm, my favorite." He took a bite, turning to her. "Okay, a Ferrari please. Red."

"Scott."

"I said, how about a Ferrari?"

She sighed, waved her hand at the window and set a red Ferrari in the back yard. "As you wish."

His eyes bugged out as he stared at the beauty of the machine, with its gleaming red paint. "Red's a bit much. Black would be better." Before his eyes, the color changed. "Hmm, better. Okay, I need to sit now." Sliding into the chair, holding his coffee in one hand, the Danish in the other, he let it all sink in.

"It's a lot to take in, I know."

"I always wanted a dog, but, being on the road, well, what would you do with a dog in a hotel? I want a dog."

"Scott."

"Indulge me, Blackie. I'm having a nervous breakdown here, might as well make it enjoyable."

At his feet landed a small, black furry puppy, yapping at him. "Cute, but what the hell is it?"

"A dog. You didn't specify, so I gave you a little of everything."

He laughed as he reached down to pet it. "A mongrel couldn't be more perfect. Let's call you…."

"No." She stopped his thoughts short. "You can't call him Satan."

He glanced up, still petting the puppy. "How did you know that was the name I was thinking of?"

"I read your mind."

Both eyebrows came up now. "You can do that?"

"Yes, though we prefer not to. I have thoughts blocked. It gives me a headache to hear all the voices, but sometimes one slips past me. Yours was very clear."

"Okay, no Satan. Tell me what I'm thinking now."

She giggled. "Behave yourself, Scott. I am not going to make my clothes disappear. But I will do this." She made his disappear, and sat back and laughed at his astonished face. "Satisfied?"

"Hardly. Put them back." He was overjoyed when his clothes reappeared on his body. "This is real." Scott lifted the puppy onto his lap, grinning as it began to lick his face. The pup really needed a name.

"Every bit of it."

"I'm not crazy, or having a mental breakdown?"

"No, you're not crazy or having a mental breakdown, Scott. I can do anything just by simply thinking of it."

"Can you make yourself human?" He regretted it the instant he'd said it.

"No, unfortunately, that I can't do."

"I'm keeping the dog, and I'm going to name him Blackie. Do you know why?" She shook her head. "To remind me of you, and to never piss you off." He broke off a piece of the Danish and fed it to the puppy.

"What will happen if we continue to see each other?" He remembered it all. Though his head was pounding, he remembered it, including why she had pushed him away.

"Uh…I would lose my powers, be punished, have to live an eternity alone."

He stroked the puppy's fur. "Hmm, that sucks, seeing as though I'm kind of liking getting anything I ask for."

"Scott—"

"Is there no way around it?"

She shook her head. "No, I tried."

He tilted his head. "You tried, how?"

She leaned against the counter, crossing her feet at the ankles. "The day you told me we couldn't be together, I'd had enough and I told Satan I wanted out, wasn't going to do his duty anymore. I wanted my life back."

"What happened?"

"He took my mother."

"He took her, how?"

She sighed, poured herself a cup of coffee. "That day in your office, when I got the call from Hunter, he was calling to tell me she was dying. The stipulation to my parents having a child was for me to serve him. If I didn't, he would take their lives, and mine."

"Harsh bastard. So it wasn't her heart?"

"No."

"Where is she now?"

"Home, alive. I had to ask for her back."

He rubbed his head. "I'm sure, in a few days when this has all sunk in and crashed down on me, I'll see how weird this is. In the meantime, tell me what you did to get her back."

"I agreed to continue working for him. As a punishment for disobeying him, he upped the ante. I gather several a night now instead of one, and he keeps a closer watch on me."

He jumped up, his head spinning around the room, his eyes wide. "Shit, is he here, now, in my house?"

"No, he's in my mind. It's complicated and hard to explain. You've had enough for one day."

"You're right. I should go, let this sink in, maybe take a nice long walk to clear my head, slap my face a few times to make sure I am really awake." He looked up at her and marveled in her beauty. "Can I keep the car?"

Laughing, she nodded. "It's all ours."

He paused as he stepped up to the door, the dog in his arms.

"I'm not sure I know what to do about all of this yet, but I know one thing hasn't changed."

"What is that?"

"I still love you."

Chapter Thirty-One

$\mathcal{H}$e was in love with a demon. In the two days since he'd seen Aurora last, since he had learned who she was, what her family was, he'd said that over and over in his mind. He was in love with a demon. Part of him accepted it. Part denied it. Then the dog would rub up against him, or bark, and he would be slapped in the face with reality.

She was a demon, she drank blood, she could make anything appear, read minds and she worked for the Devil himself. No big deal. So what if he was in love with her, so what if he'd had a demon in his bed? He laughed at that metaphor. Maybe that explained her…staying power when they made love. He shook his head clear.

I am in love with a demon.

Okay, so now what?

According to her, it was forbidden for them to be together, forbidden for them to have a life together. Despite the fact that her being a demon was a little weird, he realized one thing. He wanted her in his life, needed her there. *Think of the perks*, he thought to himself. *She could give you anything you wanted just by thinking it. You wouldn't have to drive, you could travel anywhere you wanted just by having her move you there with her mind.* The memory of how his body had felt after the first time was a definite deterrent. Okay, scratch the teleportation part. However, the rest was cool.

But it was forbidden.

How was he going to live his life without her in it?

He couldn't.

"Mark, I'm stepping out. I've got my cell if anything comes up."

"Sure thing, boss."

Scott felt a giddy sense of childish glee when he sat behind the wheel of his new car. He started the engine, revved it, and laughed as he pulled away, the dog barking beside him.

He sang along to the rock tune blasting on the radio, ignoring the howling from his new pet. Fingers tapping, he drove with a smile on his face. To hell with the Devil. He hoped he wouldn't be struck down by lightning for saying that, but he wanted her, and he wasn't letting some scary dude keep her from him. Tapping his fingers, he drove toward his love.

ೞ

Boy, was life boring without a job. Aurora wondered how she'd made it through her entire life dealing with her boredom. It was hard to think about it now that she'd had something so meaningful as gainful employment.

Wandering the house, she decided the best thing to do was occupy her time. So she set out and cleaned her entire house. She had dusted every inch, top to bottom, examining for the first time all the belongings of Scott and his father. She tinkered with the instruments that sat in the band room and, she learned, she was terrible at it. So much for her career as a famous rock star.

She went to Scott's father's old room, curiosity getting the best of her. She'd respected the privacy of the room, but figured enough time had passed for her to enter.

In the closet, where his clothing still hung, she found photo albums. Pulling them out, she sat on the floor and began poring over Scott's life. *Look at how adorable he was.* So chubby and blond. She wondered if they were to have a child, would he or she have blond hair, or her dark hair? She shook that thought off and turned the page. *This must be his mother and father. He looks like his father*, she thought, as she admired the handsome man beaming as he held his son. Though Dustin's hair was long, and his eyes weren't blue, he and Scott looked similar. He must have inherited the blue eyes from his mother. And wasn't she beautiful, with her dark red hair, blue eyes, and porcelain skin?

She turned the page, watched as Scott learned how to sit, how to crawl, got his first teeth, and stood on wobbly legs, taking his first steps. Her eyes burned with tears. He wore a cute little suit for his first school picture, and he looked absolutely adorable. Suddenly it seemed as if there was a blank in his life, no pictures until he was a teen. Was this when his mother died?

He wore a leather jacket, black, and had one foot on a beautiful gleaming silver motorcycle. He was about sixteen. She felt her body quiver with his beauty. Why was it a man in a leather jacket, standing by a motorcycle, got woman all gooey inside? She ran her fingers over the length of his body. How she wished she had known him then, had grown up with him while their love built.

She shook that off, wiped the tears that fell from her face. She wouldn't have been able to have him then, either. Taking another book, she opened it to pictures of Scott and his father's band. Scott sitting behind the drums. Scott arm and arm with the men in his father's band. They all looked so happy. The next page had graduation pictures, cap and gown, the next, Scott in a white lab coat, a stethoscope around his neck, smiling. He would have made a wonderful doctor. He had the heart of one.

She turned the page and saw him arm and arm with a beautiful blonde woman. A girlfriend? She turned that one over quickly.

Then pictures stopped.

She clutched the album to her breast and let the tears slide.

They would never have an album for themselves, no album of pictures of their children as they grew, no life at all. How was she going to go on without him? How was she going to manage being in the same city with him, knowing he was only a call away?

Maybe if she left, went somewhere else….She would still ache for him. She would always ache for him.

She hated that she had been born demon, hated that she wouldn't ever be allowed to be with the man she loved because she was a demon.

When the doorbell rang, Aurora wiped her face, set the albums away, and went down to answer it. A tiny black ball of fur ran between her legs, which meant—

She stared into the blue eyes of the man she loved with all her heart.

"Don't say anything." Stepping inside, he gave the door a shove and scooped her up into his arms. Taking her lips, kissing her until her mind went dumb, he carried her up the stairs. He pushed the door open to her room and laid her on the bed.

He kept her mouth busy while his hands tore at her dress. As he slid his lips, his mouth, along her jaw, down her neck, over her erect breasts, she shivered. He moved lower, kissing, tasting, and she moaned with each embrace. The moment he touched her, tasted her heat, she erupted like a long-dormant volcano.

She clawed at the blankets, shredding them as her body was catapulted into an earth-shaking orgasm. Breathless, she felt him slide over her, his clothing no longer a barrier. She wanted him, all of him, now.

"Let me see, Blackie. Give me all of you and let me see." Cupping her face in his hands, he drew her attention to his face. "Show me."

She hoped what she was about to give him he would accept, that he wouldn't be repulsed by her. With her eyes locked on his, she changed.

Running his fingers along the ridges of her forehead and her face, he smiled. "A true beauty."

No one aside from her parents had ever expressed how beautiful she was before. Her heart swelled with the sincerity in his voice.

He dipped down and sank his lips onto hers, making her head spin. Lifting up, he looked down at her, his blue eyes shimmering.

He slipped on a condom then eased in between her legs. She spread for him, gave herself completely. If this was wrong, she didn't give a damn.

He rocked inside of her in slow, meticulous strokes. A wave of sensations rocketed her insides. Her skin tingled, her body grew hot, her heart pounded beneath her chest. Wrapping her legs around his hips, she arched her back as he plunged deeper.

She dug her long nails into his back, totally wrapped up in the desire he brought out in her.

"Open your eyes, Blackie. I want you to look at me when we come."

Opening her eyes, she saw the bluest ocean, and dove. Crying out, her voice low, growling, she let herself go.

With eyes locked, they let the wave crash through them before collapsing onto the bed.

"You are so beautiful, utterly beautiful." He kissed her chin, nibbled lightly. "And, in case you haven't figured it out," He turned her head to face him. "I want you, you, all of you, the woman, the demon, everything that goes with it." He tilted her chin up, kissed her lightly. "I love you, all of you."

She couldn't stop them, the tears just flowed, hot burning tears.

"No, no, no don't cry! I have this strange ailment. When a woman cries, it makes me cry. Please, don't make me humiliate myself." His voice cracked with his own tears.

She cupped his face in the palms of her hands and smiled. "You are the sweetest man "We can't do this. I can't do this."

"Tell me why?"

"I've already told you why." She wiped the tears, determined.

Look at me. Look at me, Blackie." He lifted her chin. "How will he know if we're together?"

She pulled away, his touch was making it so much harder to let go. "He'll know."

"How? Does he pop in for coffee, sit at your table and say, *Hey there, so I noticed you've been sleeping with a human, bad girl?*"

She didn't find the humor in his statement. "It's not like that."

"Tell me how it is. Make me see how he'll know about us."

She wiped the tears from her face. "He knows. He's in here." She tapped her head. "He is a part of me. Please, don't do this to me, I can't do this." She pulled off the bed, grabbing the robe from her closet and wrapping it around her naked body. Her heart was breaking in two.

"I can't live without you." He took hold of her arm, held her in place. "I can't. I won't. I need you in my life. I've already lost one person I love. Don't make me grieve for another."

"Don't make me grieve, either, Scott. My parents' lives are in jeopardy. If I choose you, turn my back on my life, theirs will end."

"How can I become what you are? Tell me how I can become a demon"

She jerked away as if he had burned her with his words. "No, no I will not tell you how you could become like me. Don't ask me that."

"I am asking. Tell me how do I become you?"

"This is ridiculous." She broke his hold. "It has to stop." She wept while she spoke. "I love you, so much so I feel you inside of me and I know I will never be rid of you. But I can't do this. Too much is at stake. I'll erase your memory of me if need be."

He grabbed her wrist. "Go ahead and try, but I will never, ever forget you."

"You won't have a choice. Once the mind is stripped, all those memories are gone, permanently."

"Memories, maybe, but there will always be a hollow ache in my heart for you." He pulled her to him, one hard jerk that ended with her mouth colliding into his. "Tell me, Blackie, how will you live with my memory inside of you?" He smothered her with a kiss so hard, so demanding, it took her breath away.

She pushed him away, wishing her heart would adhere to the rules. "I'll have to." She didn't want to hurt him, didn't want to rid his mind of her, but he wasn't leaving her any choice.

He grabbed her once more, pulling her hard against him. "It will tear you up inside, day after day, not feeling me, tasting me, having me. Is that how you want to live the rest of your life? In agony, lonely, aching for me?"

She shook her head. "I can't do this. You don't know how hard this is for me. If I give in and stay with you, I lose my parents. If I chose my family over you, I lose the only man I will ever love. There is no easy answer."

"Yes, there is. Make me into you."

She pushed him away so that he stumbled back hitting the wall. "No! Never, because it isn't a life. I've hated being what I am my entire life. I would never do that to you." She walked to the door, her heart breaking. "I need you to leave, please."

"Forget it. I'm not leaving here until we resolve this."

She wiped her eyes. "You won't have a choice. I'm sorry." Closing her eyes, she sent him to his home at the shelter. Falling to her knees, raising her voice a pitch above deafening, she screamed. The windows shattered into little pieces, so much like her heart.

Chapter Thirty-Two

Talking to the illustrious Mr. Starr would get Scott nowhere, and if the guy was a demon sired by a relative of Satan, he didn't want to mess with him. So he turned to the Missus.

She was a woman. One point for him—he had always been good with women. She was also part demon, two points, and she was part human, three. He couldn't go wrong with her. She would know just how to help him. She'd sympathize with him. Still feeling giddy, he stepped from the car and walked to the huge mansion. Now he saw the intimidation of it, and yes, maybe it was a little spooky, considering who owned it, but he didn't have time to dwell on that. He was on a mission.

The rain had started shortly after Aurora had dropped him in his room. He was still smarting from that. It had affected him just as harshly as the first time. Shaking it off, he lifted the gold star knocker and tapped it hard against the dark wooden door. When Hunter pulled open the grand doors with his usual scowl, Scott didn't wait for an invitation and strolled right past him.

"I don't recall inviting you inside."

"You didn't. I'm here to see Mrs. Starr." He looked around, hoping against hope that Aurora's father wasn't lurking about, ready to jump out and devour him. "We can stand here all night if you prefer, Hunter, but I'm not leaving until I see her."

"It's all right, Hunter." Missy walked into the grand foyer, her flowing blue dress shimmering as she moved. "Hello, Scott."

"Mrs. Starr. You look nice today, and I'm glad you're well." There was an incredible resemblance between mother and daughter. The dark hair, the golden eyes, but the face wasn't completely the same. Aurora's nose was stronger, her cheek bones fuller, and her mouth wider.

"Please, call me Missy. Can Hunter get you anything to drink?"

"I won't put Hunter out more than I have already." He turned to Hunter with a smile. "Are you...you know, one of them? A demon?"

Hunter's eyes shot wide. "Uh, not exactly. I'll be around if you need me, Missy." With that said, he turned and left.

"I make him nervous." He turned back to Missy. "I've come here to talk to you about you daughter."

"I figured as much. How are you feeling today?" She led him into the grand sitting room, where they took a seat.

"This place is incredible." He turned back to Missy. "Aside from my body being churned inside out from being transported about and learning the woman I love is a demon, I'm doing pretty good." He relaxed against the back of the sofa. "In case you didn't catch that, I'm in love with your daughter."

"I know."

He leaned forward in his seat. "She told me everything."

Missy nodded, her legs crossed, looking ever the elegant lady of the manor. "Yes, she told us. Did she tell you the penalty of mating with a human?"

He nodded. "That's why I'm here." He shifted, fidgeted, not sure how to go about asking, and decided to just jump in head first. "I want you to make me into a demon."

"I see."

"I'm not sure how it's done. She wouldn't tell me, but I'm willing to do anything to be with her."

"Does that include selling your soul, Scott?"

"Yes, if that's what it takes."

"Are you willing to give up your life's work, your father's

dream, the shelter, and all it entails?"

He tilted his head. "Why would I have to give that up?" He could still work there, helping people. He would live longer, doing more good.

"You can't exactly work for Satan—and you will have to if you sell your soul—and save souls. It's a conflict of interest."

"Aurora does it."

She nodded. "Yes, and she's been punished for it several times."

He shot forward. "What did he do to her? How do you mean she was punished?"

"Since she's started working for you, she's gained a whole new perspective on life. She told you what her job is with Lucifer?"

"Yes."

"More than once she has questioned her duties, Satan's motives, his need for souls because she felt the need to help them, to rehabilitate them, instead of killing them. Lucifer doesn't take that kindly. He prefers to think himself in charge. Anyone disputing that is punished in whatever means he sees fit at that moment."

"He hurt her?"

"Yes, to show her he is still in charge. He would never allow you to save souls, Scott, when his whole goal is to gather them for his own."

He got up to pace the floor, thinking. Could he give up his father's dream, his passion? Could he walk away from something he had done for almost half his life? Could he do the exact opposite? He was a healer, had always been a healer, saving lives, not taking them.

"I won't have you resent my daughter years from now, when you realize you've made a mistake."

He turned to Missy, scowling. "I would never resent her. She doesn't even know I'm here, asking you this." He ran a hand through his hair, trying to think. "At least tell me how it's done, so I can decide on my own. Do you have to bite me or something?"

She smiled, and it was at that moment that he noticed more of a resemblance between mother and daughter. "Not unless you want me to. No, it doesn't work that way. There are two ways. You have to die, but not at the hands of a demon, and have a demon revive you and claim you as their own. You would belong to them from that day forward."

"And the second?" He had a feeling this one wasn't going to be pretty.

"You have to take your own life. When you die, and you are taken down—and you will be, having committed the ultimate sin—you wouldn't be granted access into heaven. Your soul is automatically for Lucifer's taking. If you agree to turn yourself over, completely, he will grant you the power of demon, but…" She paused, taking a deep breath. "He may not let you up at first, not until you prove you are worthy of being with the living, to do his job for him."

"And how long would that take?"

"Oh, it could be weeks, months." Her eyes grew slightly darker. "Centuries."

"Centuries?" He swallowed hard. He didn't want to wait that long to be with Aurora. And suddenly it occurred to him. Suicides didn't go to heaven. Did that mean his father was in hell, burning for his sins?

"Are you willing to give up everything, everything you have worked for, lived for, everything you believe in, for my daughter?"

"I love her," he stated softly.

"Will that love be enough?"

"I guess that's something I'll need to think about." He turned to leave, paused. "Can I ask you another question?"

"Of course." She stood.

"Is there any way that Aurora could become human?"

"You wish she was human?"

He shook her head. "No, I love her for who she is, and personally, I find it fascinating. But she doesn't. She doesn't want to be a demon anymore. How can she stop being one?"

Missy stared in shock. "She wishes not to be a demon?"

Scott tilted his head. He'd thought her parents had known.

"Yes, she said so tonight. She hates it. You didn't know?"

Missy shook her head, her bottom lip trembling. "Is this because of you?"

He lifted one shoulder. "Could be, though I got the impression it's been her feeling for a long time. Can she stop being a demon?"

"It's not a way I want my child to live."

"Even if it's what she wants, what makes her happy?"

She sighed heavily as if the question weighed heavily on her heart. "Two ways. Becoming impregnated by a human, and ending her ties to Satan, taking God into her heart." She looked squarely at Scott. "But she will be stripped of her powers."

"But she'll be human?"

"Yes, but her life would be long, and she would watch everyone around her die. She would be alone and lonely and know there would be no end unless Satan granted it of her. He would still have control over her soul. Is that what you want for her?"

"No." He rubbed a hand over his chin. "I guess the only other way is for me to give up my life for her."

"Or just walk away."

"I couldn't even if I tried. Thank you, Missy. I appreciate your candor and your help. I'll show myself out."

※

Draco waited until his wife had disappeared before he appeared. He had heard it all, the entire conversation, and he felt the love pouring from the young man so desperate to have his love. If his daughter felt half of what that young man felt, he imagined the pain she was in. It had to stop.

Turning, he nearly ran Hunter down. "How long have you been standing there?"

"Long enough. Eavesdropping, sir?" He clucked his tongue and shook his head.

Draco narrowed his eyes and gave his black jacket a quick tug, his chin angled up. "Don't you have some place else you should be?"

"Nope, this is where I need to be right now."

"Why is that?" He moved around Hunter, feeling the unease of his eyes penetrating him.

"To prevent you from doing something stupid."

Draco stopped short in his stride, Hunter nearly rammed into his back. He spun around, furious. "What makes you think I'm going to do something stupid? And might I say that was pretty ballsy of you to say that."

"So noted, and I'm not worried. I know because I know you, and I see that look in your eyes."

Draco turned away, hiding his eyes. "I have no look in my eyes." He stormed off to his office, slamming the door in Hunter's face. If the man knew anything about his employer, he would stay out. Draco was completely shocked when his office door swung open and Hunter strolled in.

"Yes, you do. It's a look that says you are about to do something really stupid."

The man had a death wish. Draco narrowed his eyes. "There once was a time you feared me."

Hunter nodded as he took a seat, examined his nails. "True, but when you met Missy you became a whipped man." He lifted laughing eyes.

"I am not whipped. I could show you whipped. We could start by making you very, very afraid of me once more."

"I'm quivering. Now, are you going to tell me what you are up to, or do I go to your wife and tell her you're planning something?"

"I despise you."

"So noted. I'm waiting."

Hunter had learned entirely too much from him in his years as his aide. "I plan on saving my daughter from heartache," he said finally.

Hunter sat forward. "How exactly do you plan on doing that?"

Draco waved his hand and held a lit cigarette and grasped a glass of wine. "The only way I know how."

"That was exactly what I was afraid of."

Chapter Thirty-Three

*E*xasperated, Aurora pulled yet another pan of burned cookies from the oven. All she'd wanted was to occupy her mind, and the only thing she could think of was baking. As she dumped the cookies on the table, several fell to the floor. In a flash, the dog was on them like…well dogs on food.

"Blackie, stop eating those. I'm telling you if you puke one more time, I'm tossing your butt outside."

"Looks like you've been busy."

Aurora spun around, spoon in hand, surprised to see her mother standing by the table. "Busy messing up. Which I seem good at. I just can't seem to get this right." She tossed the spoon on the counter and turned in time to see Blackie vomit at her feet. "Oh you are in so much trouble. Outside!" Opening the door, she scooted the dog outside, and shut the door before he could whine his protest. Grabbing the roll of paper towels, she began cleaning up the vomit.

Stupid dog.

"I'll help. Where is your recipe?" Her mother stepped over crumbled cookies to walk to her daughter.

"Somewhere under all this mess. They keep burning, and I don't know why." She gave the pan she had just filled a shove. "Maybe I'm just a lost cause."

She took Aurora's face in her hands. "You are not a lost cause, dear." She kissed her cheek before turning to the oven. "You just have the oven too high. Now, why don't you sit down and tell me what this is all about?"

"Life," Aurora grumbled as she dropped in her chair.

Her mother grabbed the garbage can and tossed the burned cookies into the trash. "And it has nothing to do with Scott Monroe?"

Aurora looked up at her mother, frowning. She was in no mood for her mother to chastise her. "I'm not in the mood, Mamma, so don't lecture me."

"I wasn't going to lecture you, Aurora."

She saw her mother was sincere, sighed. "Okay, yes, it has everything to do with Scott. Why does love have to hurt so much?"

Her mother scooped cookie dough onto a clean pan and slid it in the oven, then set the timer. "It's a misconception that love is pleasant when in actuality, it hurts like hell." She smiled at her daughter as she ran her hand over the long silky braid. "Is it the love that hurts, or not being with him?"

Aurora's shoulders dropped. "Both. He wants me, Mamma, everything about me, who I am what I am, he wants it all. But we can't be together." It hurt so bad that Aurora thought it might just swallow her whole. "It's not fair that some ancient rule should still apply. If I want to be with a human, I should be allowed to."

"If the rule wasn't in place, there would be half-human demons roaming free in the world, possibly causing mayhem and disaster. And how would we survive if people knew what we are? We wouldn't."

"You don't know that. Times have changed. People are more open. Look at Scott! After the initial shock wore off, he was fine. He accepts."

"Oh, sweetie, love has clouded your mind."

"So what if it has?" She pushed from the table to pace the floor. "Yes, I love him, and he loves me. If we want to be together, we should be allowed. And if I wasn't a damn demon we wouldn't even have to worry about it."

"Aurora—"

"No, Mamma, don't say it. I'm sorry, but this is how I feel. If I could make it go away, if I could make myself human, I would. I've never wanted it, and I would gladly give it up."

"For one man? And what if that man isn't the one?"

"It's not just for him. I've felt this way…forever." Aurora let the dog back inside. "I was never allowed to have friend, go to school, play with the kids at the playground. All I wanted was to be normal, like them." She scooped the dog up into her arms. "And he is the one. He is the only one. Didn't you know, just know, with Daddy, that he was the one?"

"And you feel this for Scott?"

"Yes." She filled a dish with water, set it down for the puppy. "But it's a moot point now, isn't it? Any way you look at it, we can't be together." The tears sneaked up on her, sending her sliding to the floor while they burned her face, her throat, her heart.

"Oh, darling." Missy went to her daughter, and simply stroked her hair while the puppy leapt up to lick her face. "I wish I could make it all better for you."

Sobbing, Aurora wished she could, too.

CS

When people thought of Hell they thought of heat, fire, brimstone, and suffering. It was really nothing like that. But people needed their fantasies. Draco figured if people knew the truth, they would be very disappointed.

It was dark, yes, warm, but not smothering. There were no flames, but there was plenty of suffering. It was a void, a dark endless void where souls lingered, with no place to settle, no place to go for peace. There was no peace at all. Being sent to Hell was akin to being locked into your own private nightmare. The sin you made in your life was the damnation after your death. Your soul, neither belonging nor not belonging, hung weightlessly to repeat your sins, over, and over, until the end of time. Now to some that might not seem so bad, but having to relive, say, a murder you committed, over and over, like a broken record…it would drive you mad. That's why the souls screamed, and they did scream, while they hung in the void.

As Draco waited in the darkness for his meeting with Satan, he could feel the pain around him. There was always so much pain.

Why have you come?

Draco didn't flinch. He had after all, grown up to that voice. "To ask a favor." The mere mention of the word *favor* would warrant a slap. Though Satan didn't use a hand to hit, you felt it just the same. As the spearing pain sliced into his chest, Draco stood strong.

I do no favors.

Draco turned to the voice and saw not a beast, but a beautiful man caught in a world that he'd been thrown into because of his rebellion in heaven. Satan had once been an angel, loved by his Father, adored by his siblings. Until he'd wanted more. He'd lashed out at God and had been banished to his own Hell. Wanting to rule as his father did, Satan began his reign of terror on earth. Only able to use his mind to control others, Lucifer lured his victims to create horrible sins. Once sent to Hell, he took them as his own. From there, his army began to build.

"You do when it benefits you, and I believe what I have to say will definitely benefit you." The air began to swirl around him. Though it couldn't be seen, it was felt.

Explain.

He kept his back straight as he prepared to barter with the Devil once more. "My daughter is in love with a human—"

FORBIDDEN.

The ground quaked around him. He could feel it despite being suspended well above the cavernous floor. "I know, I know, just hear me out." He drew in a long, careful breath. He could feel Satan over him, breathing down on him with breath that could scorch on first contact. He was pushing his luck. "She wants a life with him. If you grant her a pardon, not removing her powers, but a pardon, I would continue her work for her."

Your child's job now, per our original agreement, and not

yours any longer.

Draco felt the sweat drench his body. "I know, but she won't last. She can't handle the misery, the senselessness of it. But I can." He had, once before, long ago. He would do it again.

Draco fell to his knees not because he wanted to, but because Satan commanded it and dragged him down. He would beg, and Satan knew it, for he had begged once before. "I would give you much more. I would return to my old ways, terrorizing the humans, driving them mad and making them commit the ultimate of sins. I would do your bidding, carry out your work, I would bring you the souls of any you chose."

And what of your wife?

"She stays out of this. It is only you and me here. She need not be involved."

Draco wiped the sweat from his brow, his dark hair clinging to his forehead. He would protect Missy in any way he could, even if it meant never seeing her again.

You are a disappointment, my son. What once was a fearsome animal now quakes over the love of two women.

Draco felt his chest spread, felt the slippery hand of Lucifer slide inside and grab hold of his heart. He didn't buckle but he did feel the room waver with his pain.

Where would you be without your love?

"I would be what I once was. Isn't that what you want?" Draco could feel the dark force thinking, planning, and yes, he felt the sneer.

Prove your worth and we will talk.

The lights blinded him. It took several seconds before his eyes grew accustomed to the brightness, and Draco understood what was expected of him. He had to fight to the death, with Lucifer's most fierce warrior to prove he was worthy of asking the favor. If he survived, there was a good chance he'd be granted his wish. If he didn't...well, the consequences and was not going to be the casualty in this fight.

As the fearsome beast stomped into the room. Draco had his work cut out for him. The animal warrior was tall, twice his size, and mean-looking. He had scales, his face was that of a beast, his teeth laser sharp. *No problem*, Draco thought. He was familiar with this particular beast's weakness: the horns. Starting at the tip of his nose, dozens of them ran gradually over his face, growing larger as they trailed down his back and ending with a six-foot tail. The problem was, you had to break off at least half of them before he would be vulnerable enough to bring down with a blow. Rolling his shoulders, shifting to beast mode, Draco hoped the thirty-some-year sabbatical he had taken from fighting wouldn't be his undoing.

The beast moved in, his legs spread in a predatory stance, and the fight began.

Draco dodged the first blow, but wasn't so lucky with the second. The lash of the tail against his back slashed into him with the snap of a whip, slicing his skin. He needed to be quicker next time. Standing up, cracking his neck, Draco looked up at his opponent with perseverance. "You'll have to do better than that to bring me down, Craegon." He held his hands out, motioning with his fingers to bring it on. "Show me what you've got."

For the next two hours, they fought. Exhaustion clung to Draco, dragging him down. Still, he fought to keep up. He'd snapped off twenty-five of the beast's horns, and only had seventy-five left to go. Despite his fatigue and pain, he had to keep going. His family depended on him. Standing, Draco wiped the blood from his face, and motioned for the beast to attack.

Chapter Thirty-Four

Scott was taking a huge chance, He understood that. His plan might not even work. Well, it was too late now. The decision hadn't been that hard to come to, not when his entire heart was captured by the spell of love. Whatever life he could have with Aurora, he wanted.

He had written out his desires, instructing his father's band mates to take over the shelter. As well he'd written a note, explaining why he was doing what he was doing, explaining that the pressures had become too much to bear. He hoped everyone believed it, and understood. Oh, he had been there once, been the one who was left behind afterward. They probably hey wouldn't understand, but he hoped at least they would learn to move on. It was the only way he saw to do things. Though he would miss his father's—correction—*his* shelter, he would move on. He wasn't too sure what he would do after, but he'd figure that out when the time came.

As he stood at the door to the place he'd called home, he hoped Aurora was willing to help him. He was counting on it. Tonight, if all went according to plan, they would start their life together, as one. He knocked, his heart pounding, his head woozy.

Wearing a pair of jeans and a long work shirt, Aurora answered the door. The dog yipped at her feet. His heart began to beat just a bit faster. "Before you say anything about us not being allowed together, let me have my say. And don't even think about sending me away again. I'll just keep coming back."

"Scott—"

He silenced her with a brain-numbing kiss, kicking the door closed as he entered. "You smell like strawberries." He licked his lips. "Taste even better."

"What are—"

"Hello, boy. Have you been keeping Mommy company while I've been away?" Scratching the dog's head, he felt a pinch of dizziness. Carefully he stood and took Aurora's hand. "Let's sit. I haven't got much time. There are a few things I need to ask you." He dragged her to the sofa. "Okay, first, do you love me enough to be with me for an eternity or more?"

She sighed heavily. "Please—"

"Just answer the question, Blackie. Yes or no?"

She narrowed her eyes. "Yes, but—"

"Question two. If I were to die, would you take me as yours?"

"I am not—"

"Yes or no? It's a simple question."

"Yes. But it's a little more—"

"Question three. If I die, and you take me as your own, what happens to my soul?"

"What is this all about?"

"Just curious. Humor me, Blackie." The puppy curled up on Scott's feet and went to sleep.

"It lingers neither in nor out of Hell, but in between. Essentially up for grabs, but that—"

"Interesting. Question four. Will I live as long as you?"

"Yes, but—"

"Question five. Will I have powers?"

"Only if I grant them to you, but I—"

"Guess I'll have to convince you." He could feel himself growing sluggish, the effects starting to take over.

"What are you doing? I already told you I will not make you a demon."

He nodded, the room swayed as if little waves of heat floated about. "You won't have a choice."

She gripped his hands hard in hers, tilted her head before gasping. "Oh, Scott. What did you do?"

His eyes grew heavy. He fought it just a bit longer. "I've decided in order for us have a life together, I have to die and you make me yours." The room began to sway. His head grew heavy, so he leaned back against the sofa. His eyes fell shut, and he couldn't force them open. "I love you, Blackie."

"No, Scott, wake up!" She shook him, hard and his eyelids lifted slowly. "What did you take? Tell me, damn it, what did you take?"

He slid into her arms. As far as dying went, this wasn't so bad. He was in the arms of the woman he loved. "Sleeping pills." His speech slurred; his head fell as she cradled him in her arms. The darkness filled him, and he surrendered to its bliss.

"No, damn it! I won't let you do this. I will not let you end your life." Scooping him in her arms, she sent them both to the entrance of the hospital. She burst through the door. "I need help! Someone, please, help me." Several men dressed in green scrubs rushed to her side and took Scott out of her arms.

"What's the problem?" A tall brown-haired doctor looked down at Scott, listless in her arms.

"He took sleeping pills. I don't know how many. Enough to kill him."

"What's his name?" The doctor opened one of Scott's eyes, shined a light into it.

"Scott, Scott Monroe. Please, save him."

The doctor's head whipped up to Aurora. "Scott Monroe, from the Monroe Shelter?"

"Yes. Please, help him."

"That's what I'm here for."

They rushed him into a room and began working on him. She didn't need them to tell her he was dying. She felt it. The awful part of who she was ebbed up. He was clinging to life and she could feel the shadows in wait. She feared the doctor wouldn't be quick enough to bring him back. But she knew someone who could. She hurried to a room, making sure no one was around to see her, and sent herself home. As she stood in her living room, she called out to the void, to her Master. When she felt the block, she pushed harder. She was determined to get in, one way or another.

"Let me in, damn it!" Her head exploded in blinding pain. Not giving up, she stood strong, felt the block crack and forced her thoughts into his. "I said let me in."

You dare demand!

"Yes, I demand. You can't take him. It's not right." She stood in the darkness, her mind set.

He has chosen.

"No, his mind is clouded with love."

His decision, not yours.

"No, he doesn't know what he's doing. He thinks by doing this we'll be together forever. I don't want him to give his life for me." The darkness stirred. She felt herself shifting into a different realm.

You don't speak of your father?

"My father? No, no I speak of Scott." She was confused. "Why do you ask about my father?"

The laughter rippled around her, into her, vibrating her bones. *Watch, little one. Watch.*

The spear of light shot into her, carrying her away, taking her someplace she had never been before. When her watery eyes focused, she saw. "Daddy." But she couldn't move, couldn't run to him. She was helpless to stand, frozen in her spot and watch as her father battled a huge beast before him. His body was battered, his face bruised and bloody. She saw the exhaustion was weighing heavy on him. She felt his power draining rapidly.

"Why is he doing that?"

It seems you have two hearts willing to die for you. Ah, there he is. Scott Monroe, hmmm.

"No." She spun around. The fight her father was engaged in was behind her. She searched for the voice. "No, don't take him. You can't take him." She fought the need to cry only because it would be worse to show that much weakness.

His faith is slipping. I hear him calling to me.

"No, please don't take him." She pleaded, and didn't care if she sounded weak now. She couldn't let him have Scott. He was too pure, too good. People needed him, depended on him.

What will you give me to save him?

"My life. I'll devote everything I am, everything I have, to you."

You are your father's daughter. He bartered the same. I want more.

"What do you want? Tell me! I'll do anything, please. Tell me." The tears fell now, she simply didn't have the energy to stop them. She felt the grin slide into her, intruding inside of her, filling her, and she felt sickened by it. She was well aware that what Satan would ask would be everything and more.

Choose. Love or loyalty.

She turned in circles, searching for a face to go with the voice. "I don't understand." Once again, she felt the smile slide into her, but this time, it cut like a knife.

Will it be the father, or the man you love?"

Chapter Thirty-Five

*H*er heart felt one hundred times larger, and hurt like hell. It pounded in her and made her body shake. The air caught in her throat, and she felt her whole world tilt.

"Choose? No, no, I can't choose." How could she choose one over the other when she loved them both?

Then I take both.

"No, stop. Please, don't make me do this. Please don't make me choose." She couldn't. How could she choose?

One is calling to me, one is losing the battle. Which one do you love more?

His laughter rippled into her, like waves of ice, slicing, nipping at her skin. She covered her ears and let the tears spill out, hot and fierce. "No, I won't let you do this." Pulling in all her strength, she slammed a fireball directly into Satan. Everything she had merged into that one ball, everything she was, placed into that ball of heat. But it hardly made a dent.

You have strength. I am stronger.

Like an earthquake to her system, he proved he was still in command. Her body rippled with it. Something deep inside of her rose up. She felt it as it took control of her, empowered her. Love was a powerful thing, and she used it now.

As he shot out at her, lasers of heat and pain, she took it in, controlling it, absorbing his power. Lifting her head, she smiled.

"No, you are weak." She pushed him aside, straining with the effort to overpower him, but managed. "I have love, times three." It took almost all of her strength, but she pushed in, all the way in, and faced him.

He was neither man nor beast and yet, so much more. She didn't cower, or even so much as show any sign of repulsion. She stood tall, confronting her maker. "I have love; you have nothing." She pulled her father to her side. "I have my family." Then her mother. "And I have a man who loves me enough to sacrifice it all." She pulled Scott's energy to her side. She heard the doctors as they pushed to save his life.

"We're losing him."

"Charged. Ready."

Scott's body jerked with the surge of electricity that shot into his body.

"Still no rhythm."

"Damn it, Scott. Don't you dare do this to me." The doctor climbed over his body, straddling Scott, and began pumping his chest. "Come on, damn it! Will yourself to live."

A bright, glowing light shone around her, around her family, a protective wall that only love could produce. "You are defenseless against love, against loyalty, against the good that love instills in us all. You are defenseless, Satan. You are nothing, and you are no longer in control. I renounce thee and all you are. Release us from your hold."

The fury was ten times the strength of a hurricane, plus more. They stood strong, hand in hand, circling her, their love a shield that not even Satan could penetrate.

You will regret this.

Each of them, Draco, Missy, and Aurora, was shot back into the world they desired more than life. Her parents dropped into their home, Aurora into hers. Scott fell like a lead weight back into his body.

The room spun wildly, the nausea rolled inside of Aurora as she fell to her knees. Clasping a hand over her head, she cried out in pain. As she rode the wave of agony, she began to focus on her surroundings. She was home. Gathering her strength, feeling as if every part of her being had been drained, she stood... and began laughing madly. She had no idea why it was affecting her this way. She'd transported millions of times. Why now was it different? She didn't have time to process it.

When the laughter finally subsided, she drew in a deep breath, and immediately began coughing, choking, gasping. Her lungs were on fire, her throat raw. She felt the dizziness swamp her, and she nearly let it take her over. Remembering what Scott was enduring, she fought through the nausea and pain. She needed to see, to make sure he was okay, that he hadn't been taken. Closing her eyes, she wished herself to his room, and found she still stood in her living room.

"What the hell?" She waved her hand, nothing happened. She wished it again, still nothing. She had no powers. Maybe she'd exhausted them in her fight with Lucifer. When the telephone rang, she scooped it up, hoping it was word on Scott. "Hello?"

"Aurora. Are you all right?"

"Yeah, a little off-kilter though. Must be from using everything I had to fight him." She rubbed the ache in her chest. It felt as if she'd been sucker-punched where her heart was.

"No, no darling, it's permanent. You beat him, but he got his revenge."

"I don't understand. I need to go, Mamma—"

"You are human, love. We all are."

"Human? Are you sure?" Her brain seemed fuzzy, unclear.

"The steady beat of my heart is a dead giveaway. Darling, we need to get together, discuss this. Your father isn't well, but he refuses a doctor. Come to us."

"I can't, not now. I need to see Scott. Give Daddy a kiss for me. I love you." Setting the phone down, she grabbed her keys and hurried out the door. Her destination was love.

❧

The beeping rhythm echoed with the sound of raindrops on a

tin roof and had him stirring out of his slumber. The brightness of the room scorched his eyes. He blinked rapidly. Every damn light was on. His head felt as if he'd been hit with a crowbar. Not that he'd ever had it happen to him before, but he figured what he felt now would probably come close. He didn't care for it.

"Damn, that's bright." Wasn't Hell supposed to be dark and hot?

The nurse smiled down at him as she checked the IV attached to his arm. "It's easier for us to monitor you that way. How do you feel, Mr. Monroe?"

"Like I went a couple of rounds with the Devil." Suddenly it hit him, the reality of what had happened. He bolted up. His head exploded, his vision blurred, and his chest ached. "Crap." The dizziness swamped him and sent him falling back to the bed.

"Just relax, Mr. Monroe." She helped him to lie down, straightened out his blankets.

"Where is she? Where is Blackie?" He opened his eyes daringly and was glad the room no longer spun.

"Who?"

"Raven-haired beauty, hair nearly to her knees. Five-foot-five, golden eyes."

"Oh, the young lady that brought you in. I don't know where she is. She disappeared just after you arrived. Is there someone we can call for you, Mr. Monroe?"

"Yes, call Blackie. Uh, Aurora Starr." He recited her number. "Please hurry."

She lifted his bed into the sitting position before leaving the room.

଼

How could she be out of shape? She was a demon, for pity's sake, yet her lungs burned, her legs ached, and her chest felt as if it were being ripped open. She pressed a hand over her heart, felt the pounding rhythm, so unlike her usual heartbeat. She stopped, panted, and remembered what her mother had said.

We're human.

Was it true? Had Satan turned her human, taken her powers, and her demonic rights? It was beginning to look that way. Checking the street signs, she realized she had only run ten blocks from her home. She would never make it all the way across the city to the hospital. She needed help. Checking her pockets for money, she came up with only loose change. Well, she wasn't going to get a cab with only three dollars on her. What next?

Looking around, she saw the bus stop down the block. Taking a few deep breaths, she walked slowly to the bench that sat there. One should be around soon, she hoped. Sitting, she rubbed her legs, then her chest. She wasn't sure she liked the feeling. Closing her eyes, she wondered if Scott missed her. Had he woken? What was he thinking? She needed to believe he'd made it out safely. Her parents had. She needed to believe Scott did as well. Her mind was so completely wrapped around Scott, she didn't even hear the man approach until it was too late.

ଓ

"Mr. Monroe, I'm Dr. Marshall. How are you feeling?"

Scott scanned the doctor: middle-aged, tall, thin, dark hair, dark glasses. "I've felt better."

"It's to be expected in a near-fatal overdose. I was asked to come in and talk with you. I'm the hospital-appointed psychiatrist."

He should have pegged him. He had the look. "A shrink? Why the hell would I need a shrink?"

Dr. Marshall stood beside the bed, his hands tucked in the pockets of the white coat he wore. "It's standard procedure. Do you remember what happened? Do you know why you're here, Scott? And may I call you Scott?"

Why the hell not? "Sure, and yes, I remember, and before you ask, I've never attempted suicide before." Damn it, he didn't need this. Where the hell was Blackie? What had happened to her after he'd been sent away from wherever he'd been taken to so abruptly? It had been dark, and cold, he remembered that much. And the eyes, those glowing animal eyes that had pierced through the darkness would haunt him forever.

"Have you been feeling depressed, feeling blue?"

Scott nearly sighed. "I've been under a lot of pressure lately. I took the pills, stupidly, and regretted doing so right after." He hoped to God this guy bought it. He certainly didn't need some shrink sending him to the psych ward.

"You run the Monroe Shelter. I imagine that can be very taxing."

Great, it appeared he'd have to talk to the guy. "Yes, it can be." He heard the bustle, the nurses calling out orders, calling for an attending. God, how familiar it all seemed. That had been his life once upon a time.

"We have a single stab wound, lower left side, no exit, pressure low, pulse weak and tachy."

"Someone tie her hair back. I can't see her face with all this hair," the female instructed. "The wound's not too deep. Who's on for surgery tonight?"

"Duncan. Check out these eyes…are those contacts? You ever see gold eyes like this before?"

Scott sat straight up, ignoring the throbbing in his head and chest, and climbed out of the bed.

"Scott, what are you doing? You can't—"

He bolted before Dr. Marshall could finish the sentence. Pulling the curtain that separated him from the other room, Scott gasped. "Oh God, Blackie." Racing to her, he ignored the hands that reached out to pull him back, the IV that tugged from his arm. Why was she bleeding? "No, Blackie, no." Had Satan done this to her?

"Get him out of here. I can't work like this."

"Do you know her, Mr. Monroe?" a small nurse asked him as she tried to hold him back.

"Yes, yes, she's…Aurora Starr. What happened to her? Why is she bleeding?" Did demons bleed? Apparently they did.

"She's been stabbed. You'll have to stay back so we can help her."

"Does she have family?" Another nurse asked.

"Yes, her parents. I need to call them." They would know what to do, how to help her.

"Scott, let the nurses call. You need to lie back down."

Scott pulled his arm away from Dr. Marshall. "No, I'm fine. I need to get them here. They can help her."

"The doctors are doing their best. They'll fix her up, but you need to sit down."

He whipped around. "No, damn it. That woman lying there is the reason I'm still alive. She's the love of my life. Now let me go so I can call her family." Pulling away, he ran to the nurse's station, ignoring the dizziness and the pain.

Chapter Thirty-Six

$\mathcal{D}$espite Draco's snarls and insistence that he could walk on his own, Hunter helped him down the corridor, limping his way down the hall. Missy raced to the nurse's desk, her eyes burning from the tears she'd shed.

"I'm told my daughter is here. Aurora Starr." All Scott had said was that she'd been stabbed.

"Yes, your daughter is being looked after, but I need you to sign a few papers. If you could take a seat in the lounge, I'll inform her doctor that you're here."

Taking the form, Missy walked to the chairs. "The doctor will be by to tell us how she is." Missy stroked her husband's battered face. Not even bruises could diminish his handsomeness. "You should have a doctor take a look at you."

Draco shook his head. "I'll be fine."

"Your leg is torn up and the way you're holding your side, I suspect your ribs might be broken."

"Enough." Draco scowled at Hunter. "I'm well aware of my condition. I'm not going anywhere until I hear from my daughter."

"I'm so glad you're here."

All three heads turned, flicked a gaze over Scott's attire and the IV. "Scott?"

"She's in surgery, has been since I called you. The stab wound isn't critical, no major organs were damaged, and her chances are good."

"Stab wound? I'm confused. She didn't receive any wound from her fight with…Satan." Missy whispered the last, her eyes checking for listeners.

"From what I heard, someone stabbed her while waiting for a bus, though I haven't a clue why she was waiting for a bus."

"Oh, my baby." Missy reached a hand out to her husband, feeling the warmth in his touch.

"She's strong, but I thought maybe you both could, you know, use your powers on her and heal her up properly."

"We have no powers to use." Draco grunted.

"Come again?"

Missy laid her hand on Scott's, baffled as to why he wore a hospital pajamas and was hooked up to an IV. "We've been punished for disobeying Lucifer. He's stripped us all of our powers."

Scott's forehead scrunched up. "That whole thing has me confused. One minute I'm in the hospital room, falling endlessly, then *boom*, I'm standing beside Blackie, facing…I don't know what the hell I saw."

"She needed you, your love. She gathered up all her strength to bring us all to her. Our love, the all-encompassing love we feel for her helped to fight him off. In return, we were cast away. We're now human. Including Aurora."

"She's human? Oh my God." He worried even more for her now. He prayed the doctors did their jobs well and kept her alive.

"I don't understand why she did that, why she went to see—I am assuming that was him, the…Devil?" Scott got an affirmative from both Draco and Missy. "I had it all planned."

Missy tilted her head. "Had what planned?"

"I took a bottle of sleeping pills after I left you. I planned to sell my soul for her. I went to her because I wanted to be with her when the end came, and to make sure she would claim me after I died. It all kind of gets blurry after that."

After the initial shock had worn off, Missy had been amazed he'd actually carried through with it. She shook her head and gave her husband a steely glare. "It seems both you and my husband were inflicted with stupidity."

"I am not stupid. What I did, I did for the love of my child," Draco shot back, and immediately went into a rush of coughing spasms that had Missy clutching his hand. "I'm fine."

"You are not fine, but we'll deal with you later." She turned back to Scott. "Draco went to Lucifer to barter for our daughter, to allow her to be with you. He was in the midst of proving his worth when Aurora pulled him to her."

"I didn't think you approved, let alone cared about me."

Draco bared his teeth in what no one mistook as a smile. "I didn't, but now, knowing what you attempted to do to be with her, I guess I could upgrade you to tolerable."

Scott smirked. "I guess I probably should thank you for not killing me when I came to see you. I'm sure you could have."

Draco started to laugh, but ended up with another bout of coughing. "Without a doubt."

"Get him to a doctor already, Hunter."

Draco snarled at his wife. "After I see my daughter."

"How long do you think this will last, the human aspect?"

"This isn't a slap on the wrist, Scott. This is permanent."

His eyes went a little wider as he looked at Draco. "Permanent?"

"Yes. Will you still love her, Scott, now that she is human?"

"It pisses me off that you would even ask that, but I'll answer you. Yes, I love her, whoever, whatever she is."

"Mr. and Mrs. Starr?"

Their heads turned to look up at the tall, red-haired doctor wearing hospital scrubs and looking rather ragged. "Yes, how is our daughter?"

"Stable. Mind if I sit? My sacrum is killing me." He sat, cradling his back. "The surgery went fine, no complications. We managed to seal the wound. It wasn't too deep, didn't hit any major organs, but I have to tell you." He leaned a little closer. "I'm not sure if the baby will survive."

"She's pregnant?" Missy asked quickly.

"Yes. She's in the early stages. I would suggest the father be called in, just in case."

"He's already here." Scott managed in a whispered and very shocked tone. "I'm the father. What would you say her chances are for going full-term?"

"The next twenty four hours will tell." He looked over at Draco. "Were you examined?"

Draco shook his head. "My daughter came first."

"I would suggest you go down to Emergency and have them look at you immediately. I don't like how fluid your lungs sounds. Were you in an accident?"

"Something like that. Thank you, Doctor. I'll take into consideration what you've said."

The doctor stood, bracing his back. "She's in ICU. Only two at a time, and only for fifteen minutes."

"Thank you, Doctor." Missy nodded as the doctor hurried off.

"Well, do I have any color in my face?" Scott asked as he rubbed a hand over his cheek.

"If you're thinking of cutting and running now—"

"Okay, I was polite the first time, this time not so much. Get it through your dark and formerly dangerous head, Mr. Starr. I love your daughter, love 'til death us do part. The fact that she's carrying my child is a surprise, but not a disappointment. And just so you know, yes, I plan on marrying her, and having a dozen more children with her. Like it or not, I'll be your son-in-law, *Dad*," he remarked snidely.

Missy fought the smirk and thought how lucky Scott was that Draco had no power now. There wouldn't be anything left of Scott if he had tried that attitude a day ago.

Draco narrowed dark eyes. "You're slipping back down to intolerable."

"So be it."

"Boys, let's stop this pissing match and concentrate on the real problem at hand here."

Scott tilted his head in confusion. "What problem?"

Missy leaned in closer so only the four of them heard her.

"How do you suppose you'll handle it when the child is born demon?"

"It won't matter. It's my child, and I'll love it no matter what." Scott got to his feet, wobbled before righting himself. "I need to see her first." He walked off before Missy or Draco could respond.

"What if it isn't his child?"

Missy turned to her husband, a stern look of disapproval on her face. "Enough, Draco. He loves her, she loves him. Accept it already."

He shook his head. "I meant what if it isn't his? What if…Satan planted it after the fight?"

Missy's eyes went wide in horror. "You don't think—"

"Time will tell." Getting to his feet, he stumbled, losing his balance and nearly tumbling over. If it hadn't been for Hunter, he might have hit the floor.

"That's it. You're coming with me." Holding him tight, Hunter shifted so he had a better grip.

"Remove your hands."

Hunter merely laughed, tightened his grip. "Well, well, this is a day I won't soon forget. I've become the stronger one. I now hold the power."

Draco snarled. "I still hold the paycheck."

"That's not entirely true, dear." Missy hooked her arm under her husband's to help Hunter keep him still. "I do the payroll for the staff."

"Traitor." Draco snarled at his wife.

Smiling up at her husband, Missy decided payback was going to be a pleasant one. "Oh, you know I love you, and to show you how much, I'll guide you into humanity as smoothly as you guided me as a demon."

His eyes rolled back. "Wonderful. I'm doomed."

ଔ

She looked so pale, Scott thought, as he stroked the dark hair from her face. The nurses had tied it up in some odd kind of twist, but a few stray hairs had managed to wriggle free. He wondered if she even knew of her condition. Would she have told him if she had? He liked to think she would have. It didn't matter now. They were together.

He caressed her face, looking down at her beauty and didn't see any difference in her at all. Shouldn't she look different now that she'd been turned into a human? His hand slid down, rested on her flat belly. And what if their child wasn't human? How would she feel looking at it, knowing she had lost her abilities? Would she resent it? Resent him? Remembering her wish not to have powers, he knew better. She would love the child no matter what. And so would he.

"I've finally got you, Blackie," he whispered as he laid his head on her arm. "And I'm never letting you go." Closing his eyes, he drifted off to sleep.

CS

While she slept, she dreamed. She felt an unbearable pain, slicing into her, ripping her apart. She panted, cursed, then panted some more. When the pain speared, the wave engulfing her, she grunted as she pushed.

"A little more, Blackie. You can do it."

"No, no I can't. I'm too tired."

"You're doing fine, sweetie. Just a few more pushes."

"You said that a dozen pushes ago."

"I can see the head. Come on, Aurora, one big push."

Clamping tight onto Scott's hand, she pulled herself up and pushed. She felt the release, the contraction ending, as her child was born. Laughing gleefully she fell back down to the bed. "What is it? Please, tell me. What did I have?" When no one answered, she opened her eyes and the darkness engulfed her. "Mamma? Scott?" Out of the darkness, he came. In his arms lay a child, small, pink and crying with lungs incredibly strong.

"My baby. I want my baby."

He smiled at her as he pulled the child to his face. *He is my son.*

She sat up, clawing, reaching out to her child. "No, no—he's mine. Give him to me."

Mine now. He held up the crying child, and the tears suddenly stopped. As the tiny head turned to her, his eyes opened, and she screamed. He bore the face of Satan.

"No! What have you done to him?"

He is my creation. I warned you. You would regret what you've done.

Chapter Thirty-Seven

*A*urora ached, deep in the darkness of sleep. She felt it stir her awake. Mind groggy, she tried to shift, and moaned when the pain sliced into her. The darkness seemed to fade and the light began to seep in. Glancing over to her right, she looked on at the most beautiful blue eyes she'd ever seen. "Scott?"

"Yeah, baby, I'm here." He leaned in to press his lips to hers.

Had it all been a dream? Scott's attempt at suicide? Her fight with Satan? "Is it time to get up?"

He laughed, kissed her forehead. "You won't be getting up any time soon, Blackie. How do you feel?"

She frowned, her mouth dry as a bone. "Terrible. I feel really terrible." Deep down, utterly horrible.

"Are you in pain?"

"Unbelievably. Why am I in pain?" She saw the room, the unfamiliarity of it, and the bland walls. "Where am I?"

He leaned his cheek on her head. "To answer the first, you had surgery a few hours ago. The second, you're in the hospital. They just moved you out of the ICU."

The last thing she remembered she'd been waiting for a bus, when suddenly a blinding pain shot into her side. "Why did I have surgery?"

"You were stabbed, nothing major. They stitched you up good as new."

He looked tired, she thought, with bags under his eyes, those deep blue eyes. "You didn't die." She felt her eyes burn with happiness for him. "Never do that again."

He laughed, gave her a quick kiss. "Okay, once is enough."

"We won, didn't we?" Something inside of her felt different, a little hollow, but not an uncomfortable hollow.

"Yes, well, if you ask your father, he might think differently." He continued to stroke her face.

She tried to shift, but the pain forced her back down. "Is he all right?"

"Yes, he's pretty banged up, a few cracked ribs, a femur fracture, bruises over most of his body. He's in a pisser of a mood."

She imagined so, and if she remembered correctly, they had all lost their powers. They were all human now. Would her parents hate her for what she'd done to them? "I need to see them."

"In a minute. I need to talk to you first. Is it okay if I lift you a bit so I can see you better?" She nodded, so he carefully raised the bed. "Too much?"

"No, that's fine." She felt a little dizzy, but it would pass, she hoped. "What's up?"

He sat next to her, taking her hand in his and stroked her knuckles lightly. "There's no other way to start this but to ask right out." He drew in a deep breath. "Did you know you're pregnant?"

Her dream. Oh God, her dream. Her baby. "No, am I?"

He nodded, kissed her palm. "The doctors weren't sure if you would continue carrying it, after the surgery and all, but the kid's a stubborn one. It's strong, very strong."

She closed her eyes as fear danced along her spin. "How far?"

"Not far. We created a baby out of our love." He kissed her face several times before settling on her lips. "And, as soon as you're up to it, I want to make you my wife, not just because of the baby. I wanted you as my wife even before I found out you were pregnant."

She closed her eyes, wanting nothing more than that as well. But something wasn't right. "Scott, I want to be your wife, but it won't be as easy as that."

He cupped her face in his hands and held her eyes captive. "After what we've been through, everything else will be a piece of cake. And if you're worried that our baby might be half demon, don't be. Your parents already discussed this with me and whatever it is, whoever it is, it's ours. I will love it no matter what."

Silently, tears slid down her cheeks. If her dream meant anything, the baby wasn't his. "Hold me, please, just hold me."

Lifting her carefully, he pulled her into her arms. "What did I say tears did to me?"

She snickered as she stroked his face. "Sorry. I was so scared that I would lose you. When Satan told me I had to choose between you and my father…I couldn't."

He lifted her face and kissed away her tears. "It's over. Everything is over and all we have now is our future." Kissing her head, he wiped her damp cheeks. "That is, if the shrink says I can have one."

Her brow furrowed as she tilted her head to him. "Shrink?"

He handed her a tissue. "Being that I attempted suicide, the hospital won't release me until the hospital-appointed shrink gives me the okay." He lifted one shoulder sluggishly. "It's not a problem, though. I've got Claire, the shelter's psychiatrist, coming by to verify that I am not a risk and have them release me in her custody. What a mess."

"Oh Scott, why did you do something so foolish?"

"Hey, I'm a fool in love. What can I say?"

"Why pills, though?"

"I needed something that wouldn't work instantly. I needed time to get to you."

She cupped his face in her hands, squeezed. "Don't ever do that again."

"I think you already said that, and I won't. I have no reason to now that I have you." He kissed her head and slid off the bed. "I'll go get your family."

Resting her head on the pillow, Aurora let out a long breath.

She had fought for the men she loved, and by all accounts they had won, though she wasn't sure her parents would feel the same as she did.

She and Scott could be together now, and she was pregnant. She laid a hand on her belly, felt the bandage over her wound, and wanted to weep endlessly. It had to be Scott's.

Her room door swung open and her parents rushed into the room, Scott trailing behind them. "Oh darling, it is so good to see you awake." Her mother hurried to her, taking her in her arms. "My baby. I feared I would lose you."

"I'm too stubborn to give in." She took her mother's hand as she sat on the edge of the bed. "How are you?"

"I'm fine, now."

The door swung open once more, and she nearly gasped. It wasn't just the condition of her father that shocked her, though the battered face, the bandages, cuts, and the cast on his leg were enough to surprise her. But being wheeled in by Hunter shocked her to her core. "Daddy, you look like hell."

"I think it gives me character." Swiping Hunter's arm away, her father pushed himself up from the chair. He wobbled as he grabbed the bed and leaned down to kiss her head. "You are all I need to feel better, my sweet."

"Why did you do that? You never should have gone to him and fought for me."

"I don't believe I have ever needed your permission to do anything, and as if you should talk, young lady, going to the Master, fighting him alone."

She squeezed his hand. She hated seeing him bruised and battered, looking weak. "I didn't know what else to do. I had no idea what you were doing. If I had…I still would have been furious with you." She leaned against his arm, sighing. What he'd done for her, she would never forget. "I need to know, and please don't spare me, thinking I'm too frail now." Aurora looked from her father to her mother. "Do you hate me for what I've done?"

"Never." Her mother stated firmly. "We did the same with your life now, didn't we?"

"Daddy?" Their eyes met, held and she feared he wouldn't tell her the truth. She couldn't read his mind any longer.

"Well, I can't say I appreciate Hunter's constant mockery of me, or his treating me as an invalid, but I'll find a way to get even." His lips curved, only slightly, but enough to show her a smile. "I love you, my sweet. I know what you did, you did for love." His gaze met his wife's. "I'm no stranger to what love can make you do."

"Does that mean you're accepting this...us...him?"

"All of the above, darling." He kissed her hand again. "What can I say? He grows on you, and, he'd been willing to give up his life for you. I suppose I could give him a break."

"You're too generous," Scott snarled.

She took Scott's hand as he sat next to her on the bed. She thought about him, about them, about the child she was carrying. "Scott tells me you were discussing the baby and the possibility of it being...demon."

"I said that it didn't matter if it's human or not. It's my child. Our child." Scott kissed her hand, his face beaming.

"Scott, there's something we need to talk about in regards to the baby."

"Come on now, Blackie, if I can accept you for what you were, do you think I wouldn't be able to accept my child if is a demon?"

"What if it isn't even demon, but worse?"

His brow scrunched up. "I don't understand."

With Hunter's help, her mother eased Draco back into his chair. "You've thought about it as well?"

"I have. It's hard not to."

"What's going on?" Scott asked, looking around at each person.

"Would you care for me to explain it to him, dear?"

She shook her head at her mother's question. "No, I'll do it." She looked up at Scott, his beautiful deep blue eyes. She would give anything to have a child that resembled him. "There is nothing more that I want than to carry your child, but I fear the child I am carrying isn't yours."

"If you expect me to believe you slept with another man, Blackie, I won't humiliate you by laughing at that. We both know I was your first, and only."

She shook her head, clasped onto his hand. "You are the only man I've ever been with. What I fear is much worse." She cleared her throat, took a cautious, deep breath. "I'm worried I might have been implanted with the Devil's seed as punishment for disobeying him."

Scott burst out laughing, then cleared his throat when he saw no one else found it funny. "Okay, are you trying to tell me that Satan, the Devil himself, got you pregnant?"

"Not in the sense you mean, but yes, I think he planted his seed in me before he sent me away." She saw the shock in his face. "Scott, I had a dream. Well, it wasn't really a dream as much as a message from Satan. In it, I was in labor. I gave birth with you and my mother helping me. We had a son." Her voice wavered. "But he wasn't human."

He literally felt the color draining from his face. "That can't be. I know this child is mine." He laid his hand on her belly. "Mine, not the big bad guy's. Mine."

"Scott, there is the possibility it isn't."

He turned to Missy, shook his head. "No, it's mine."

"What if it isn't, Scott? Do you want to take the chance that it might be Satan's?"

He looked back at her with horror in his voice. "You aren't suggesting what I think you are?"

"Maybe terminating it would be for the best." Her father suggested, leaning his good arm on the bed.

"No, no that wouldn't be the best." Scott turned back to Aurora. "We went through Hell, literally, to be together, because we love each other more than life itself. I don't believe for one minute that this child you are carrying is anything but mine. Thinking back on it now, I know when you conceived. Remember when the condom broke?" He held his hands out.

"Scott—"

"Please tell me you don't want to terminate it."

She wanted to believe as strongly as he did. "I won't give my son to Satan, Scott. I will not let him have him."

"Then fight with me, once again." He lifted her hand to his lips, pressed a long, slow kiss to her fingers. "Fight for our child."

"Scott—"

"Come on. We won. We beat him. He's just using this to scare you. It's his last revenge. Using the child we created in love as a toy for his evil sense of humor. He can't hurt you, us, or the baby." He kissed her hard before she could protest. "Okay? No more talk of terminating the child. We can deal with whatever comes our way."

He was right, in a sense, but he had no idea how hard that fight might be. Looking into his deep blue eyes, the sincerity, the love, she knew without a doubt that they would fight. "Okay."

"Excellent. Wow, I'm feeling a little woozy."

"You should go back to bed, Scott. You've been through a lot." And she'd nearly lost him once. She wasn't about to go through that again.

"In a bit. I want to spend some time with you first.

"And that's our cue to leave." Taking the handles on the wheel chair, her mother turned her father toward the door. "We'll stop in and see you a little later, dear."

As her parents left, Aurora noticed Hunter standing off to the side. He'd been quiet during the whole discussion, and she wondered what was on his mind—and it suddenly occurred to her how quiet her mind finally was.

"Are you all right, Hunter?"

He pushed from the wall where he'd been leaning and walked to her bed. Taking her hand in his, he ran a thumb over her knuckles. "I'm glad you're all right, and congratulations, but there's something I need to say."

Aurora swallowed hard, expecting the worst.

"I am going to take great pleasure in getting even with you for turning me into a donkey. That child of yours will be taught all the nastiest tricks just to irritate you."

Aurora burst out in laughter, clutching her side. "That was just mean." She'd been sure he had some choice words to say to her about screwing up her life, facing off with Satan, giving up everything, sacrificing her parents for one man. Instead, he smiled down at her.

"And so my revenge begins." He kissed her hand before leaving the room.

"You turned him into a donkey?"

Hunter couldn't have said anything better to bring her mood up. "Only once, but he holds a grudge."

"I can understand why." Scott took her chin in his hand, looked down at her as his voice grew serious. "Will you regret this, regret giving up your powers and all that went with it, for me?"

"Never." She took his hand in hers. "I love you, and I've always hated being a demon. Sure, being a human will take some getting used to, especially since I've come to realize I despise pain, but I'll manage."

"Lots of drugs it is when you go into labor. We'll be all right. All three of us, and however many more we decide to bring into this world."

She so desperately wanted to believe that. "I want lots of kids."

"Define lots."

"Under ten."

He laughed, gave her hair a tug. "That's pretty brave coming from someone who despises pain. Okay, Blackie, we'll have less than ten kids."

"I love you, Scott, more than I ever thought possible."

Kissing her, holding her mouth captive, she felt all the pain, the stress, simply float away.

"I love you too, and I'm damn grateful you won't ever be able to turn me into a donkey."

Laughing, she cursed him violently. "Jerk, that hurts."

"Sorry. I love you. Forever and for always."

Epilogue

$\mathcal{H}$is eyes were blue, just like his father's. He had golden blond hair, and his skin was fair. He was a good baby. He only cried when he needed feeding or soiled himself. He slept like an angel and was always happy. Yet when she looked at him, she couldn't help but wonder. Was the Devil hiding in him somewhere?

She stroked her fingers along his delicate baby face while he slept soundly in his crib. Three weeks earlier, she had brought Michael Scott Monroe into the world, screaming and showing his fists. When he'd finally come out, much to her relief, she'd waited for the Devil to call. But when he'd been placed on her breast and began to suckle, she felt a sense of relief that could be matched by nothing else. They had bonded instantly. In the three weeks since his birth on that stormy night, she'd kept him as close to her as possible. Inside, she always had a tiny nagging fear that the moment she left him, the moment she turned her back, Satan would snatch him up. So he slept beside her at night, and during the day. When Scott would work and she needed to shower or get some work done, she kept a baby monitor close at all times.

She kissed his tiny blond head and he smiled. He belonged to them, her and Scott, and she would fight to the death before she gave him up. She took comfort in the fact that he looked a great deal like Scott. She had no doubt he was Scott's child. Yet still she worried.

"I should have known I would find you here." Putting his hands on her shoulders, Scott kissed her head. "He's beautiful, isn't he?" As always, Scott slid his finger into his son's tiny hand and smiled when he gripped him tight.

Aurora, filled with so much love, turned to her husband. "And he's all ours."

Scott stroked a finger along her jaw and up to the hair curling over her forehead. "You're still worried, aren't you? He's our son, Blackie. Anyone looking at him can clearly see that."

She sighed, nodded, but the fear didn't subside. "I know. I can't help but worry, though."

"It's over." He kissed her in the slow passionate way. "We beat him, and we won. It's time to move on." Sliding his finger from his son's grip, he leaned down, kissed his head again. Slipping his hand in hers, he dragged her from the room. "Everyone's been wondering where you went, though your father's been preoccupied with a jar of pickles."

Aurora stopped short before they started down the stairs. "On Scott, you didn't. Not again?"

It was a running joke, one her father had yet to figure out. Scott and Hunter were having a field day with it.

"It was Hunter's idea," Scott admitted.

Shaking her head, she started down. "When are the two of you going to stop making fun of my father over his fragility?" In the months since he had lost his powers, her father had learned to cope with the fact that he wasn't as strong as he once had been. Aurora felt sorry for him, but certainly wasn't about to say so to his face.

"It's all in good fun."

Yeah, at her father's expense, still—and she would never admit this to either Scott or Hunter—she did find it amusing. And there he was, at the kitchen sink, jar in hand, grunting as he attempted to open it.

She wondered what would happen if her father figured out that they'd glued it shut.

"I could run it under some warm water for you if you like, sir."

"Go to Hell, Hunter. I'll get it, sooner or later."

Despite the humor, Aurora had enough. "Give me that." Snatching up the jar, despite the snarl from her father, Aurora set it in the sink and shot Hunter a nasty scowl. "Hunter and Scott have been playing with you, Daddy. They glued the lid down." She aimed a heated look at her husband.

Her father's eyes narrowed, and she knew if he had his powers back, both Hunter and Scott would pay dearly. "Are the two of you enjoying yourself?" he asked as they bent over with laughter.

"I know I am. How about you, Hunter?"

"Completely."

"You," her father aimed a long, narrow finger at Hunter, "are lucky my wife won't allow me to kill you. And you," he turned the pointed finger at Scott, "are damn lucky you bore me a grandson."

"Who bore you a grandson?" Aurora asked, giving her father's ear a twist. "Last time I checked it was my body that carried him, my body that went through twelve hours of agony and my body that delivered him, not my husband."

"If I could—"

Aurora shot Scott a steely look.

"I'll shut up now, dear."

"My sweet." Her father hobbled toward her using a cane to help him walk. "We all know how you labored to bring that dear child into the world." He kissed the top of her head and smiled. "For that, you will always be my favorite child."

She gave him a gentle slug to the arm. "Very nice, Daddy. I feel so privileged that you would choose me out of all…wait, I'm an only child." She scowled at him, her tone sarcastic and laced with heat that only got worse when her father grinned.

"Hey, he has a son now." Scott waved his hand in the air.

"You keep up the funny antics, and you won't even be considered an in-law and will be stricken from my will."

The mediator that she'd become, her mother patted Scott on the back. "I'll keep you in mine, and you will always be a son to me."

"You are all so hilarious. I'll go spend time with my grandson. At least he loves me."

"We love you, Daddy." Reaching up on her tiptoes, Aurora kissed his cheek.

She clutched a hand to her breasts when she felt the tingle. "Oh, it's feeding time. I'll be just a bit. Go ahead and start dinner without me."

"Do you want me to come with you?"

She smiled at her husband and shook her head. "No, you can stay here and irritate Daddy." Smiling, she left the room and went to her screaming son. "Is my little man hungry?"

Lifting him from the crib, she nuzzled his neck with her nose. "So mad. Come now, let's put an end to that temper." Carrying her son to the rocking chair set up by the window, Aurora unbuttoned her blouse and laid Michael to her nipple. "There now, isn't that better?"

Smiling as her son drew the milk from her breast, Aurora rocked and sang. He was the most perfect child she had ever seen. Okay, so she hadn't seen many babies, and so what if she was a little biased, he was perfect to her. Holding him close, his tiny fist kneaded her breast. Aurora reveled in the moment.

☙

In the darkened room, he stood in protection, in admiration. The boy was perfect, as he'd expected him to be.

Soon, my son. Soon.

~ABOUT THE AUTHOR~

Raised on a rural farm in Saskatchewan, Shiela Stewart relied on her vivid imagination to fill her days. Never did she realize that her need to tell a story would someday lead to becoming a published romance author. In the fall of two thousand and six, Shiela published her very first book and hasn't stopped since.

When not writing, Shiela spends time with the love of her life, William and their three children. She has a strong affection for animals which is evident in the five cats, one dog, three turtles and ten fish she owns. Some of her passions aside from writing are drawing and painting and proudly displays her artwork in murals in her home.

Her favorite time of day is sunset and loves to stargaze.

You can visit Shiela at:
www.shielasbooks.ca

Awaken the Demon

The Demon Series – Book One
By Shiela Stewart

Abused for years by a sadistic fiancé, Missy Green has finally had enough. Running away is her only recourse. Wanting a new life, she takes refuge with a group known as the Stargazers. Taken in by the illustrious Draco Starr, Missy is elated to finally find peace. Yet, something doesn't seem right about her host.

Born in the pits of hell, Draco Starr was once a fearsome Demon. For centuries, he collected soul s for Satan. Having done his time, Draco sets out to start a new life. Even with more wealth and prestige than anyone could ever want, something is missing in his life.

Love.

Missy is about to have her world turned upside down. Discovering Draco is a demon is terrifying enough, but finding out she too is a demon is more than she can handle.

Can Missy deal with her new life, and the affection she is beginning to feel for Draco, or will her past come back to haunt her?

Available in ebook or print

Decadent Publishing Company
www.decadentpublishing.com